In memory of Gerald Pollinger, my agent, without whom this book would not have been written.

THE LION *and* THE LILY

PETER TALLON

authorHOUSE®

AuthorHouse™ UK
1663 Liberty Drive
Bloomington, IN 47403 USA
www.authorhouse.co.uk
Phone: 0800.197.4150

Published by AuthorHouse 12/21/2016

ISBN: 978-1-5246-6550-0 (sc)
ISBN: 978-1-5246-6551-7 (hc)
ISBN: 978-1-5246-6549-4 (e)

Print information available on the last page.

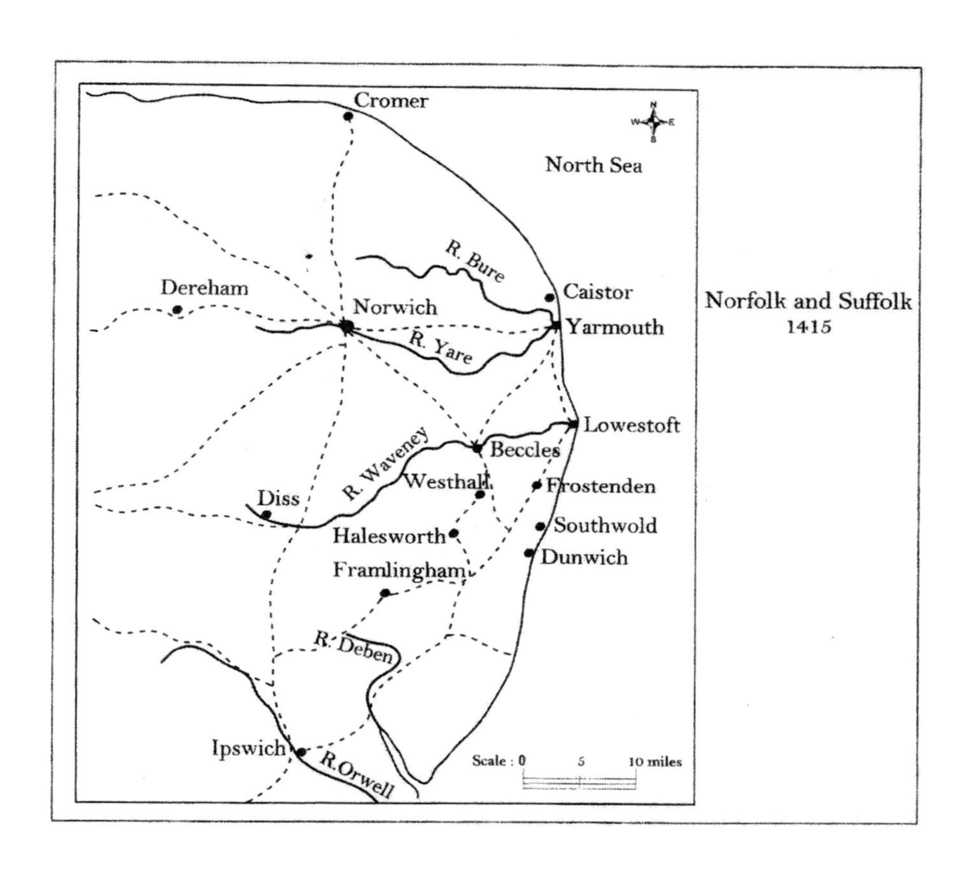

Norfolk and Suffolk
1415

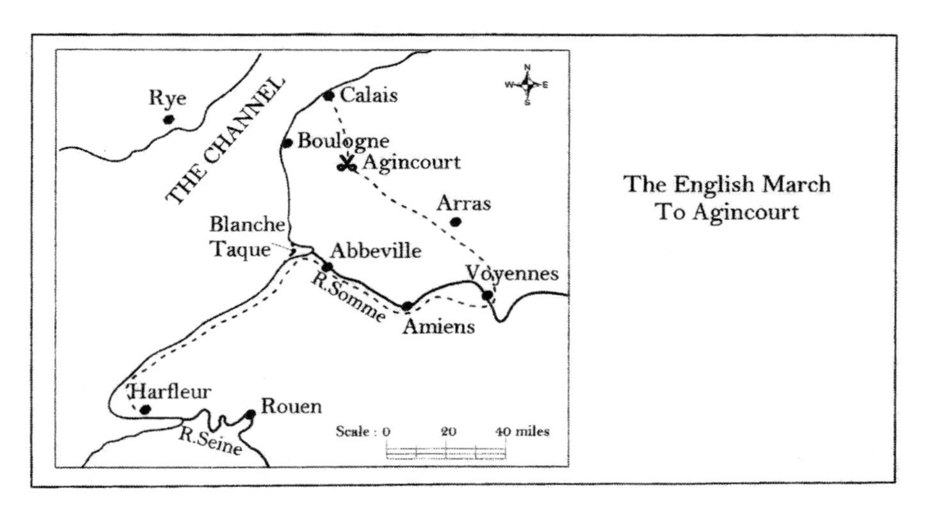

The English March
To Agincourt

CHAPTER ONE

The square was crowded. It was market day in Beccles and a crisp September sun warmed the robust Suffolk folk as they began to gather round the wooden platform at the north side of the square for the highlight of the day; the auction. The church of Saint Michael, which walled off one entire side of the market, tolled two o'clock and, as everyone knew, that heralded the commencement of the sale.

There was a sudden surge of people towards the platform, for an auction was second only to hanging as public entertainment. The amount bid and, more importantly, the identity of the bidders would serve as a reliable indicator of the current fortunes of the wealthier local families, for this was no ordinary auction. It involved land, the most treasured currency in the kingdom, the bridge between yeoman and gentleman and the greatest social divider in the realm.

A rotund, balding man of middle years ascended the platform. The crowd hushed in anticipation. His red face and unsteady legs suggested an overlong stay in the White Boar tavern just behind him, but years of well honed technique overcame the influence of ale as soon as he began to address his eager listeners.

"Good people of Beccles, I have today a special contract for your consideration." He wobbled, but only slightly, as he bent down to take a rolled and sealed parchment from a well dressed notary who was standing at the foot of the platform. Holding the parchment above his head as if it were a piece of the true cross, the auctioneer announced grandly, "This document bears the seal of Sir John Satterley, a well respected knight of these parts. It authorises me to sell to the highest bidder eighty acres of prime land in the parish of Westhall, five miles south of here. The terms of the holding are to supply five archers and one fully mounted man at arms or the equivalent in specie each year, plus one day of labour on Sir John's own land annually during the harvest."

The auctioneer lowered the pitch of his voice slightly in order to achieve a conversational, more intimate tone; he was one of the best in the business.

"Friends, these terms are indeed generous. Before the Great Plague a demesne such as this would have borne three times the terms now on offer. Who will bid me fifty pounds?" Ten or eleven hands were raised but, by the time the bidding reached sixty five pounds, the auction seemed all but over. A broad shouldered, stout man of medium height and unweathered skin held the initiative. He smiled confidently at his older companion, who was scanning the crowd for any further signs of opposition, and whispered, "Less than a pound an acre. You have done your work well this day Titus." The lean, cadaverous Titus exposed a row of yellow, decaying teeth as he grinned, "Do I get an extra reward then?" His master, never one to part with money needlessly, said coldly, "Let us see. It's not over yet."

The auctioneer knew his client's land should be fetching at least a hundred pounds, never mind sixty five. He could smell a crooked auction a mile away and, at the very least, he determined to identify publicly the source of the false price. To no-one's great surprise he shouted, "The bid lies with Master Geoffrey Calverley of Holton. Is there no-one who will bid me sixty six pounds for this prime plot of Suffolk farmland? No? Well in that case -Aha! Well done sir! I am bid sixty six pounds down here on my right." Geoffrey span round but could see nothing over the heads of the crowd. Elbowing his taller companion in the ribs, he said angrily, "Who is it Titus? Tell me who it is if he raises the bid again." Geoffrey raised his hand only to have his bid topped once more. His opponent was a tall, raven haired man dressed in a green, quilt tunic and smart, buckskin breeches. He looked across the crowd to Titus Scrope and nodded an acknowledgement. Trying not to smile, Titus turned back to his master and whispered, "It's your cousin Richard." The reaction was predictable.

"God's balls! What's he doing here!"

"Bidding against you," replied Titus in a neutral voice.

"Do not be clever with me Scrope or you'll pay for it." Titus knew what is master was capable of when thwarted. Geoffrey enjoyed the protection of Michael de la Pole, Earl of Suffolk which effectively put him beyond the reach of the law in civil matters. Even the criminal law was not beyond de la Pole's purse.

Geoffrey hissed, "I told you to scare off the opposition Scrope. You have failed me."

"But your cousin too? You did not tell me he would be here."

"It's your job to find these things out. That's why you are so well paid. You'd better sort this mess out or it'll be the worse for you."

"But why do you not just outbid Richard? You are far wealthier than he is."

"Fool Scrope! You know it's not as simple as that. Richard is stubborn to a fault; I'll end up paying double the true price if I follow your advice."

Titus looked into his master's baleful, grey eyes; he knew he must do something to retrieve the lost sale. Although he was the nearest thing to a friend Geoffrey had, even Titus was not safe when his master's greed was unfulfilled.

"I want that land Titus," whispered Geoffrey. "Fix it. Fix it by tonight. If you fail this time don't come back."

"Sold! Sold to Richard Calveley of Westhall!" exclaimed the auctioneer joyfully. Seventy pounds was still cheap but it seemed to matter less now because Geoffrey had been foiled. "Give the notary your money Master Calveley and place your mark here." The auctioneer pointed to a blank space at the foot of the sale document but Richard said, "I can sign if you prefer."

"Indeed yes, that would be capital and I shall be your witness." Richard carefully signed his name and dated the signature to the twenty fourth day of September in the Year of Our Lord 1414, then handed the quill back to the auctioneer who gave him the counterpart complete with the Satterley seal to keep. As Richard carefully stowed the precious document inside his tunic a voice from behind him said, "Well done sir." Richard turned round and beheld a small, well groomed man wearing a rich, fur lined, leather jacket.

"From your accent I assume you are not from these parts," said Richard.

"Indeed not sir. I first saw the light of day in God's own county of Yorkshire. John Smith of Beverley at your service."

"Well then John Smith, what brings you so far from home?"

The small stranger smiled, "Wool, what else? I had hoped to secure the holding that is now yours to graze sheep."

"Then why did you not bid?"

"In Yorkshire land sells for less than in Suffolk. I am not yet accustomed to your steep southern prices. Now if you would consider an underlease I would pay you a good rent."

Richard shook his head, "No, I intend to work the land myself and in three or four years, God willing, I should be able to buy out the lease terms and turn the land into a freeholding. Then when my two sons come of age, they will be true gentlemen and my newly born daughter shall have a worthy dowry."

"A right worthy cause to be sure," acknowledged the Yorkshireman, "and in token of which I would deem it an honour to buy you a drink or two in yonder tavern." Richard hesitated. He still had fifteen pounds in the leather pouch attached to his belt and the White Boar had a fearsome reputation.

"I thank you for your offer Master Smith, but I think I should return home; my wife will be expecting me." Clapping Richard's mighty shoulder with the palm of his hand, the Yorkshireman said, "Come, come Richard, a drink to celebrate a new friendship between Suffolk and Yorkshire. Surely you would not refuse that?" Richard thought that John was offering friendship rather too freely, especially for a Yorkshireman, but one drink could do no harm and, after all, he did have cause to celebrate."

"Very well," agreed Richard, "I'll drink to that."

It was a decision that changed his life.

★ ★ ★

II

"Wake up Richard! Come on now. Don't you have a home to go to." Richard opened his bleary eyes to the formidable sight of the White Boar's owner. Mary Bradby was almost as tall lying down as standing up and had never required assistance to eject drunken patrons when the need arose. On one well remembered occasion she removed two belligerent archers by the simple expedient of grabbing the contents of their cod pieces in her vice like grip and leading them howling like children into the market square where she unceremoniously dumped them into the steaming midden beside the stock pens. Afterwards it was said that if the French had possessed two dozen Mary Bradbys, the outcome at Crecy and Poitiers might well have been different.

Richard struggled to his feet, rubbed his eyes and felt for his money pouch. Mary placed it in his hand and said, "Don't worry Richard, it's all there. I took it off you before that scheming little Yorkshireman did. Why did you let him get you drunk?"

"I don't know. I didn't mean to. God's teeth! My head hurts. What time is it?"

"Just past six. I let you sleep it off. You were in no fit state to be moved last night."

"I've been here all night! What will Ann say?"

"Ann need have no fears on your account. You were too ill to get up to any mischief. I'll bear witness to that."

Richard tried to straighten his creased tunic. "She'll be worried though. I must leave at once."

Mary chuckled, "Knowing your Ann you'll be in for a warm welcome."

"She's entitled to be angry," said Richard. "A man should not leave his family all night unprotected."

Mary's chuckle expanded into a laugh, "Ann Calveley may be the handsomest wench in Suffolk but she's also the fieriest. God help anyone who crosses her and that includes me!"

Richard nodded, "True, but when I tell her about the inside bathing room I shall build for her and the extensions I plan for the house now that we are true landholders, I think her temper will moderate."

"I am pleased for you both but be careful. From what I hear the auction did not go as planned."

"You mean my cousin?"

"He may be your cousin but he's not out of the same mould as you Richard."

Richard pressed a florin into Mary's large, red hand and said, "Thank's for looking out for me last night. Now I shall be on my way."

A few minutes later, Richard was cantering out of Beccles on his stocky, grey palfrey. He was not really concerned about his wife's temper. She had never used it on him in eight years of contented marriage and from now on he would be able to look after her in the way her devotion deserved. Ann was of gentle stock and had moved below her class to marry Richard, but during the struggle of their early years together when there was little food and no coin in the house, she never mentioned the difference in their births. Richard had always been aware of it though, even without the constant reminders from his father in law, but now years of toil combined with three consecutive bountiful harvests, had at last given him the chance to achieve his dream of being a landholder in his own right. The future seemed assured.

Richard quickly covered four of the five miles to Westhall, but as he breasted one of the many low hills which separated his village from Beccles, he saw a plume of smoke rising like a dark stain in the clear blue, autumn sky. It was not the pale grey colour of burning vegetation, so common at this time of year, but an ominous black. A feeling of unease began to penetrate Richard's mind but he tried to ignore it as he descended into the next shallow valley assuring himself that when he re-emerged a simple, harmless explanation for the smoke would reveal itself.

It was not to be. As soon as he saw the smoke again he realised it came from a source just south of Westhall village; his was the only property there. He spurred on his palfrey and galloped through Westhall; there was no-one about, which was unusual for this time of day. Either the villagers had been driven away or they had shut themselves up in their dwellings too frightened to come out. With panic welling up inside him, Richard cut off the last bend in the road by riding along the track through the oak copse which formed part of the land he had just bought, but when he came out on the other side his stomach churned as his fears were confirmed.

The simple, single storey, timber building that had been his home was a smoking ruin. The thatch had burned out and charred beams stuck up like broken black fingers where the roof had been. The heavy oak door was smashed off its hinges and through the gaping doorway Richard saw the fruits of eight years toil reduced to smouldering ashes. But this was of secondary importance compared to the fate of his family. He dismounted leaving his horse untethered and ran into the house kicking aside a scorched, upended chair.

"Ann! Ann!" he shouted. But there was no reply. Frantically he searched amongst the debris promising the Almighty anything in his power to give if only his wife and children were safe and, after a few minutes, hope began to flicker as it became apparent that there was nothing in the house save blackened furnishings. Perhaps Ann and the children had escaped and found sanctuary, possibly in the parish church. Richard had almost decided to go to the church when, through a broken leaded window, something in the grass field at the back of his house caught his eye; it was a crumpled, brown blanket.

Instinctively his blood ran cold. He opened the back door, which oddly was still in place, and walked towards the blanket. A sense of dread began to build in his heart which deadened all feeling in his limbs.

He wanted to run but his legs would not obey. He guessed what awaited him but, until he was sure, hope would last a precious moment longer.

At last Richard reached the blanket. He stopped and looked down at the three shapes, one tall and two short, which lay beneath it. Slowly, deliberately, he knelt down and pulled it back. There, still not yet cold, were the battered and broken bodies of his wife and two sons, Robert and John. The boys had both been killed by a single heavy blow to the head; they would have died quickly. But not so Ann. Her clothes were torn, her fingernails ripped and her body was covered in deep lacerations, bruises and bite marks. There could be no doubt what had happened to her; she had been brutally raped, probably more than once, but she had fought back like a wildcat and her assailants would surely bear the marks of the struggle. Their time would come later but for now the search was not yet finished; there was no sign of baby Joan.

Richard's guts heaved and he was violently sick. After recovering himself somewhat, he pathetically tried to straighten Ann's clothing but within a few moments he had to stop to be sick again. He had just enough time to rearrange Ann's hair into some sort of order before the tears came. Richard Calveley of Westhall grieved over the three bodies from the very depth of his soul. The purpose of his life seemed ended.

⋆ ⋆ ⋆

III

It was almost noon before Richard was able to stand up and consider what to do next.

His grisly ordeal was not yet over for he still had to find Joan and, after scouring the area outside the house, he re-entered the still smoking ruin to begin a more thorough search there. He had not been in the house many minutes when he was startled by a voice at the broken front door.

"Is this what you seek?" Richard span round. Framed in the doorway was a fresh faced young man of about middle height clad in the grey robes of the friars of the Franciscan Order. The Franciscan held out a small bundle and once more the tears welled up in Richard's eyes as he clasped his tiny daughter to his chest, "Joan, Joan, Joan," he kept repeating quietly to himself.

"The child is well," said the friar. "I found her sleeping in a basket in the stable."

Richard nodded, "Ann must have hidden her there to escape the murderers. She was ever resourceful. Who are you?"

"Brother Hugh from the Franciscan priory at Dunwich."

"Was it you that covered the bodies of my family?"

"Yes."

"Then I thank you for that. Do you know who is responsible for this vile crime?"

"No, but it cannot have been the result of one of the spontaneous affrays that have afflicted this land so much in recent years else the village would have suffered also. There was purpose behind this violence. You were singled out for some reason. I have already made enquiries in the village but no-one knows anything; at least that is what they would have me believe."

Richard said, "Affrays do not normally happen in the middle of the night, but when I got here this morning the embers were already cool."

"Do you have many enemies?" asked Brother Hugh.

"Not that I know of. There is no love lost between me and my cousin Geoffrey but he would never stoop to this sort of thing."

"Well if you are sure about that I suggest you look in the local markets for items stolen from your house and begin your enquiries there. Halesworth's market day is tomorrow and I'd be willing to bet a few pence, if my vow of poverty would allow me, that something will turn up there."

"That is good advice Brother Hugh," agreed Richard. "I will strike while the trail is still warm but for now I must make burial arrangements for my family."

"I have already been to the church in Westhall but the priest is not there or he is still too frightened to come out."

"But Ann and the boys must have the last rites. Can you not administer them?"

Hugh shook his head sadly, "I have not yet received the blessed sacrament of Holy Orders but I have my horse and wagon nearby. Let us salvage what goods we can, return to the priory with your family and intern them there."

"There is bitter irony in that," sighed Richard as he felt the tears welling up again. "My own father and mother are already buried there."

It was with some difficulty that Richard managed to persuade the Dunwich friars to bury his family on the afternoon of the murders. He could not bear the thought of some red faced coroner prodding and poking the bodies. In any event, there was nothing a coroner could tell him that he did not already know. To the friars, Richard's haste appeared unseemly and barely legal, but the old prior finally ruled in his favour and provided three lead lined coffins from the priory stores.

After the requiem mass, Richard stood silently over the open grave watching the coffins being lowered into the ground. The afternoon sun looked down from a clear blue sky on the sombre little gathering, and although Richard had always appreciated nature's simple beauty, especially the warm, golden brown colours of autumn, everything now seemed dulled by the grey shadow of his misery. The thought of a future without his beloved Ann was unbearable. He recalled small things such as the way Robert and John would always come running into his arms when he returned to the house after toiling in the fields while she would look on, smiling at her exuberant menfolk with maternal pride. Or the mock scoldings she would give him when he forgot to remove his muddy boots after a hard day behind his plough. Yet how could he have imagined that his perfect happiness would prove to be so fragile, swept away by one cruel twist of fate? And now there was nothing except little Joan. If Joan had not been spared he felt he would have done away with himself, but now he must go on somehow for her sake.

There was of course another reason to go on. As two lay brothers started to shovel soil over the coffins, a new feeling began to make its presence felt in Richard's mind. It was encompassed in a single word, a single concept that identified itself in his thoughts quietly at first, but then it grew stronger and louder forcing out for a while at least every other emotion in his consciousness, even his abject grief, until it seemed to scream throughout his soul. Vengeance! vengeance! vengeance!

Father Anselm had been Prior of the Dunwich Franciscans for almost twenty years. Now his kindly, old heart was saddened as he sat in his flint walled chapter house listening to his favourite student quietly describing the terrible events at Westhall. Richard's voice was expressionless, numbed by his despair and sense of guilt for not being at Ann's side when she needed him most. Tragedy had struck the Calveley family again thought Anselm wistfully, though the Holton branch seems to have escaped as usual. John and Eleanor Calveley had died of plague in Dunwich when Richard was still young. They had provided a benefice to the priory for the upbringing of their son, and Father Anselm had become a surrogate parent for Richard in their stead. The old cleric looked through his west facing, glass window at the blood red sunset and said, "And what will you do now?" A bitter Richard leaned against the oak mantel beneath which a log fire burned to keep out the evening chill, "I shall find out who the murderers are."

"But that might take some time. What about your land?"

"I have no heart for it now."

"But if you default on the rent it will return to the original landowner."

"Then let it."

"Come now Richard, I know it is difficult but these things must be thought about. Why not sublet to your cousin for a year or two and then resume the tenancy yourself or sell it on, whichever seems best at the time. It is what Ann would wish you to do." Anselm knew that last sentence would hit the mark.

"Of course you are right Father," agreed Richard, "and I must keep in mind a suitable inheritance for Joan. Ann lives on in her and I vow she will marry a gentleman." He paused for a moment and a strange look came into his green eyes as he added, "On the subject of vows Father, I wish you to solemnise an oath for me."

"What oath my son?"

"An oath of vengeance for I shall not rest until the murderers are dead and their souls burning in Hell." Apart from the crackle of the fire the room went quiet; the atmosphere became leaden. Anselm was disturbed and shifted uncomfortably, "You know Richard I cannot accept an oath like that. Vengeance is reserved to God and to God alone."

"But I shall be his instrument on earth. I need to make this oath." Anselm had seen something of the world before entering the Franciscan Order and understood that a man must sometimes break the Christian ethic if only to maintain his sanity at times of crisis. His surrogate son needed help; he could not refuse.

"Listen Richard. Although I cannot accept your oath, there is someone else who might but first you should discover who is responsible for the destruction of your family. When you have done that I will make arrangements for solemnising your oath. Is that agreed?"

"Yes Father. I shall begin my investigation in Halesworth tomorrow and on the way there I can call in at Holton to see my cousin and make arrangements for my land."

"Good," replied Anselm, relieved that he had postponed the oath taking, for the person he had in mind was someone he ought not to have dealings with, someone outside the accepted mainstream of Roman Catholic society. "Perhaps you would take Brother Hugh with you," he added. "He did not reach Beccles market today so he can go to Halesworth tomorrow instead. Some of our provisions are running low and Hugh never misses an opportunity to get out of the confines of the priory. Fond as I am of him, I sometimes have my doubts about the strength of his vocation."

"I should welcome his company Father."

"As for your little daughter," continued Anselm, "we will look after her here for as long as you wish. I can easily arrange for a wetnurse to stay in the guest house; Joan will not lack for homely comforts while you reorganise your life."

Richard looked at the old, grey priest and smiled, "I shall always remember your kindness Father."

* * *

IV

Geoffrey Calveley nursed ambitions to the gentry though like his cousin he came from yeoman stock. Through careful management and ruthless business practices he now held the freehold of two hundred and fifty acres of prime farmland around Holton and lived in a large house built in brick, the fashionable new building material, inherited from his father Robert, which he had grandly renamed Calveley Hall. This morning, two mornings after Ann Calveley's murder, Geoffrey sat in his study having just returned from a visit to Ipswich, the main purpose of which was to be seen well away from Westhall while the vile deed was done. But he was an unhappy man and berated his steward who stood uncomfortably with his back to the door ready to beat a swift retreat as soon as the opportunity arose.

"You fool Scrope!" bellowed Geoffrey. "What can you have been thinking of! Burning the place down is one thing but murdering my kin is quite another!"

"You said fix it," answered Scrope truculently.

"Yes but not like that you idiot! You did not have to murder them. Burning them out would have been quite sufficient."

"Murder was not intended. Some of the lads got a bit out of hand because of that woman."

"Ann?"

"Yes. She fought like a tiger and injured two of us with her claws. That stirred the lads up and before I could stop them they'd stripped her and taken their revenge."

"Are you sure you weren't one of them Titus; your appetite for women is well known," said Geoffrey threateningly. Titus nervously licked his lips and remained expressionless as he thought back to the pleasure of penetrating high and mighty Ann Calveley while he denied any part in her violation.

"What me! Of course not, I've got more sense than that. But after she'd been raped we could hardly let her live could we. Just think what her husband would have done when she told him who was responsible."

"She identified you! How? Were you not masked?" Titus gulped and struggled for an answer. During the one sided fight Ann had torn off his hood and threatened dire revenge on him and his master. She had to die. Titus inadvertently touched the scratch on his cheek and said, "I don't know how she knew but she knew. Her children heard her promise to avenge herself on you so they had to die too." His hooded eyelids widened and the hint of a grin revealed his rotting, yellow teeth as he added hoarsely, "We were carrying out your orders, all the lads know it to be so." The threat was not lost on Geoffrey. He reached for his purse and pulled out five silver shillings and a single gold coin, "Your story is inconsistent Titus but we shall leave it for now. Give your men a shilling each for their trouble and their silence. The pound is for you."

"Is that all I'm worth?" As soon as the words were uttered Titus regretted them. He had pushed his master too far. Geoffrey's face reddened. He jumped to his feet, knocking over his chair as he did so, but before he could release his fury there was a knock at the study door.

"What is it!" snapped Geoffrey. A servant entered warily and said, "Your cousin, Richard, is in the reception room sir. He wishes to see you." Geoffrey suddenly felt faint and had to grip his desk to stop himself falling.

"Er, very well" he stammered. "Tell him I'll be down shortly."

As soon as the servant departed Geoffrey hissed, "God's teeth he knows! What's to be done!"

Titus purred menacingly, "He is but one man and he's in your house. You have nothing to fear. Anyway, he cannot know; we left no witnesses."

"Then what's he doing here! He's not visited me in ten years."

"What is more natural than to seek help from your kin in times of need?"

Geoffrey was not convinced, "You do not know Richard like I do. He is too proud to beg."

Titus, irritated by his master's blatant cowardice said shortly, "Just go and see what he wants." Geoffrey walked reluctantly to the study door and slowly turned the large, bronze handle. "Get four of our strongest men within easy hailing distance and make sure you're one of them. I may need you."

"Cousin Richard, welcome!" said Geoffrey effusively. "I have just returned from Ipswich. I heard what happened not ten minutes ago. I am so sorry. I know we have not always seen eye to eye over the years but if there is anything I can do to help, you have only to ask. Blood is thicker than water eh."

"Thank you for your sympathy," answered Richard, trying hard to keep the contempt he felt for his plump, well fed cousin out of his voice, "though it is the murderers who will need sympathy when I have finished with them."

"Of course, of course," agreed Geoffrey shakily, still unsure of how much Richard knew. "Have you made any progress in catching the villains?"

"Not as yet but I will. You can wager your life on that." Geoffrey felt his knees weakening again and sat down in a padded, high backed, oak chair.

"Sit down Richard and tell me how I can be of service to you." Richard ignored the request and remained standing. His jade green eyes looked down at his fidgeting cousin but as yet they were untouched by suspicion. He said, "You recall that land of Sir John Satterley's I secured at the Beccles auction?"

"Certainly, you outbid me for it."

"Well I am no longer in a position to work it properly but I do not wish to forfeit it for failure to pay the rent."

"That is understandable," agreed Geoffrey, his nose for a deal beginning to suppress his fear. "Go on."

"I will need two years to get back on my feet again. Until then my land must be worked and the rent paid. Will you take it on for that time?"

"Perhaps," said Geoffrey. "But what will you be doing in the meantime?"

"Hiring out my labour for money to buy tools for farming and materials to build a new cottage. And hunting the murderers of course."

Geoffrey rubbed his chin appraisingly, "So we are talking about a sublet at no extra charge for two years. Well that seems fair enough but with one condition."

"Which is?"

"If you are not in a position to resume the tenancy two years from today, the headlease will revert to me in perpetuity."

Richard smiled sardonically, "What was that about blood being thicker than water?" Geoffrey, confident now that his evil-doing remained undiscovered, shrugged, "Business is business but to show willing I will pay for all the notary's costs in drawing up the agreement."

"Agreement? Will a handshake not suffice between cousins?"

"Don't be ridiculous Richard. My notary will call on you tomorrow morning. Where are you residing?"

"Dunwich Priory."

"Very well then, be ready to sign tomorrow," said Geoffrey. His ill temper of five minutes ago was quite forgotten, for eighty acres of prime Suffolk farmland had just fallen neatly into his hand. Even if Richard was able to resume the tenancy within the allotted time, Geoffrey would make sure that the fine detail of the agreement would prevent it reverting to his cousin.

Richard walked towards Brother Hugh who sat on the wagon outside Calveley Hall waiting to continue the journey to Halesworth. Geoffrey had surpassed himself in base greed but Richard had expected nothing less and, as he mounted up beside Hugh, he felt a great relief that the audience with his cousin was over.

"Come on Brother Hugh, flick the reins and take us away from this place."

"Your cousin refused to help?"

"He's helping himself first as usual, but I'm in no position to bargain. At least I shall retain my land."

"Then we have cause to celebrate," said Hugh. "By the time we reach the King's Head it will be past noon and Father Anselm has provided me with a few pence to purchase our wayside needs."

Richard glanced at his young companion and smiled, "You will appreciate Brother Hugh that I am hardly in the mood to celebrate anything just now, but I will gladly join you in some bread and cheese and a tankard of ale. Does the Franciscan Order approve of strong drink?"

"In moderation. Ale is at the top of my shopping list."

"But your vows?"

"Poverty, chastity and obedience. No-one said anything about abstinence!" laughed Hugh as he urged his pony into a smart trot."

The King's Head was well patronised. Late September was a popular time of year with farm workers, especially when the harvest had been good and money was plentiful. The harvest of 1414 had been a bumper crop and the inkeepers appeared to be reaping the benefit too judging from the numerous inebriated revellers that littered the road to the King's Head. Hugh tied up the pony outside the inn and walked with Richard towards the door, but before they had gone more than a few yards the door flew open and a drunkard staggered out followed closely by his woman, who was in an even worse state. Richard and Hugh stood gingerly to one side to allow the couple to pass, but Hugh's eyes widened and his mouth fell open as his companion suddenly stepped in front of the drunken pair and stopped them in their tracks.

The drunkard blinked and shouted aggressively, "Whashamatter!"

"Nothing," replied Richard mildly, "but I could not help noticing that brooch your wife is wearing."

"That hag's not my wife!"

Richard frowned, "She is not a hag and she is wearing a fine brooch." The woman gave Richard a gap toothed smile in response to his compliment.

"I gave it 'er," said the drunk proudly.

"But why if she's not your wife?"

"For a good rogering o'course."

"She commands a high price then," said Richard. "Your master must pay you well."

"Hah!" scoffed the drunk swaying backwards and forwards, "Old Calveley's as tight as a duck's arshehole."

Richard's throat tightened. He had to whisper the name, "Geoffrey Calveley?"

"Course, who elshe?"

Turning to the woman Richard enquired politely, "Would you consider selling your brooch to me?"

"Praps," said the hag.

"Two pounds?"

"Five, not a penny lesh."

"Three?"

"Done!"

As the drunken couple tottered back up the road to Holton, Richard stood outside the inn and stared fixedly at the round brooch he held in his hand. Inside the outer ring of green jade there was a representation in white calcite of a triangular shield. Etched into the shield were thin, elongated, garnet crystals which formed the red cross of Saint George. Hugh saw the distress in his companion's face and asked, "What is it Richard? Did you pay too much?"

"I would have paid far more if necessary," said Richard softly. "This is Ann's brooch."

"Really? Can you be certain?"

"It was my wedding gift to her. I had it made to my own design by a jeweller in Norwich."

"Then that drunken sot must be one of the murderers! Quick, let's go after him."

Richard put a restraining hand on Hugh's shoulder, "Not so fast young Hugh. Although I would happily poleaxe the bastard here and now, the time is not right. It appears that my dear cousin is the root cause of my family's destruction, so there can be no satisfaction in taking retribution on his minions without taking it on him too. My vengeance must be slow and thorough, a knife between the shoulder blades would be too merciful."

Hugh pointed an agitated finger up the Holton road, "But why let that rogue walk free?"

"His reprieve is only temporary. If I take action now it will serve to warn Geoffrey that I have discovered his guilt. He will then take precautions and make my task more difficult. As it is, he made sure he was in Ipswich when the murders took place but for now he does not know that I know, nor must he find out until I decide otherwise. This way the initiative lies with me."

Hugh shook his head in disgust, "Your own cousin! How could he do such a terrible thing?"

"I confess I too am surprised," agreed Richard bitterly. "And to think that less than an hour ago I offered to rent him the very land he determined to steal anyway. He must have been laughing at me all the time I was with him."

"So what do we do now?" Richard was pleased at the young Franciscan's eagerness to help and said, "We carry on to Halesworth and buy the provisions for the priory. We cannot allow your worthy bretheren to spend another evening without their ale."

★ ★ ★

V

Father Anselm rubbed his forefinger absentmindedly around the rim of his ale mug and watched Richard enjoying his first proper meal since the tragedy two days before. The change in young Calveley was remarkable now that he had a purpose in life again; few emotions drive a man harder than revenge. The old cleric quietly thanked God for the security of his own life, the discipline of his days and the structured regularity of his work. The homely plainsong from evening benediction wafted its way into the guesthouse where Anselm and Richard were just finishing supper together, but as he contemplated their differences, a voice from somewhere in the darker recesses of the Franciscan's mind asked if he had really lived life to the full if, by avoiding the depths of a secular existence, he might also have missed out on the heights. He quickly brushed such uncomfortable thoughts aside and said, "Well, you did not waste much time."

"It was sheer luck seeing Ann's brooch pinned on that woman at the King's Head," acknowledged Richard.

"Luck or the work of God," murmured Anselm contemplatively.

"Whichever, but even without the brooch I should have realised that Cousin Geoffrey would be the source of the evil that has come upon my family."

"Why so?"

"Because he hates to lose. I thwarted him at the auction. In hindsight it's obvious that he would not simply have left things unresolved to his satisfaction."

"But to murder your own cousin's family?"

Richard shrugged, "The kings of England and France have been doing exactly that for centuries. Why should yeomen and peasants be any different?"

"I had not thought of it that way," agreed Anselm, "but it still surprises me how your father and his brother could produce such different offspring as you and Geoffrey."

Richard took a long pull at his ale and asked, "Did you ever know Geoffrey's father?"

"No."

"I am told that he died in France in the same year that my mother and father were taken by the plague, but there is no record of his burial place. Robert Calveley was the elder brother and had better fortune in the wars. He captured a high ranking French knight and used the ransom money to buy what is now Calveley Hall. Geoffrey is, like me, an only child and was brought up by his mother after Robert died until she too was taken by the plague. That happened when he was twelve. Afterwards his steward, Titus Scrope, took over Geoffrey's education which probably explains a great deal."

"This Titus Scrope, is he a bad influence?"

"Certainly Father. Scrope is pure evil. His relationship with my cousin is based on mutual fear." Richard frowned and looked Anselm directly in the eyes, "When can I take my oath of revenge?"

"I will arrange it for tomorrow," sighed Anselm.

"Who will solemnise it?"

"Mary Hoccleve."

"A woman!"

"Yes, she is a Lollard. They have women priests."

Richard raised his eyebrows, "A Lollard! But did not Archbishop Arundel condemn all Lollards as heretics?"

"He did, but he was an intolerant man. Much depends on your point of view. It is true that some of their beliefs are heretical but there is also much good in what they preach. The established church fears the

Lollards because they criticise the wealth of the hierarchy and compare it with the poverty of the common people."

"You seem to sympathise with these Lollards."

"They do not threaten the great preaching orders. The Franciscans, Dominicans, Augustinians and Carmelites operate outside the established church structure. You see the Lollards say that all that is necessary for salvation is written in holy scripture. They have even translated the bible into English to make it directly accessible to the literate lay folk. The great church hierarchy of parish priest, bishop, archbishop, cardinal and even the pope is unnecessary and unwanted by the Lollards. They also point to the corruption that exists within the church, which cannot be denied, the selling of indulgences and so on. Not surprisingly therefore, they find much support amongst the poor people; even some of the poorer priests sympathise with them."

"So that is why they are persecuted."

"I believe so Richard. Mary Hoccleve will solemnise your oath because you, like a Lollard, have little hope of gaining justice through the courts. Your cousin is the Earl of Suffolk's man is he not?"

Richard nodded, "You are remarkably well informed on secular matters Father."

"Franciscans are not a closed order. We well know how things work in the secular world. You need a powerful supporter yourself, someone who can counter Suffolk's influence."

"I suspect you already have that person in mind."

"I do. Squire John Fastolf of Caistor Manor near Yarmouth. He is young Lord Mowbray's man and no lover of Suffolk. I was his confessor for some years."

"I have heard of John Fastolf. Was he not the old king's lieutenant in Aquitaine?"

"For a brief period. I will write a letter of introduction for you to take should you wish to offer him your services." Richard paused for thought. Pledging himself to another man was contrary to his instincts as a free yeoman, but upon reflection he realised that it was no more or less than the act of homage a duke gives his sovereign, or a baron his duke.

"Very well Father, I shall follow your advice but I have heard that John Fastolf is a hard man."

"Hard but fair. He has a strong sense of justice, especially where money is concerned. He pays all his creditors on time but he is implacable in collecting his own debts, no matter how small or whatever the cost. In his way he is very pious but he tends to picture God as the Great Accountant. Provided his good deeds outweigh his bad ones, Fastolf believes he will ultimately end up on the credit side of the celestial balance sheet. But if you serve him loyally he will reward you well."

"I shall endeavour to do so Father. Now about my oath........."

CHAPTER TWO

Mary Hoccleve lived in a small Lollard community on the Yarmouth Road near Frostenden, five miles south of Lowestoft. Father Anselm wrote another letter for Richard to take which would introduce him to the Lollard priest and explain the purpose of his visit; Lollards had learned to be suspicious of uninvited guests. As he watched his charge mount up outside the priory on the morning after the decision to seek service with John Fastolf, Anselm wondered if he would ever see Richard again.

"Cheer up Father," said Richard as he turned his palfrey's head northwards. "I shall be back soon." Anselm smiled through the drizzle that had set in during the night and handed Richard the leading rein of the pack pony which the priory had provided to carry spare clothes, provisions and the old fashioned armour once used by Richard's father in France.

"Do not worry about Joan," said the old priest. "We will take good care of her for as long as needs be."

"I know Father. You will deal with Cousin Geoffrey's notary when he comes today?"

"Of course."

"Then all that remains is to thank you once more and bid you farewell." Richard spurred his horse into a brisk trot and headed down the track towards Blythburgh where he would join the main road to Yarmouth.

"Don't forget to write!" called Anselm after him. He was answered by a cheery wave and, just as Richard reached the bend that would take him out of sight of Dunwich Priory, Anselm raised his hand in a blessing and offered up a prayer to Saint Christopher, the patron saint of travellers.

A cold easterly blew the drizzle in from the sea, and even before Richard had covered the two miles to Blythburgh, both palfrey and pack pony were spattered up to the girths in mud. He looked wistfully at the White Hart inn where men would be sitting by the warm, log fire topping up the ale in their stomachs from the night before though it was not yet ten o'clock. In fairness they needed to feel well disposed because today was Sunday and the Blythburgh curate, John Hidyngham, would have prepared another interminable, boring sermon for the edification of his long suffering parishioners at the eleven o'clock mass. The village harbour was cluttered with small cogs and fishing smacks waiting for the tide to take them downriver to the sea at Southwold, so Richard stopped to purchase some of the salted herrings which had made Blythburgh famous.

North of Blythburgh, Suffolk was still well forested and the tall oaks and elms provided some protection from the raw east wind as far as the little village of Frostenden. Following Anselm's instructions, Richard left the main road here and took a small track deep into the dark forest nervously looking all around. This was ideal terrain for the highway robbers who still infested the more remote parts of the countryside.

"Where be you going friend?" The voice that came from a clump of bushes beside the track sounded anything but friendly. Richard reined in and gripped the handle of his father's great sword which he always carried on journeys in unfamiliar territory.

"Who wants to know?" he replied truculently. Two tall men stepped onto the path in front of him and, hearing a noise behind, Richard turned to see two more standing behind his pack pony. He relaxed slightly for all four were well dressed in the simple, functional style of woodmen; vagabonds were usually ragged. Nonetheless he was clearly disadvantaged. One of the men in front stepped forward, "You are the stranger here. It is for you to speak first." There was no point in arguing so Richard replied in a more conciliatory tone, "I seek Mistress Mary Hoccleve."

"On what business?"

"Private business."

"If you have been sent by the magistrates to plague us then leave now while you may."

"And if you are Lollards you need have no fear of me. My name is Richard Calveley of Westhall. I have a letter for Mary Hoccleve from Father Anselm, Prior of the Dunwich Franciscans."

The tall woodman seemed satisfied and said, "The Franciscans are no enemies of ours. Follow me friend and I will take you to Mary." At a signal the other three melted back into the forest and Richard followed his long striding escort for another hundred paces or so until they reached a clearing which contained about fifteen small, well founded, timber dwellings.

It was immediately apparent to Richard that the Lollard community was well organised. Each house was enclosed by carefully tended gardens where vegetables grew in rows, chickens scratched and pecked the ground, and neatly ordered piles of seasoned firewood awaited the onset of winter. Manure was provided by swine that grunted happily in a compound placed to one side of the settlement, and the children playing between the houses were clean and well clad.

Richard's escort halted in front of a small, ivy fronted, single storey dwelling which was flanked by a well planned herb garden. He turned to Richard and pointed, "This be Mary's house friend. I will see if she will speak with you while you dismount and tether your beasts. Hand me the Franciscan's letter." Inwardly smiling at the Lollard's archaic rendering of English, Richard did as instructed while the woodman entered Mary's house without knocking; clearly Lollards felt no need for locks. Within a minute Richard was ushered into a simple, whitewashed reception room where he was greeted by a small, soberly dressed woman who stood beside a log fire. She was not at all what he had expected. Far from being a hard faced zealot, Mary Hoccleve was a young, open faced woman who combined an unusual blend of fair hair and dark brown eyes. The hair, which was full and straight, fell to her shoulders and was cut above the eyes in a low fringe rather than the shaven forehead style currently in favour with ladies of fashion. Her soft, educated voice was pleasant to the ear as she enquired demurely, "Is there something the matter Master Calveley?" Richard realised he was staring at her and said, "No, nothing at all. Please call me Richard." She glanced at the woodman who hovered protectively near her, "That will be all John. Stay nearby if you please. I will call you if I need you. When they were alone, Mary touched the letter on the table beside her, "I see from Anselm's letter that you hope to solemnise an oath of revenge which he will not accept."

"That is true."

"Then why should I?" The question had a touch of aggression which caught Richard by surprise.

"I do not know except Father Anselm thought you might." Mary seemed uncertain about what she should do so Richard tried to balance the scales in his favour by adding, "My wife and children were cruelly murdered. There is nothing left for me to live for but revenge."

"Anselm says as much in his letter, but why must there be an oath?"

"Because it is my way of telling Ann and the boys that I love them."

Mary nodded, "Then I agree, but I do not think it is really necessary and nor will you when you understand the meaning of a Lollard oath. It is a terrible thing and utterly binding."

"That is just what I want," said Richard eagerly, "but ..." he hesitated.

"What is it?" asked Mary.

"Are you really a priest?"

Mary smiled. Her generous mouth revealed regular white teeth. "Not in the sense you understand the word Richard. I have not been ordained. I am a pastor, a preacher. We do not acknowledge the authority or the need of a parasitic clergy."

"Then how is it that Father Anselm seems to hold you in some esteem?"

"The friars lead the intellectual argument against us but ironically they also follow the simple life we aspire to. Both Lollards and friars despise the worldly wealth and corruption of the episcopate. We and the friars may not agree, but that does not mean we lack respect for each other."

"I see, at least I think I do," said Richard. "Let me see the Lollard oath."

"Do you read?"

"Yes."

"Then sit down by the fire and dry your surcoat while I bring the oath to you." Mary walked to a chest which occupied a corner of the room behind the table. She opened the lid and took out a small, yellowed scroll of parchment, which was worn at the edges, and handed it to Richard saying, "Before we begin, look at the penalties you must accept should you break the oath." He unrolled the scroll and started to read. At first he was unconcerned. There were the usual strictures for oath breaking; praying that his tongue would be torn from his mouth, his body consumed by fire and his soul condemned to everlasting torment but suddenly he stopped, aghast at what came next.

"I cannot swear to that!" he gasped.

"To what in particular," asked Mary mildly.

"This part here," said Richard, anxiously pointing to the last few lines on the scroll. "The oath requires me to pray for the plague to take me and my offspring should I break it. How can I wish the Black Death on my little daughter!"

"Are you not serious about the oath?"

"Of course I am."

"Then it should not trouble you."

"I will not do it. It would not be right."

Mary smiled again, satisfied that she had made her point. "As I said before, the oath is not necessary. Be content with your own determination for revenge. Ann would have been satisfied with that."

"How can you know?"

"Because I knew your wife." Richard's eyes widened in surprise as Mary continued, "Ann Calveley was one of many thinking women who identified with our cause."

"But she attended church every Sunday. Why did she not tell me she was a Lollard?"

"She was not a Lollard. She would not become one out of respect for you."

"I would not have minded."

Mary raised her eyebrows, "Really? Perhaps you would not mind now, but Ann must have judged that you would have until three days ago. One of the central Lollard beliefs is complete equality between men and women. Could you have coped with that?"

Richard looked into the fire and replied quietly, "Ann was a good judge of character. I would not argue with her view."

Mary took the parchment and rolled it up again. "You loved her very much."

Richard felt his throat tighten and his eyes moisten. He whispered hoarsely, "I adored her. She was the finest wife a man could wish for." He surreptitiously brushed a tear away from his eye and got to his feet, "Thank you for your time Mary Hoccleve. I will be on my way now."

"It is past noon. Why not share a meal with us before you leave and meet the rest of our little community? Your coat could do with more time to dry out."

"Well, I am in a hurry but …." Richard's hesitation seemed to amuse Mary, "I promise not to try and convert you," she said with mock solemnity.

Richard, entering into the spirit of the invitation, answered, "Then I will take a chance."

"Good, our fare is but simple. I hope it will suffice."

Remembering his Blythburgh Herrings Richard said, "Then may I make a contribution?"

* * *

II

The meal in the high vaulted moot building was a revelation to Richard, not so much for the universal popularity of his herrings, but for the attitude displayed by the whole community to Mary Hoccleve. Including children there were about forty Lollards, all of whom seemed to hold Mary in near veneration. Her opinion was sought on all matters, even the most trivial in a way that might usually have been expected of a village elder, yet Richard estimated Mary's age at no more than twenty five. In part this was because she was educated to a higher standard than her companions but there was something else, less easily defined, that seemed to give her the natural air of authority with which a few fortunate people are born.

The meal was followed by a reading by Mary from the bible in English which told the story of the prodigal son. The audience was spellbound, and when Mary concluded by saying, "These are the actual words of Our Lord Jesus Christ, the very words he spoke to his apostles," even Richard felt a sense of awe, for until that moment he had only heard clerical interpretations of the biblical classics. To hear the words as Jesus spoke them seemed to put him in direct contact with his God in a way that had been unimaginable before. Fourteen hundred years of separation from the Christ suddenly closed. He would not forget this day.

After the reading, the congregation dispersed to resume its duties and Mary approached Richard accompanied by the man who had first accosted him in the forest.

She said, "John Fletcher will accompany you part of the way to the Yarmouth Road. It is wise to be cautious."

"Thank you," replied Richard.

"And where do you go now?" she asked.

"To offer my services to Squire John Fastolf of Caistor Manor. It is near Yarmouth."

"I know Caistor and Squire John," said Mary reflectively. "Do you hope to use his help to achieve your vengeance?"

"Indirectly, yes."

"Richard, you must handle him with care. He is honest and true by his own standards but do not expect too much of him or you might be disappointed."

"I will heed your warning Mary, and if there is ever anything I can do for you or your community you have only to ask."

Mary smiled, "The time may come when I have to hold you to that. Farewell Richard Calveley."

Mary's parting words disturbed Richard, and as he led his horses through the Frostenden forest he asked John who was walking by his side, "What did Mary mean about holding me to my word? Is she expecting trouble?" John Fletcher had warmed to Richard since his acceptance by Mary and was happy to talk.

"We of the Lollard persuasion have long been under pressure from the church authorities, but since Lord Cobham's abortive uprising in January we have felt the full rigour of secular persecution."

"But everyone knows Cobham was only representing himself. The espousal of the Lollard cause was a matter of convenience to give his treason moral justification."

"Aye Richard," sighed John, "that be true, but it also gave our enemies the means to use the criminal law to persecute us. To many good, but easily led people, Lollardy and treason mean the same thing. That be why we are forced to live in our own isolated communities; it be less out of choice than protection. My own brother, a Richard like yourself, was driven out of Beccles earlier this year. His only crime was to preach the word of the good book in the language the people of this country do ken."

"That might have been a little provocative. Sometimes fervour must give place to common sense."

John did not seem to hear Richard's mild criticism and continued, "And Mary herself, there be a case in point. She comes from a well respected family in London. Her father held high office in government and should have known better, but when he found her in possession of an English bible he demanded she recant her Lollard heresies or depart from his household."

Richard said, "I cannot imagine Mary bowing to that sort of pressure."

"Indeed not," agreed John, "but Thomas Hoccleve's loss was our gain, praise be to the Lord."

By the time Richard bade farewell to John it was past two o'clock and, not wanting to arrive at Squire John's manor too late in the day, he dug his heels into his palfrey and followed the Yarmouth Road at a smart trot. The drizzle had lifted and the cloud had broken up enough to permit an occasional glimpse of the sun. It had been a strange morning. Richard's oath remained unsworn but he no longer minded because Mary had shown it to be unnecessary; his own determination would be sufficient to see his retribution through. He would have liked to have stayed longer at Frostenden speaking with Mary about Ann, for there is sometimes comfort to be drawn from talking about one's bereavement and, as he reflected upon this, he realised that for the first time since the murders he had been able to put his anger to the back of his mind while he listened to Mary reading the bible. He felt a natural empathy towards the Lollards and their ideas, but he was sure he could never become one himself. They were too worthy for his taste and he sensed that given a position of power, they could be just as intolerant as their episcopal persecutors.

The westering sun promised a dramatic twilight as Richard approached Caistor Manor. His long shadow preceded him across the drawbridge, which linked the gravelled access road to the entrance cut into the flint curtain wall, and although he could hear the barking of large dogs nearby, there was no sentinel on duty to challenge visitors at the gate; a confident or a careless man this Squire John. He dismounted in the courtyard, and while he was tethering his palfrey and pack pony to a post by the horse trough, a servant came out of the large, two storey manor house. He bowed stiffly rather than respectfully and asked, "Are you here as a supplicant or by appointment?"

"Neither," answered Richard. "My name is Richard Calveley. I wish to see Squire John on a matter of mutual interest." The servant, who would never see sixty again, raised a contemptuous eyebrow and returned to the house. Richard followed without waiting to be asked and entered the hallway which alone was almost as big as his house in Westhall had been. A finely woven tapestry hung from one of the walls, but other than that the furnishings were simple. Richard leaned against a low rectangular table where a bowl of dried lavender provided a delicious fragrance which greeted the visitor with a flush of summer.

The servant opened the large, oak door at the far end of the hall and stood half in and half out as he addressed his master on the other side.

"Excuse me sir. A stranger has just arrived, neither a supplicant nor by appointment so he says, who wishes to speak with you."

A deep, strong voice replied, "Does this stranger have a name?"

"Richard Cavley or Clavery I think he said."

"Tell him to come back after making an appointment. It's too late for visitors today." Before the delighted servant could pull the heavy door closed, Richard wedged his foot in the gap and gently eased the old man to one side. Then pushing the door open again he stepped into the great hall and said, "Your servant has cloth ears. I am Richard Calveley of Westhall and I have ridden twenty miles this day to see you."

The great hall was an impressive room, the living quarters of a man of power and influence. Here there was no upper floor, the room extended upwards into a tall, vaulted roof whose height was necessary to absorb the smoke from the fire which burned in a grate in a recess in one of the side walls. Daylight entered through six lead lined windows, and the whitewashed flint walls sprouted numerous sockets for candles and braziers to provide illumination at night. Close to the fire were two high backed chairs in which Fastolf and his wife were sitting. The squire, unimpressed by Richard's startling entrance, said quietly, "What nerve you have sir to burst in upon us without invitation."

"For that I crave your forgiveness," replied Richard, "but after my long journey I did not wish to be sent away for ignorance of my identity." Fastolf's broad, weathered face remained unmoved and Richard began to fear his impatience would count against him. The brown haired squire was in his late thirties, about ten years older than Richard, and sported a short beard of the type that had been fashionable at the turn of the century. His wife was of a similar age with eyes of deepest brown. The laughter lines around them hinted at a witty and intelligent mind. Fastolf reflected for a moment and said, "Calveley, I seem to have heard of the name."

"My father, John, was a sergeant in the French wars," explained Richard. "He and his brother Robert fought in the company of a distant kinsman from Cheshire, Sir Hugh Calveley."

"Ah, that's where I have heard it. William, I will see Master Calveley after all. You may leave us." The old servant exhaled a disapproving sigh and closed the door. Richard took out the envelope from his tunic and handed it to Fastolf.

"This letter is from Father Anselm at Dunwich Priory. It explains why I am here." The squire opened the letter, and while he read it his wife spoke for the first time, "As my husband seems determined to ignore me, it appears I shall have to introduce myself. I am Millicent Fastolf, previously Millicent Tiptoft."

Her husband grunted, "Sorry dear," and resumed reading Anselm's letter. Richard bowed and Millicent pointed to a stool near the door, "Bring that over here and sit down beside us. Perhaps you will take a little wine while we wait for my husband?"

"That would be most welcome." Millicent picked up the green bottle on the small table beside her and poured some wine into one of the goblets that were stacked up next to the fire. She poured herself a goblet too and said, "Best clairet from Aquitaine. It brings out the flavour if the goblet is warmed slightly."

Richard's wine was half drunk by the time Fastolf had finished reading Anselm's long letter. He handed the letter to Millicent, who could also read, and turned his bright blue eyes on Richard, "It appears you have suffered considerable misfortune, but I do not see how I can be of help to you. Surely your best course is to gather what evidence you can and take your cousin to court. If you win he will be hanged along with his accomplices."

"I do not have the money for that Squire John, nor have I sufficient evidence at present for a jury to convict. Knowing is not the same as proving." Fastolf poured himself some clairet, looked into the fire and frowned as if coming to a major decision, "I could lend you the money if you wish to try your luck in court."

"That would be a waste of time," said Richard, "though I thank you for your generosity." Fastolf could not disguise the relief that swept across his face as Richard continued, "My cousin is Suffolk's man. The jury would in any case be filled with his creatures."

Fastolf's attitude suddenly changed, "Suffolk! That upstart! Anslem did not say that in his letter. De la Pole, Earl of Suffolk, what a nonsense! Do you know his grandfather was a Hull fish merchant! My dogs have got more noble blood than he has. This puts a different light on things."

"You do not approve of the Earl of Suffolk," said Richard mildly.

"Hah! Do you approve of the plague? It is men like that who lost us our lands in France which young King Henry has sworn to recover. De la Pole! I would sooner give the ermine to old William!" As if regretting his outburst, Fastolf quickly became business like again. "But what exactly is the nature of the help you need and what is in it for me Master Calveley?"

Richard felt a surge of excitement. If he put his case well now, there was every chance he might secure the patronage of one of the most powerful men in Norfolk. He spoke slowly, and he hoped succinctly. "Squire John, the driving force in my life is revenge but I understand that on my own the scales are too heavily weighted against me. Take me as your man. I am literate, I can speak French and know how to work hard. In due course I shall assuredly gather enough evidence to see my cousin hanged provided the jury is not fixed against me. You are a magistrate. You will see the trial is fair."

Fastolf took a drink from his goblet and said, "War is coming. I am looking for soldiers not legal battles. Can you fight?"

"War is in my family's blood though my father hoped I would lead a different sort of life. But he died young and as soon as my education at Dunwich Priory was over, I joined a small company of Suffolk yeomen who were due to march north to fight the Scots with Harry Hotspur's army."

The squire seemed impressed. He poured himself another drink and asked, "Were you at Homildon Hill?"

"Yes. It was hard fight but we eventually put the Scots to flight."

"How old were you?"

"Sixteen."

"Were you an archer?"

"No, though I can draw the longbow as any true Englishman should. I fought as a hobelar."

Fastolf was delighted. He slapped his thigh and exclaimed, "A hobelar! Excellent! I have always thought we should make more use of light horsemen."

"That's because they cost you less than a man at arms dear," said Millicent who had now finished reading Anselm's letter. Her husband glared at her, "Well there is that of course but in my opinion, if I am allowed to have one, the days of heavily armoured mounted men at arms are strictly numbered."

"Is that for military or financial reasons?" chided Millicent sweetly.

"Wars cannot be fought without money," answered Fastolf pompously. "I cannot fight for the King of England if I am unable to pay my soldiers."

"I thought you fought for ransom money dear." Richard could not stop himself smiling as he witnessed Fastolf's discomfiture. The squire, who was no match for his wife in debate, ended the matter by muttering, "God preserve us from intelligent women."

Richard raised his goblet to Millicent and said, "You will excuse me from sharing those sentiments Squire John."

"I suppose so," acknowledged Fastolf, "but as we happen to be on the subject of money, I cannot afford to pay you anything more than your living expenses."

The humour left Millicent's eyes and a steely edge hardened her voice, "John that is hardly fair. You pay your humblest archer six pence a day."

"Monetary payment is unnecessary," interrupted Richard. "I have a proposal which will actually pay your husband to employ me." The frown left Fastolf's brow, "Go on Master Calveley, you have my full attention."

"I hold the lease for eighty acres of prime farmland at Westhall but I cannot farm it myself now. My cousin was going to farm it for me until I found out about his part in my misfortunes. Why not put some of your retainers to work on it, and after the costs have been met we can split the profits equally until I can afford to resume occupation?"

Fastolf sighed, "The principle sounds well enough but I am not sure about splitting the profits." He saw Millicent glowering at him out of the corner of his eye and quickly added, "but provided all my costs are met including administration costs, which will be assessed by my own steward, I am prepared to accept your offer." He stood up. "Here is my hand on it."

"You will not require legal documentation?" asked Richard.

"Pay lawyers more money? What for? A handshake is my bond and yours also I trust." Richard was surprised to find Fastolf almost as tall as himself and his vice like hand had the strength of a man accustomed to hard physical toil.

"We must think of a title for you," said Fastolf as both men resumed their seats, "for I shall want you to represent me on occasion. I already have a steward who takes care of the accounts and general administration, so your role will be more as a deputy or an assistant."

"How about lieutenant?" suggested Millicent. "Was that not your title John when you deputised for the old king in Aquitaine two years ago?"

"Indeed it was. Lieutenant of Caistor Manor; it has a certain ring to it. Richard, I shall arrange your quarters after dinner. Millicent my dear, would you tell William to set another place for our new lieutenant?"

Richard was delighted. His course for revenge upon his cousin was firmly set though the day of judgement was still some way away. First a war must be fought which would decide the future of the kings of England and France.

* * *

III

At the very moment Richard agreed terms with John Fastolf, twenty five miles away at Calveley Hall, Geoffrey was in conference with his steward. The two men were sitting in the study where so recently Geoffrey had been making plans for the acquisition of his cousin's landholding.

"You are reading too much into it," said Titus. "Richard just changed his mind. Perhaps he got better terms from someone else."

Geoffrey shook his head, "How could he in so short a time? My notary returned from Dunwich Priory with no other explanation than Richard had left leaving no instructions about signing a document. I think Richard might have found out."

"About what?"

"Your bit of business with his wife."

"Impossible," said Titus. "There were no witnesses. I made doubly sure of it."

"What about your men Titus? People talk."

"Not my men," replied the steward silkily. "They would not wish to incur my displeasure." Geoffrey looked at his sinister, cadaverous companion and agreed, "Maybe not, but I still think we should find out where my cousin has gone. Tomorrow send your men to Dunwich and start asking questions."

"Now that would arouse suspicion."

Geoffrey, smarting at this direct challenge to his instructions, said, "So what would you suggest my clever steward?"

"Wait. Sooner or later someone will occupy Richard's land. As sure as I am sitting here, that someone will lead us to the whereabouts of your cousin. All that is required is a little patience."

CHAPTER THREE

The Lieutenant of Caistor Manor soon found his duties more than enough to keep him busy. In addition to his land in Norfolk, Fastolf also owned large estates in Yorkshire and Wiltshire through his marriage to Millicent, and during the winter months Richard found himself riding hundreds of miles on rain soaked tracks between the Fastolf properties searching out suitable recruits for the war.

"Ten archers from each of the counties," Fastolf had said, "and only volunteers. I want no pressed men at my back when we face the French."

In the event Richard had no difficulty in securing the volunteers he needed; he could have presented many times more than the thirty archers required by Fastolf's liege terms had the squire been prepared to pay for them, because the coming war was popular in England. Most Englishmen felt that the French should be honoured to have an English king instead of ungratefully rejecting Henry V's claim to their throne. Had not Crecy, Poitiers and a host of other engagements proven that one Englishman was at least as good as four Frenchmen?

The spring of 1415 was warm and dry which enabled the estate labourers to sow promptly for an early harvest and thus extend the campaigning season. No civilized country went to war until the harvest was safely gathered in. Richard spent this time arranging the supplies to support his master's little army and getting to know the staff and retainers of the Caistor household, not the least of which were Fastolf's two huge, fawn mastiffs, Hector and Ajax. They were the reason for there being no cause to draw up the manor bridge at night.

But always close to the forefront of Richard's mind was Cousin Geoffrey. As the months passed, Richard found that the easiest way to cope without Ann and the boys was to contemplate his revenge. Anger helped to drive out the pain, which would always return uninvited during his brief moments of relaxation, but hatred was no real substitute for love and Richard was sure he would never be able to love again. His regret was accentuated when he saw how the crusty Fastolf adored Millicent, the one person in the world to whom he refused nothing. Her attitude towards him was less easy to gauge but the squire's love seemed to be returned in full measure, though with the hint of a maternal streak.

At last the seventh day of July arrived, the day appointed for the assembly of the Fastolf forces. Richard, dressed in his father's armour, looked out of the window of his upstairs room down on to the manor courtyard where thirty archers and their horses milled around waiting for his appearance. The old fashioned armour, more chain mail than plate, weighed heavily round Richard's shoulders, but there was plenty of room inside, for his father had also been a big man. He picked up the red and blue plumed basinet, which still bore a small indentation near the crown where John Calveley had let a French mace through his guard during a skirmish near Tours, and looked inside it. There was something particularly personal about a helmet and as he rubbed his forefinger along the soft brown leather which formed the padded lining, Richard felt especially close to his father. This was the lining John had worn thin during years of campaigning. His face, his head, his neck had rubbed against and gradually refashioned the leather to the unique, individual shape that most suited. Now the son was about to follow the father.

Richard had never worn this armour to war, a padded jerkin and open helmet had sufficed for the company of hobelars he had joined to fight the Scots, yet although his father had wanted him to follow a peaceful life, Richard was certain that John would have been proud of him this day. He could hardly remember the tall, long limbed man who had bounced him on his knee, but there were still occasions when Richard felt strangely near him, almost as if his spirit was standing close by. Richard looked round, half hoping to see him, and whispered, "I will not let you down."

A warm, kindly voice in his mind answered, "Fear not my son for I shall always be near you." Richard put the helmet under his arm and strode out into the morning sun to parade his men. He felt invincible.

"An excellent body of men," said Fastolf to his lieutenant as they walked between the ranks of archers. "You have chosen well Richard. They must all be over five and a half feet tall."

"Thank you Squire John, I am glad they're on our side. You already know Thomas Riches your Norfolk sergeant." A stocky, square jawed marshman nodded as they passed. "But these two men at the end of the line may be unknown to you. The bearded, one eyed man is Henry Hawkswood, your Wiltshire sergeant, and the tall, fair haired man beside him is John Thorpe, sergeant of the Yorkshire archers."

Fastolf stopped in front of Henry Hawkswood and asked, "How can you shoot straight with only one eye?"

The sergeant unslung his bow and replied in a soft, west country burr, "See that small pine tree." He pointed through the courtyard gateway to a tree with a trunk the width of a man which was at least a hundred paces away. Then taking a battle arrow from his quiver, he drew it the full cloth yard length, pushing the bow away from his body in true English style rather than pulling the string to the ear like other nations, and let fly. The arrow buried itself six inches into the pine tree.

"Bravo!" laughed Fastolf. "A perfect answer by God!"

John Thorpe, the Yorkshire sergeant said, "Aye Squire John, but would you like to see what a Yorkshireman can do?"

"No need. You will all be excellent marksmen I'll warrant. Save your arrows for the French." The Yorkshireman scowled at his Wiltshire counterpart; there was already rivalry between the three counties which was all to the good provided it was properly controlled. Richard wondered fleetingly if he had made a mistake choosing Thorpe. He instinctively disliked Thorpe but logic dictated his selection based on the Yorkshireman's obvious powers of leadership. Events were to prove that Richard's instinct was more reliable than his logic.

The parade was dismissed and Richard strolled around the kitchen garden with Fastolf to receive his final instructions. Now that the campaign was about to start, the squire seemed to have put his constant financial concerns to the back of his mind, temporarily at least, and spoke with relish about the war.

"It is high time we reminded the French who is master. Young King Harry might only be twenty six, but he is experienced in war and will assuredly lead us to victory."

Richard smiled, "And ransom money."

"Aye and that too," agreed Fastolf, looking over his shoulder in case Millicent was in earshot, "but we must also consider the men's spiritual welfare. Father Anselm has agreed to provide us with our own priest, so I want you to march our archers down the coast road past Dunwich to collect him. I will take the men at arms along the direct route to Framlingham castle where we are due to meet My Lord Mowbray's division in two days' time. From there we march to Southampton where King Harry has decreed the entire army should assemble before we set sail for France."

"Then I will bid you farewell," said Richard "until we meet at Framlingham."

★ ★ ★

II

Everything seemed to bode well as Richard cantered at the head of his mounted archers under the warm July sun. As they passed through the villages, which clustered round the parish churches on the road south, they were greeted with cheers from the men and coy waves from the women, and when they chose to stop in order to rest the horses, food and ale was brought out to help them on their way. Such treatment was hardly surprising, for Richard's men looked the very essence of brave warriors on the trail of glory. The king had ordered that all those not entitled to wear a coat of arms should instead wear a white surcoat bearing the red cross of Saint George front and back to make identification easier. In addition Fastolf had belied his parsimonious reputation by equipping his archers in brigandine jackets, expensive sallet helmets which protected the neck as well as the head, and smart red hose from his Wiltshire estate at Castle Combe. The men's uniform appearance augmented their martial image in Richard's eyes. He was proud to be leading them.

The fresh, well fed palfreys that Fastolf had provided covered the ground quickly, and noon was still an hour away when they entered the sandy heathland south of Lowestoft. Although the gorse had finished blooming, the open, green countryside was spotted pink with campion, and along the forest fringes purple and while foxgloves grew tall and stately in the mottled shadow of the woodland eaves. But the trouble free part of the journey ended when the little company entered Frostenden village.

Richard had intended to pass straight through Frostenden but a commotion on the village green made him change his mind. He held up his arm to call a halt and spoke to John Thorpe who was riding beside him.

"John, I do not like the look of that group of men on the green. Ride over and see what's happening." A few minutes later, the Yorkshireman came back grinning from ear to ear.

"It's all right; they're just having a bit of fun with a Lollard. No harm done though, just a few cuts and bruises and a broken arm I think." Richard loosened his huge sword. He knew he ought not to interfere but he could not help himself. He ordered his company to remain mounted while he trotted across to the men on the green.

"What goes on here!" he bellowed. The men, who were mostly farm labourers and unemployed marshmen, were kicking and punching a prostrate figure which lay face down on the grass. They stopped in response to Richard's stentorian command and one of them, a marshman clearly the worse for drink, answered truculently, "It's only a preaching

Lollard. I already told your henchman to mind his own business, so you can mind yours too." The man on the ground groaned and rolled over. Richard's temper began to fray as he recognised beneath the bruised, swollen face, John Fletcher.

"You will disperse at once and leave this man with me," said Richard menacingly.

"By my holy arse!" jeered the marshman to his companions, "Saint George here thinks he can see us all off, all twenty of us!" Richard did not argue. Instead he drew his sword and struck his antagonist on the head with the pommel. The marshman hit the ground heavily and lay still, barely conscious. All of a sudden the mob parted in front of Richard as if cloven in two by an invisible axe. He gesticulated at them angrily with his sword, "Get back to your homes while my patience still holds or by God it will be the worse for all of you!"

Someone muttered, "It was only a Lollard. Everyone knows they're fair game." But whoever it was that spoke had not the courage to stand his ground.

As soon as the mob was a safe distance away, Richard dismounted and knelt beside the stricken Lollard. He poured some cold water over Fletcher's bruised face and wiped away the blood. "John, John, can you hear me? It is Richard Calveley of Westhall."

The Lollard could only speak in a whisper, "I thank the good Lord for sending you this way Richard. He has not deserted his chosen folk."

"Squire John Fastolf sent me this way, not the good Lord, but that does not matter. We must get you back to your companions."

Fletcher's faith was remarkable. "The Lord works through us all Richard. We are but his instruments. It was he who sent you."

"This is not the time to argue philosophy. Can you mount my horse?"

As soon as Fletcher struggled shakily to his feet it was obvious to Richard that his left arm had been broken at the elbow. Tearing off a strip from his new, white surcoat, Richard made a sling to support the injured arm though without the attention of a skilled physician it would soon reset incorrectly. With some difficulty he helped the large Lollard into the saddle and asked, "Where is the nearest doctor?"

Fletcher looked down at Richard and smiled through broken, bloodied teeth, "We need look no further than Mary. She has the knowledge. Will you take me to her friend?"

Richard led Fletcher back to the company of archers and called the three sergeants to him. "I will take one of the spare palfreys and return this man to his community. You take the company to Dunwich Priory and wait there until I rejoin you."

"How long will you be?" asked Henry Hawkswood, the one eyed sergeant from Wiltshire.

"Less than three hours behind you," answered Richard.

John Thorpe shook his head and said, "You did wrong there Master Calveley. Lollards are traitors and heretics; everyone knows it." Richard had already been irritated by the Yorkshireman's blunt manner and snapped back, "You are under my command Sergeant Thorpe. Do as you are told and keep your opinions to yourself." Thorpe said no more but a glance from his bright blue eyes told Richard that the man from God's own county was unafraid as he spurred his horse back to his men.

Henry Hawkswood whispered, "Watch him Master Calveley. He is no friend of yours."

"Should I have let those louts murder the Lollard?"

"Of course not," replied Hawkswood, "Every man is entitled to a trial whatever he has done."

For the first time Thomas Riches, the dark Norfolk sergeant spoke, "Not all Lollards are traitors."

When Richard, leading the injured John Fletcher, reached the Lollard settlement, Mary Hoccleve herself came out to greet them. Richard had forgotten how pretty she was. Perhaps that was because he had been in no state to appreciate such things when he had last seen her.

"I warned John not to go out preaching today," she said. "There is always trouble when the marshmen are in Frostenden."

"But the Lord sent a deliverer," said an unbowed John Fletcher as he was helped from the saddle.

Mary shrugged her shoulders, "Sometimes John you expect too much from the Lord."

John was taken into his house to have his wounds washed before his arm was reset, a painful operation which could entail breaking more bones to do it properly. While he was being made ready for the treatment, Mary and Richard were left briefly alone at the entrance to the Lollard settlement.

Richard asked, "Are you sure you do not need medical help?"

"I shall be all right," replied Mary. "John Fletcher's is not the first broken bone I have tended." She touched Richard's arm, her large, brown eyes looking up at him, and said, "You know you have put yourself at risk because of us."

"The ignorant have been encouraged to persecute you by those who should know better."

"Yes, but you have publicly sided with people who are virtually outlaws. Your enemies could exploit that." Richard thought of his scheming cousin and congratulated himself for playing a waiting game. If Geoffrey knew Richard had found out about his evil deeds, a well timed accusation of Lollardy could easily put him beyond Richard's vengeance.

"I am in your debt for saving John," continued Mary, "but even so I would try to persuade you to abandon fighting your fellow Christians."

"You mean the French?"

"Yes."

"To me Mary, the French are England's enemies. I am English first and Christian second."

"And a mere woman can have no say in the matter?" The gentle sarcasm was not lost on Richard. He said softly, "You are no mere woman Mary Hoccleve." For the first time she saw a tall, smiling warrior not through the eyes of a preacher but through those of a woman. Richard did indeed look remarkably handsome in his armour and white surcoat with the red cross emblazoned upon it, a re-incarnation of a crusading Knight Templar of old. But the Templars were warrior monks; there was nothing monk like about Richard Calveley. Richard saw her distraction but did not understand the reason.

"I am sorry if my profession offends you Mary but had the good Lord, as John Fletcher calls him, protected my family from evil men I would not now be standing before you ready for war. A farmer I was and a farmer I would have stayed." The mention of Richard's family helped Mary to dismiss her superficial womanly thoughts. Her vocation was clear and she was immediately ashamed of her moment of earthly weakness.

"I am not offended Richard, just saddened. Now I must go and see to poor John's arm. May God preserve you wherever the war takes you." Richard watched her until she entered John's house, mounted his palfrey and said under his breath, "Aye, and you too Mary. I have a feeling that you will be in greater need of protection than I."

John Fletcher sang praises to the Lord, hardly faltering as Mary reset his arm and bandaged his cuts; such fervour was unusual even amongst the Lollards. At the end of the operation one of the Lollard wives began clearing away the bloodied rags. Mary said, "Leave the sling." The other woman looked at it and answered, "But Mary, it is stained past redemption."

"Even so we cannot afford to throw anything away."

"But there are better pieces of rag we can save than this." For the first and only time, Mary Hoccleve was heard to be brusque with one of her flock, "Kindly stop arguing and do as I say mistress."

Within three hours Mary had washed and scrubbed all traces of John's blood from the white cloth which was now neatly folded and stowed away in her private room. A small patch of red abutting the torn edge marked the base of a Saint George's cross. The rest was on the surcoat being carried to war by Richard Calveley.

★ ★ ★

III

Richard was within half a mile of Dunwich when a mounted friar came jogging unsteadily towards him. It was Brother Hugh. The Franciscan tried to wave but quickly grabbed his pony again as he almost slid from the saddle. He called out, "Richard! Richard! I have good news." The two men drew rein side by side, Richard grabbing the Franciscan's shoulder just before he toppled over his pony's head.

"I shall have to teach you how to ride Brother Hugh."

"Father Hugh now. I was ordained last month."

Richard laughed, "Congratulations! I had my doubts about your vocation but I am glad you proved me wrong."

"Yes, but that is not my news. Father Anselm has selected me to be the confessor of Squire John's company. I shall be accompanying you to France."

"Then I really must teach you to ride and soon. In your present state you would be lucky to reach Blythburgh, never mind Paris." The Franciscan carefully turned his pony's head towards Dunwich and walked his mount alongside Richard's.

"Richard, it is fortunate that I can speak to you before your arrival at the priory. A certain Master Scrope has been asking questions about you." The mention of Scrope's name brought back the pain and anger which was never far from the front of Richard's mind. He growled, "What sort of questions?"

"Just after you left us last year he arrived at the priory to find out why your cousin's notary was sent away with the land transfer document still unsigned. Father Anselm told him that you had simply changed your mind and we thought no more about it. But recently we found out that Scrope had been talking to the tenants Squire John put on your land, so we can now assume your whereabouts is known to your cousin."

"I do not see that it matters very much."

"Perhaps not," agreed Hugh, "but such interest is unlikely to benefit you. Under the circumstances Father Anselm decided that Joan's identity should remain a secret. So far as the outside world is concerned she is just an orphan."

"She is well?" asked Richard.

"Certainly. She is already walking and a great favourite at the priory. We will miss her when she goes."

"When we have beaten the French I shall return for her. Next month will be her first birthday. I will leave some money for a present. Father Anselm will know..."

Richard was halted in mid sentence as Hugh began to slide off his pony again. He grabbed the cleric's hood and hauled him back into the saddle.

"And now for your first riding lesson Father Hugh. Leave the pony's mane alone and try holding the reins instead."

★ ★ ★

IV

The shell keep of Framlingham castle stood tall and proud as Richard's company approached at a leisurely pace; the pace had to be steady to accommodate Father Hugh who was trying to keep as much weight as possible off his sore buttocks. The afternoon sun shone brightly on the royal standard which flapped languidly atop the battlements. The castle had once been the ancestral home of the Mowbray family as dukes of Norfolk until it was forfeited to the crown when Thomas Mowbray was beheaded eleven years before for plotting treason against the old king. Thomas' younger brother John now headed the family, and although only seventeen, he had already found favour with King Harry who had allowed him to retain one of the family's traditional titles; Earl Marshal of England. Fastolf had told Richard that it could only be a matter of time before John Mowbray resumed his full title and the political influence that was his by right.

The fields outside the castle were a sea of multi-coloured standards and tents, amongst which more than five hundred archers and men at arms were gathered in preparation for the march south. Richard spoke to one of the well dressed clerks, who were stationed on all access routes to the castle, to give directions to the new arrivals and limit the confusion that usually attended a gathering of wilful warriors. The clerk glanced at his map and pointed to a group of red and white striped tents close to the main drawbridge.

"Tell Squire John that he has taken up more than his allotted space," he said officiously. Richard chose to ignore the clerk but Father Hugh, who was riding just behind him, called out, "Tell him yourself if you dare my fine peacock." Richard smiled; their confessor had mettle which could be no bad thing where they were going.

As soon as Richard halted his men in front of Fastolf's quarters, a groom came out from the largest tent and said to him, "Squire John's orders are that you should attend on him as soon as you arrive. He is in his tent." Richard sensed trouble. Such a formal summons did not bode well. He entered the tent to find the squire seated behind his light campaign table reading from a small scroll. Although a chair was available beside him, Richard was not asked to sit down so he stood in silence waiting for Fastolf to finish. While he waited, Richard looked wistfully at Fastolf's armour which was mounted on a wooden frame in the corner of the tent. It was the latest design, entirely plate with surfaces angled to deflect bolts and arrows, and weighing less than two thirds of Richard's part mail part plate armour. The white triangular shield was small compared to Richard's because modern armour had made the need for a shield almost superfluous; even the fearsome English longbow could no longer penetrate armour like Fastolf's except at close range.

At last Fastolf looked up and tossed the scroll onto the table, "This report says you prevented a Lollard from being arrested. Is it true Richard?"

"I stopped a man from being murdered because he was a Lollard."

"The report says nothing of that." Richard felt his pulse quicken as a surge of anger passed through him, but he knew he must be patient with his benefactor who was also a man quick to anger. He tried to keep his voice calm, "That report, whatever its source, is inaccurate. A mob was beating a Lollard to death in Frostenden. I stopped them."

"Did you use my men?"

"No."

Fastolf seem relieved, "That is well, but why did you not arrest the Lollard? You must know that Lollardy is now a secular offence."

"He was half dead! I judged he needed medical help before anything else."

"And where did this medical help come from?" Richard reddened. He had no wish to bring Mary and the rest of the Lollard community to the attention of the law but he knew Fastolf would detect a falsehood; lying was not part of Richard's nature. He stammered, "I left the Lollard in the care of a local woman."

"Another Lollard?"

"I did not ask. It did not seem to matter at the time."

Fastolf sat back in his chair and said, "Sit down Richard and listen to me. You know I am a magistrate do you not?" Richard nodded and the squire continued, "As such it is my duty to enforce the law. It matters not a jot whether I agree with it or not, I am merely the instrument of the king and his parliament. You must understand that it is not sufficient for a man in my position to do his duty; he must be seen to do his duty. Your action yesterday was doubtless well intentioned but I cannot afford to have a man in my service who might be regarded as a Lollard sympathiser."

Richard replied coldly, "I am not a Lollard."

"I did not say so," replied Fastolf, barely controlling his own irritation, "but I insist you give me your word that you will not support or assist a Lollard again." Richard knew he could not give such an unconditional commitment, but without Fastolf's influence he would never avenge Ann. Choosing his words carefully he said, "Squire John, I regret that a misjudgement on my part should have caused you embarrassment. I therefore give you my word that as long as I am in your service, or until an unjust law is changed, I will give no succour, assistance or help in any way to those who follow the Lollard heresy." Fastolf's brow furrowed as he tried to detect a loophole in Richard's statement, but finding none he relaxed a little and smiled, "Well that's all right then. I know full well that attacks on Lollards are frequently excuses to vent jealousy or revenge for more mundane reasons than heresy, but we must always be on our guard. Now let us discuss the order of march for tomorrow. We depart at dawn."

That night Richard slept fitfully. Pictures of Fastolf, Mary Hoccleve, Cousin Geoffrey and Father Anselm, the people who now most influenced his life, kept appearing in his mind in a series of unconnected images. He felt as though he was being bounced between these four like a football with no power to determine his own destiny, yet all he lived for was to avenge his beloved Ann. Ann! He sat up in blind panic, his blanket damp with sweat. He could not remember her face! For an anxious moment Richard did not know where he was, but the snores and mumbles of the sleeping men around him quickly brought him back to full consciousness. He was wide awake. There was no point in trying to get back to sleep, to dreams beyond his control, so he carefully stepped over two or three supine archers and pulled back the tent flap.

Outside, the pitch black silhouette of Framlingham castle loomed above him. The clear sky was illuminated by a half moon which had not quite set below the western horizon, and in the east a slight greying heralded the dawn. Richard estimated the time at about five o'clock. He stepped outside the tent and looked around. The perimeter of the camp was marked at fifty yard intervals by fires, around which huddled the dark shapes of the dawn watch talking to each other in hushed voices to keep themselves awake. Otherwise all was still. The sea of pale tents crowding around Richard in the darkness seemed like ghostly images of all the men who were to die in this campaign. He offered up a quick prayer that he was not to be one of them; he had too much unfinished business to see to before departing this earth.

Then, for the first time since the murder of his family nearly a year ago, he found himself questioning his motives. There was no doubt concerning the retribution he intended to wreak upon his cousin, but his momentary failure to recall Ann's face, if only in a dream, made him wonder whether the sheer lust for revenge might be overwhelming the original reason for it. Living with the thought of vengeance day in day out was becoming an obsession, an end in itself. If he were to allow this to happen, the moment of final revenge might be followed by a purposeless void instead of ultimate satisfaction. Perhaps Ann was sending him a message, a warning that life has more to offer than the pure, but self destructive emotion of revenge.

Apart from arranging a fine dowry for little Joan, Richard remembered he had given no thought to what he would do once Cousin

Geoffrey had been brought down. Although he had kept hold of his land through the offices of John Fastolf, he could not now imagine himself returning to farming. What would Ann have advised? He did not know, but of one thing he was certain; no decision need be made for a while yet. For the next few months he must concentrate on fighting the French and winning back the throne of France for young King Harry of England.

CHAPTER FOUR

Richard's first sight of Southampton water remained forever etched in his memory. Standing on the town walls facing south he was able to see most of the king's mighty fleet riding at anchor in the golden afternoon sun. The short, broad beamed cogs were crowded in the narrow channel so tightly that the multi-oared skiffs, which ferried supplies back and forth from the shore like hundreds of busy water beetles, had difficulty maneouvering between them. It was the seventh of August; the king was expected to join his army at any moment. Father Hugh, who was standing beside Richard gasped, "What a magnificent sight! There must be a hundred ships out there."

"More like a hundred and fifty," said Richard.

"From here they look like a swarm of wooden clogs bobbing up and down on the waves. If only the French could see this they would beg for terms without a fight." Richard looked sidelong at his awe struck companion and smiled, "I think not Father Hugh. Our army is small for the great task expected of it and I have no doubt that there are French spies in Southampton at this very moment preparing reports to that effect."

"How many are we then?"

"About twelve thousand so I am told. The great King Edward left these shores for the Crecy campaign with at least four thousand more than that."

Undaunted, the cleric shrugged, "Twelve thousand Englishmen will be sufficient."

"I am sure your confidence is justified Father," acknowledged Richard, "even though you have never seen a sword drawn in anger." The gentle sarcasm was wasted on the Franciscan, who seemed transfixed by the impressive spectacle spread out before him. He said, "Do you think Squire John might let me take part in the battles?"

Richard laughed, "For a priest you are somewhat bellicose Father. Can you draw a longbow?"

"I have never tried but I'm sure I can learn."

"Perhaps, but not in a few weeks. It takes years of constant practice to use the great English longbow properly. You need to build muscle around the neck, chest and shoulders before you can draw the battle arrow to its full yard shaft. That is why Englishmen are so much stronger than Frenchmen, Scots, Germans, Burgundians or any other nation you care to name. It's not a God given gift but simply the extra body strength we develop from practicing archery from the cradle to the grave."

"Perhaps I could join the ranks of the men at arms?" suggested Hugh hopefully.

"Not without armour my friend. Once upon a time there was a place for ferocious priests such as you. They joined the Order of the Knights Templar but now those bold warrior monks are no more. Perhaps when you experience the blood and guts of battle your enthusiasm for the fight may wane a little."

"Perhaps," said Hugh unconvinced.

Richard put a hand on the disappointed Franciscan's shoulder, "Listen to me Father. Your greatest service will be saving men's souls and ministering to their wounded bodies. Each time you treat a soldier successfully you will be making just as great a contribution to our victory as fighting the French. Far too many men die unnecessarily because their wounds are inadequately treated."

Richard's discourse upon Father Hugh's place in the campaign was interrupted by an eruption of cheering from the north end of the town near the Bar Gate. Both men turned round and looked towards the main street, but the church of Saint Michael obscured their view.

"Come with me Father," said Richard as he began walking towards the stone steps which led from the walls down into the town, "and let us see what all the commotion is about."

The main street was crowded. Richard and Hugh forced their way through the press towards the cheering until they were pushed to one side by a group of burly archers clad in the Plantagenet coat of arms who were clearing the way for their master. A few moments later the cheering suddenly became louder as a group of horsemen appeared led by King Henry himself. This was Richard's first sight of the young king, known affectionately as Harry to the English. He had removed his helmet so that his subjects could see him better. The king sat his mount easily like the veteran horseman he was, and waved happily to the adoring Southampton townsfolk. His straight, brown hair wafted in the gentle breeze revealing a long, almost delicate face more like a priest's than a conqueror's, but the confident smile and noble expression left Richard in no doubt that here was a monarch men would happily follow. He began to cheer as wildly as any of the crowd around him. The king, seeing a man at arms isolated amongst the civilian townsfolk, reined in his charger and called down, "Who are you?" The voice, hard and metallic, was a voice that would carry above the din of battle.

Richard answered, "Your Majesty, I am Richard Calveley of Westhall in Suffolk. I am part of Squire John Fastolf's company which forms part of My Lord Mowbray's array." The king turned in his saddle and called to a young noble behind him, "One of your men John."

"Yes Sire," replied Mowbray.

The king turned back to Richard, "You are not with your company."

"No Your Majesty, I have been observing the fleet."

"Indeed, that is what I am about to do. Your name is familiar to me."

"A kinsman of mine, Sir Hugh Calveley, led a company for the Black Prince. My father and uncle also fought in the French wars."

"Then right glad am I that you are with us Master Richard," said the king. "May the Good Lord preserve you. And by the way, any man who fights for me may call me Sire rather than Your Majesty"

"May the Lord preserve you too Sire." King Harry spurred on his horse leaving Richard open mouthed at the honour just bestowed upon him. Young John Mowbray also acknowledged him as he trotted past with the rest of the king's bodyguard.

Hugh gasped, "God's teeth! Any man would follow our king to hell and back!"

"That is true," answered Richard, "though I suspect the French intend to make France a hell for us."

"But compare out noble warrior king to theirs. It is said that Charles the Sixth spends more time in the madhouse than on his throne."

"Aye, therein lies our best hope. Even the best troops soon become discouraged if badly led, but if the French ever find a leader like our King Harry, we will be hard pressed."

Hugh shrugged his shoulders and said dismissively, "That would require nothing short of a miracle."

⋆ ⋆ ⋆

II

The fleet embarked, or rather began to embark, on the eleventh of August, but the departure of so great a force meant that the vanguard was already over a day out of Southampton before the rearguard weighed anchor. Fastolf's force of forty men was carried in a small cog the *Nicholas* which, with the king's own flagship the *Trinite Royal*, led the fleet on a southerly course towards the French coast. As soon as the *Nicholas* set sail, Fastolf was free to tell his company that their destination was the fortified port of Harfleur on the north side of the estuary of the Seine. Harfleur was to form the base for English operations in France.

Richard's initial exhilaration at sea travel was quickly terminated when his ship left the Solent and passed out of the lee of the Isle of Wight. Although the swell in the English Channel was only moderate, most of the soldiers, including Richard, spent the next two days in various degrees of seasickness, only recovering somewhat when the fleet rounded the Harfleur headland and entered the sheltered waters of the

Seine estuary. There the vanguard dropped anchor to await the main force which was strung out behind them.

It was dawn on the fifteenth day of August. Richard had already woken and was looking wistfully over the cog's beam at the grey, French shore when he was tapped on the shoulder.

"I've had enough of bobbing up and down on this bucket of rotting splinters," said a pale faced Squire John. "There's no sign of the enemy so I'm going ashore to have a look round. Would you care to join me in the first boat?"

"I can think of nothing I would like more even if there were ten thousand Frenchmen waiting for us on the beach fully armed and ready for war," answered Richard. "But what about the king? There has been no signal from his ship."

"Has there not? Well I can't see in this light and we are surely not going to beat the French from here."

Fastolf span round and bellowed, "Ship's master! Lower the rowing boat!" A ragged hurrah went up from those well enough to cheer, and before the sun was clear of the eastern horizon the *Nicholas*' skiff was being winched into the sullen grey sea. Apart from a sailor at each oar, it contained Fastolf, Richard and eight archers.

It was a two hundred yard pull to the shore and the swell, which had looked gentle enough from the deck of the cog, began to throw around the occupants of the skiff as the shallowing sea turned into choppy waves. The master's mate, who was piloting the skiff, called out, "Squire John! I dare not try to beach the skiff in this swell or we'll all be tumbled out."

Fastolf looked at the breakers, now only twenty paces away, and shouted, "What depth are we here?"

The mate tested the sea bed with his oar, "Three or four feet, no more."

"That will do. Come on my noble lads!" Without a moment's hesitation, John Fastolf leaped out of the skiff in full armour and splashed chest deep into the sea. Seconds later, Richard and the eight archers followed his example cheering and yelling as the shock of the cold water met them, and even before the mate was able to turn his boat's bow back towards the *Nicholas*, ten sodden Englishmen were laughing and prancing like excited children on the sandy French beach, all distinctions of rank for the moment forgotten. The invasion had begun.

Richard pointed out to sea and shouted, "Squire John, look!" As far as the eye could see, hundreds of rowing boats, oars beating rhythmically like insects' legs, were scattered across the grey Seine estuary.

"God's holy balls!" laughed Fastolf, "They're following us in! We've led the invasion. Hurrah!" Another bout of excited capering followed, and when they had finally exhausted themselves, Fastolf's men sat down on a shingle bank contentedly cheering as each boatload of new arrivals splashed ashore.

By noon most of the men were on dry land, but that was the easy part because the horses and artillery still had to be unloaded. Richard watched in fascination as one of the twelve great bombards arrived in a large rowing boat which was so low in the water that reaching the beach seemed impossible. Fortunately the height of the waves had diminished during the day and the sturdy sailors were able to beach their boat before it foundered. Then, with well practiced efficiency, they erected a small winch and lifting gear which they used to heave the massive bombard out of the boat to the merry tune of a sea shanty. The shanty helped the sailors to work as a team, pulling in unison at certain points in the song, usually at the moment of a particularly bawdy word which caused a deal of merriment to all those within earshot.

As well as the bombards, huge, round stone projectiles each weighing about five hundred pounds had to be landed, because starvation, the usual deciding factor in siege warfare, was not a favourable option for King Harry. A French army might be expected at any moment and the inhabitants of Harfleur would have plenty of opportunity to provision their town before the English completely encircled them.

On the morning of the sixteenth day of August the entire English army had landed, and before summoning the town to surrender the king carried out the dubbing of new knights on the foreshore which customarily preceded a campaign in hostile land. Richard and Fastolf looked on as the young squires were given their knighthoods until an equerry bearing Lord Mowbray's dark blue and tawny livery approached them and said, "Squire John, My Lord Mowbray wishes to see you at once. Follow me."

Fastolf whispered to Richard, "You come too. I do not like the sound of this."

"Why ever not?" said Richard as they followed the equerry, "Your dashing action on the beach might have earned you a knighthood."

"Exactly," sighed Fastolf.

"What's the matter with that?"

"It costs money. Knighthood brings with it responsibilities. I would prefer to earn some money from this war before incurring further expenditure from it."

The equerry stopped in front of a large, white tent at the entrance of which was planted a banner bearing the Mowbray coat of arms; Gules a Lion rampant Argent. Fastolf and Richard entered to find young John Mowbray being dressed in full plate armour for battle. His high pitched voice was more that of a boy than a man, but authority sat well on his youthful shoulders.

"Well Squire John," he said. "The king was well pleased by your daring yesterday. He tells me you will be rewarded in due course."

"Will you thank him for me My Lord?"

"Yes, but I doubt not that you will have the opportunity yourself before this campaign is over."

"I shall look forward to the moment," said Fastolf.

Mowbray glanced at Richard and asked, "I saw you at Southampton?"

"You did My Lord. I am Squire John's lieutenant."

"Good, good." Addressing Fastolf again, Mowbray continued, "The French knew we were coming. Harfleur has already been reinforced. They have about five hundred men at arms in the town and as much fresh water as they want because a small stream flows through it."

"Then an assault might be necessary," suggested Fastolf.

"Mayhap, but our hobelars report that a supply convoy is heading towards Harfleur along the Rouen road. The Duke of Clarence has been ordered to intercept it and we are to accompany him. We march in one hour." Richard's mouth suddenly went dry. Until now the war had been a game, a great adventure. He had assumed that the fighting would not begin in earnest for a few weeks yet and that August would be spent in camp with like minded wandering spirits while the bombards did their deadly work on Harfleur's massive fortifications. But now he was confronted with the spectre of serious fighting just hours after landing. It did not seem quite fair. Mowbray had not finished.

"There is one most important point you must impress upon your men Squire John. The king says that the inhabitants of France are soon to become his subjects as is their right and his. Consequently there is to be no ill discipline towards French non-combatants; no plundering, looting or violation of women. Any such behaviour will be met with summary execution."

Fastolf replied in a neutral voice, "I shall inform them My Lord, though I must say the order is unexpected. Loot and plunder is what drives the common soldier on."

Mowbray raised his young eyebrows, "Surely not Squire John. The righteous quarrel of the King of England is why we are all here."

Fastolf threw a sidelong glance towards Richard and then bowed to his liege, "It is as you say My Lord."

It was an hour after noon when Clarence's force of a thousand men, nearly two thirds of them mounted archers, cantered slowly out of the English camp. They skirted round the southern edge of Harfleur because the French had already flooded the low lying land to the north, and rejoined the Rouen road a mile east of the town. Richard, along with the rest of Fastolf's men, formed the rearguard of the column and as a consequence, had to endure the dust kicked up from the dry road by the horses in front. Now that he had had some time to prepare himself, Richard felt a little better though his stomach was still knotted with nerves. He recalled feeling this way as a young man before the fight with the Scots at Homildon Hill, but then less was expected of him and the Scots were already on the run before his company was brought into action. He tried to draw strength by thinking that Ann would be watching him from her heavenly estate, but unless he concentrated hard he found the image of Mary Hoccleve appearing in his mind's eye instead. This was disconcerting though not unpleasant, and Richard began to understand that the little Lollard preacher had impressed him more than he had realised. But he could not let this train of thought develop; his loyalty to Ann forbade it.

A commotion at the front of Clarence's force quickly transmitted itself down the column which came to an unsteady and confused halt. No-one in the rearguard could see a thing because of the dust, so Fastolf himself trotted forward to find out what was happening. A buzz of excitement developed within the column and Richard looked enviously at the archers behind him who, unlike himself, seemed to feel no fear at the prospect of battle. Ten minutes later Fastolf came galloping back and summoned Richard and the three archer sergeants to one side.

"The French have been sighted dead ahead," he said breathlessly, "just outside a village called Bolbec. The column is going to attack immediately but there is a small road which branches to the north and might provide an escape route for some of the enemy. Our orders are to gallop across country and block the road."

John Thorpe grumbled, "That means we're likely to miss the fighting."

"At least we'll get away from all this dust," said Henry Hawkswood.

Fastolf snapped, "There is no room for discussion. Our orders are clear. I will lead with the Norfolk men, the Yorkshire men will be in the centre. Richard, you bring up the rear with the Wiltshire men."

Just seconds later, Fastolf's company of archers was galloping across open, rolling fields which had only recently been harvested. The palfreys pinned back their ears and gave vent to the frustration which had built up during the slow, dusty march of the previous three hours; it was exhilarating. Richard had mixed feelings about their new role. Galloping over the French countryside with fresh air instead of dust to breathe was pleasant enough, but having prepared himself to face battle he felt thwarted now that the likelihood of combat had receded. He was also relieved and was ashamed for feeling thus.

"Richard, you seem deep in thought." The voice belonged to Father Hugh who was accompanying Fastolf's men in his capacity as physician. "Is aught troubling you? Do you need to confess?"

"I should concentrate on staying in the saddle Father," replied Richard. "Your riding has improved but little since we left Dunwich."

"Tut, you are unfair Master Calveley. I am no longer in pain."

"I was thinking of your horse Father." Hugh laughed, satisfied that Richard's preoccupation had not affected his sense of humour and asked, "Do you think we shall get a blow in at the French today?"

"It is possible but unlikely. I suspect your herbs and poultices will remain unused. We will soon know, here is the road."

The company slowed and descended a shallow slope to the narrow, dusty road. A few minutes were lost hunting for a gap in the thick hawthorn hedge which flanked both sides of the road, but soon the company was in position at the far end of a long straight where the archers had a clear field of fire for two hundred yards. The Norfolk men stood astride the road with the Wiltshire and Yorkshire men occupying the hedges on either side. Allowing for the one man in five who was appointed to stand guard over the horses in the rear, twenty four English longbows were trained southwards in the direction of Bolbec.

The shadows began to lengthen and the tension eased as the sound of battle in the south faded away. The engagement had not lasted long which suggested that Clarence had secured an easy victory.

Fastolf, who was standing with the Norfolk men, turned to Richard and said, "Well, it looks as though we will not be needed today. We shall wait a few more minutes then head towards Bolbec in case My Lord Clarence has forgotten about us." Richard was about to reply but Thomas Riches, the quiet Norfolk sergeant, knelt down, took off his helmet and placed his ear to the ground.

"What is it Tom?" asked Fastolf.

The sergeant looked up, "Horses Squire John, coming this way fast."

"How many?"

"More than three, less than ten." A tingle of excitement ran down Richard's spine. Fastolf remained unruffled. "Probably sent by Clarence to fetch us but we had better be prepared. Richard, stand the men to arms again."

A cloud of dust appeared moving rapidly towards Fastolf's company, but the bend at the far end of the straight obscured the identity of the horsemen. Richard's mouth went dry again. He looked at his hands; they were sweaty but steady enough. The chattering archers were silent now, peering intently southwards. Everyone was sure the horses would be French. Suddenly they appeared, five of them, galloping as if all the devils in hell were after them. Fastolf nodded to Richard whose voice wavered slightly as he shouted, "We will shoot at one hundred yards on my command. Prepare!"

Twenty four steel pointed, ash battle arrows were notched into their bow strings.

At one hundred and fifty yards the horsemen drew rein and briefly consulted amongst themselves. Four of them were hobelars. The fifth, the leader, was a well mounted man at arms. His blue surcoat, sporting three large, gold Fleur de Lys, identified him as French. Apparently deciding that the danger behind was greater, he drew a mace and spurred his big war horse forward again closely followed by the hobelars.

"Draw your bows!" Richard's voice was steadier now. He waited until the charging horsemen were approximately a hundred paces away and bellowed, "Shoot! Prepare!" The discharge sounded like the hiss of scores of angry snakes. Some of the better archers had already notched their next arrows when the first volley of ash yard shafts struck home. About half found targets. Three of the four hobelars crashed to the ground as their mounts fell, pierced by the fearsome missiles. The horses screamed and kicked uselessly as their lifeblood pumped from their veins, staining the dusty road a dull brown, while their riders lay still, concussed by the fall and shot through with English ash. Incredibly the fourth hobelar and his mount escaped the deadly volley as did the man at arms, whose horse was armoured almost as well as he was. But they would not survive a close range volley.

Fastolf, sensing the possibility of ransom, shouted, "Arretez! Arretez! For God's sake arretez!" Either the man at arms did not hear or he was unable to understand Fastolf's atrocious accent for his spurs dug deep and his horse pounded onward.

"A brave bastard," muttered Fastolf.

The next volley was loosed at barely twenty paces. The last hobelar was killed outright but the man at arms survived though badly wounded and pinned under the weight of his fallen, screaming mount. The archers cheered and a few of them dropped their bows and ran towards the stricken Frenchman. One of them sat astride the struggling, thrashing victim and carefully placed the point of his dagger at the visor slit. The Frenchman knew what was coming and desperately tried to displace his assailant with his free arm. But it was hopeless. The archer thrust his needle sharp misericord through the visor, the man at arms jerked and twitched for a moment, then lay still.

While other archers dispatched the wounded horses, Fastolf called the sergeants to him. "Make sure all that is worth having is collected for the common pot. We want no pilfering of plunder." The distribution of plunder was a subject close to every man's heart and to prevent disagreement Fastolf, like many other indentured captains, had decided that all booty taken by his men would go into a pot from which it would be redistributed in shares. He would take three quarters with the rest being divided into equal shares; one for an archer, two for a man at arms, four for a sergeant and eight for Richard as the lieutenant. Fastolf's share was not as greedy as it seemed because apart from the cost of fitting out his men, he would have to pay a significant portion to his own commander Lord Mowbray, the Earl Marshal.

"I think it's time to give the last rites to the slain," said Fastolf to a white faced Father Hugh. "Not quite what you expected eh?" The encounter had been far from Hugh's ideal of war. No flying pennons, no dashing charges, no deeds of honour and chivalry for the troubadours to recount in years to come; just butchery in a small, French country lane. The Franciscan was unable to answer for his stomach was about to regurgitate its contents, so he walked unsteadily towards the dead man at arms, who had now been stripped, threw up violently in the middle of the road, and shakily started to implement the sacrament of Extreme Unction.

Fastolf turned to Richard with a twinkle in his eye, "I think our bellicose cleric might be a little less warlike from now on."

"True," replied Richard, who felt more like a murderer than a warrior, "but it was hardly a glorious episode."

"If that is really what you think then you're as simple as our poor priest. It was a victory, a small one, but a victory nonetheless. That is all that matters. It'll put the men in good heart."

Richard said quietly, "I feel ashamed. Those Frenchmen had no chance."

"Do not be a fool Richard. They could have surrendered if they chose -."

"Squire John! Squire John!" It was Thomas Riches who interrupted them. He was running towards them carrying three broad brimmed hobelar helmets and a saddle. "Squire John! More horses coming, dozens of them!"

Richard shouted, "To arms! To arms!" It said much for the discipline of Fastolf's men that the plundering immediately stopped and within a minute everyone was back in position, but the alarm gave way to cheering as the horsemen came into view, for they cantered under the Mowbray coat of arms.

Young John Mowbray drew rein beside the mangled corpse of the man at arms and raised his visor, "Complete victory Squire John! The entire supply column has been captured. You had trouble here?"

"Nothing we could not handle My Lord," said Fastolf urbanely.

"Excellent! First blood to us. No-one escaped. This should throw the defenders of Harfleur into a depression. I would not be surprised if they surrender within days."

★ ★ ★

III

The Earl Marshal's prediction was sadly inaccurate for the commanders of Harfleur, the Sieur d'Estouteville and the Sieur de Gaucourt proved to be brave and resourceful knights. As well as being a thriving port, Harfleur was a formidable fortress. It was protected by high walls, two and a half miles in circumference which were strengthened with the addition of twenty six towers. An invitation by the English king to surrender after the convoy had been intercepted was refused, so Harry was obliged to settle down outside the walls and begin a full scale siege.

Operations started with the sappers digging oblique slit trenches which approached the town at an angle to prevent the French being able to fire into them. Then the great bombards were dragged along the trenches. They were carefully manhandled by the artillerymen who referred to the great weapons of death as 'she' and stroked and preened them as they might their lovers. Ramparts were built at the end of the trenches to protect the bombards, which opened fire in the last week in August.

There was not much for the army to do at this time except scout and forage, but though there was no sign of a relieving French force, a far deadlier enemy soon made its presence felt. The month of August and the first half of September were hot and dry in 1415, and in such circumstances an immobile concentration of thousands of men was an ideal target for the flux. The disease quickly spread. The stench in the English camp was almost unbearable and inevitably the toll soon began to mount. After a fourth archer in his company died, Fastolf ordered that no water should be drunk which had not first been boiled. This advice came from Father Hugh, who remembered a successful treatment for the flux at Dunwich Priory the previous summer. A similar order was issued throughout the army but in hot weather it was difficult to enforce and the casualties continued to mount.

The nobility was not immune. First Michael de la Pole, Earl of Suffolk died. His young son, another Michael, survived to carry on the title for a while at least, but the senior cleric, Bishop Courtenay quickly followed Suffolk to the grave. The Duke of Clarence, the Earls of Arundel and March, and John Mowbray the Earl Marshal were invalided home too sick to carry on the campaign. Mowbray's departure was not entirely unfortunate because Fastolf's command was transferred to the grizzled, grey haired veteran Sir Thomas Erpingham, a Norfolk knight from Blickling and an old friend of Fastolf.

In all, two thousand men of all ranks died and many more were sent home leaving, by the middle of September, fewer than seven thousand men to continue the siege. But at last Harfleur's proud defence began to totter.

On the fourteenth day of September, the bombards finally made a breach in the southwest wall which was so large that the townsfolk were unable to repair it during the night as had been their wont. There was still no evidence of a relieving French army, which left the English free to assault the breach unhindered by a threat to their rear. It seemed that the Dauphin Louis, who was commander in chief of the French forces now that his father Charles VI was more or less permanently insane, had abandoned Harfleur to its fate.

The watch in the southwest trench during the night of the fourteenth was assigned to Fastolf's men. The squire himself was suffering from a mild bout of flux so Richard took command of the Wiltshire archers and the seven fit men at arms and led them up the sap to the two great bombards which had opened up the heart of the town to the English. The men fanned out along the rampart which gave cover to the artillerymen during the day, and settled in for the night. Richard placed himself in the centre with one eyed Henry Hawkswood beside him and looked at the dark, threatening town walls looming above them. A clear sky and a near full moon illuminated the breach which stood out as a great gash in the opaque, black walls less than a hundred paces away. Soon, the area of open ground between the sap and the breach would be drenched in blood, most of it English, and Richard prayed that Fastolf's company would not be awarded the honour of leading the assault.

"Thinking about the attack Master Richard?" whispered Hawkswood.

"Aye, a quick way to promotion I dare say."

"A quick way to the next world," chuckled the Wiltshireman.

Richard asked, "Are the men in good heart now that the end of the siege is near?"

"Mine are and so are the Norfolk lads, but you can never tell with the Yorkshire men."

"I have noticed they do not chatter like you Wiltshire magpies."

"They dare not for fear of their sergeant. John Thorpe rules them with a rod of iron. He combines a powerful body with the temperament of a bully."

"I selected him because of his skill with the longbow and his qualities of leadership. It appears I made a mistake."

"That you did Master Richard, for John bears no fondness towards you. He says you made a fool of him in front of his men when you saved that Lollard in Frostenden. He has sworn to get even with you."

"Then I had better watch my back when the fighting starts," said Richard thoughtfully.

"No need for that. There are others watching it for you. You have gained the respect of the men and John Thorpe knows it. He will try something less obvious, but what it might be I cannot guess. Stay on your guard."

"Thank you for the warning Henry. I shall – " A hoarse whisper from his right interrupted Richard as the archer on the outer flank of the rampart came scurrying back to the centre. His voice wavered with tension, "There's movement just in front of us sir. Might be a dog but it seemed sort of deliberate if you take my meaning. Couldn't see anything though."

Richard turned to Hawkswood, "What do you think Henry?"

"Could be a sally."

"That would explain why the French are making no attempt to repair the breach tonight." Addressing the archer Richard continued,

"Well done Stephen, you shall have an extra shilling for tonight's work. Now return to Squire John as quickly as you can and tell him the French are sallying out. Hurry!"

As the archer ran back down the sap, Richard whispered, "Henry, stand the men to arms but quietly. We do not wish the French to know we are expecting them."

"Yes Master Richard. Hand weapons only?"

"Maces and mauls for the archers, swords and axes for the men at arms."

Ten minutes passed. Peering into the darkness Richard could see nothing. If the French did not come soon they would lose the cover of night, for dawn was not far away. He began to have second thoughts. Perhaps it had only been a dog that had alerted the watch after all. Soon the support troops would arrive, but while Richard was considering the recriminations that were bound to occur if he had sent a false alarm, a muffled cry to his right announced the arrival of the French.

They came in force. In seconds the rampart was swarming with French men at arms desperately trying to overrun and destroy the English bombards. It was a frantic, confused struggle. The English, standing on top of the rampart for more elbow room, swung their heavy, two handed weapons to deadly effect but the French were equally determined and quickly pushed their way into the sap. The melee within the confined trench walls deteriorated into brutal, gutter fighting. There was no room to wield a sword so Richard instinctively used the pommel as a bludgeon and the rim of his shield as a blade. Worst of all it was almost impossible to tell who was friend or foe, and more than one English man at arms was felled by an archer in the confusion.

The struggle continued for two or three minutes. Richard, temporarily isolated from his comrades, found himself backed up against one of the bombards by two well armoured men at arms. He knew he had not yet struck a telling blow against the enemy, yet now his own life was in the balance. All three paused for a moment to summon up the strength to continue the fight. Richard could hear his opponents breathing heavily inside their helmets. Guessing they were probably more exhausted than he was, he lunged at the man to his left with his shield, knocking him off balance, and swung his sword at the man on his right. The sword blow was easily parried but the riposte glanced harmlessly off Richard's breastplate. The uneven duel was ended almost before it had begun by the arrival of cheering English reinforcements who speedily drove off all the French able to escape. Richard's two opponents were cut off from their friends and raised their arms in the gesture of surrender.

A familiar voice called down from the top of the trench, "God's balls Richard! What have you there?"

"I do not know as yet Squire John." Fastolf scrambled down the earthen wall and peered closely at the two prisoners.

"Holy Saint George!" he gasped. "One of them wears a coat of arms. You have captured a knight."

Richard said, "I was hard pressed until the support came."

"Say nothing of that," whispered Fastolf, "or we will have to share the ransom with Huntingdon's men. They were your prisoners before help arrived. Is that clear?"

"Yes Squire John."

"Excellent. You have done well this night Master Calveley. I shall not forget. Now you will excuse me. I must go. The damned flux is coming on again."

* * *

IV

Fierce though the fighting had been, the English losses were not heavy; three killed and five wounded. The French casualties were similar though their main loss was in prisoners, of which there were fifteen. It was the emaciated state of the prisoners which persuaded King Harry to proceed with a full scale assault on Harfleur as soon as possible, but just before the attack went in, a French herald emerged from the town requesting a parley. After a brief discussion with the

Sieur de Gaucourt, it was agreed that the town would surrender if no relieving French army appeared by the twenty second day of September. The agreed date duly arrived, and as there was no French army in sight, Harfleur opened its gates to the English.

During this time, Fastolf concluded ransom negotiations with Richard's captured knight. The Sieur de Freuchin came from Picardy. He was only nineteen, and his youthful ardour to impress his peers led directly to his capture along with one of his sergeants by Richard. Both were ransomable, and a delighted Fastolf eventually secured a promise of the French equivalent of two hundred and fifty pounds for the brace. The young knight's unspoilt friendliness charmed everyone in the company, and when he left the English camp having given his parole to collect the ransom money before engaging in any further hostilities, his boyish chatter was missed by Fastolf's men even though most of them spoke no French.

On the morning of the twenty third day of September Fastolf came bustling into Richard's tent full of excitement.

"The king has called for a Royal Council this afternoon in the hotel de ville in Harfleur. I am to go with Sir Thomas Erpingham."

"Congratulations Squire John," said Richard, "your knighthood cannot be far away now."

Fastolf beamed, "Thanks to you Richard I can afford it. Sir Thomas asked me to bring someone to wait upon us at the council. It is only an equerry's job, but I wondered if you might like to come instead. Seeing a Royal Council is an experience not given to most of us."

"I will look forward to it Squire John."

As he rode through Harfleur with Sir Thomas and Fastolf, Richard was surprised at how little damage had been caused by the siege. As well as bombards, the English had used mangonels and catapults but only a few houses had suffered serious damage. In line with his policy, King Harry had forbidden his men to loot the town so most of the army remained encamped outside the walls. Those townsfolk who agreed to acknowledge his overlordship were allowed to remain but the king ordered the rest to depart. Harfleur, like Calais, was to be a thoroughly English town.

The main hall of the hotel de ville was the largest room Richard had seen. Its high vaulted ceiling and big windows gave it more space and light than English town halls, and the rows of unfurled French coats of arms, which lined the whitewashed walls, provided a welcome reminder to the English of the large sums of ransom money that would come their way in due course. Around the long oak table, which occupied the centre of the hall, sat all the leading commanders of the army. They included the king's fat cousin, Richard Duke of York, the Earls of Huntingdon, Oxford, Dorset and Suffolk, and the experienced knight commanders Erpingham, Cornwall, Camoys and Umfraville. Richard stood behind Erpingham and Fastolf wondering what the ransom value of the assembled company would be if the dauphin were to turn up unexpectedly with twenty thousand men at his back.

The king sat on his own at one end of the oblong table still dressed in full armour, unlike the rest of the council who had taken the opportunity of divesting themselves of their armour as soon as Harfleur fell. There was a steely determination about King Harry, a toughness which convinced all who met him that his cause, whether just or not, would succeed. He raised his hand to speak, and in the hush that followed Richard understood the king was, amongst all his other qualities, something of a showman. Henry V was a great leader, he knew it and intended to show it, act up to it almost. He looked at each of the council members in turn, knowing they were willing him to speak, but making them wait just a little longer thus increasing their anticipation. When at last he spoke, there was no mention of deeds past such as the fall of Harfleur. That was over now. Only the future course of the campaign mattered to the king. Any other thoughts were irrelevant. The hard, metallic voice echoed round the hall, "My Lords, it is time to consider what to do next. To our certain knowledge three French armies are gathering, one at Rouen, another in Picardy and another in Artois. Our spies tell us that each one is larger than ours, yet the French commanders seem unwilling to face us in battle or they would surely have confronted us by now. Our army is weakened by disease though in good heart, but it is late in the year and the fine weather cannot hold much longer. I would be grateful to know your views. Perhaps you would begin cousin."

The red faced Duke of York's jowels wobbled as he nodded an acknowledgement to his sovereign, "Sire, you have won a great victory here. The costs of the campaign will be well covered by the ransom money we have secured," he waved a plump hand at the colourful coats of arms that surrounded them, "and the French have refused to face us even though they outnumber us by many thousands. We have done more than enough this year. Let us refortify Harfleur, leave a strong garrison and return home for the winter. Next year we can come back to a secure base with a fresh, disease free army and try conclusions with the French once more."

"Thank you cousin," replied the king in a neutral voice. "What do you say Huntingdon?"

Huntingdon was much younger than York and, as might be expected, took a more aggressive view. "Sire there is still some campaigning time left. Let us remain here a little longer and send out lightly armed flying columns to plunder the countryside. That way the French will be made more aware of your kingly presence before you return to England, and we may yet provoke their armies into attacking us and fight the battle we came for."

"You forget Huntingdon that we would be plundering my own subjects," said the king, "but from the nods of some of you round this table I see that My Lord Huntingdon's proposal is not unpopular. What about you Sir Thomas? You do not appear to agree with York or Huntingdon. What do you say?"

Erpingham glanced at Fastolf beside him and then turned his attention back to King Harry, "Sire may I speak plainly?"

"By my troth," smiled the king, "you know no other way Sir Thomas. Speak as plainly as you will. That is why you are here."

"Sire, I have already discussed this matter with some of your other captains including Squire John Fastolf, the first man ashore here. We are all of one mind. Sire, you claim to be King of France but if we return to England now, what will the French think? Certainly they will not be shaking in their boots, for all we have achieved with a large invasion force is the capture of a single town. It is an easy thing to claim to be king, but it is quite another to be king in the hearts and minds of the French as you are in ours. You must prove your claim to them the way King Edward and the Black Prince did by marching through France as if it belongs to you and destroying any force the dauphin sends against you. That way the French will see their interests lie in acknowledging you as their sovereign instead of their lunatic king."

"This is preposterous Sire," spluttered Richard of York. "Sir Thomas' proposal is reckless in the extreme. He would throw away everything we have gained, and our lives and liberty as well." The king seemed content for the moment to let the debate continue without him as young Michael de la Pole, the new Earl of Suffolk said, "Sire, none of us fears defeat as much as dishonour. Let us follow Sir Thomas' advice. We came here to fight for your just cause, not a paltry French town."

"Brave but inexperienced words," smiled Dorset patronisingly. "My Lord York does not counsel abandoning the cause but merely delaying its conclusion until next year."

"What do you say Squire John Fastolf?" asked Harry, who seemed to be enjoying the argument. "Do you think we should go home?" Fastolf had rehearsed what he would say if required to speak. He was not prepared to compromise.

"Sire, Sir Thomas and My Lord Suffolk have pointed the way by asking why we came here. Are we men of lesser mettle than those who marched to Crecy and Poitiers? They would not have hesitated now. If we abandon the campaign the French will rightly conclude that the English of our fathers' and grandfathers' day were greater men than we. Let us march into France and take what fortune God sends us."

"This madness is spreading," scoffed York but before he could add any more, the king brought the debate to a close by announcing his decision.

"I am gratified to hear there is at least some support for what I have already done. Sir Thomas, you will be interested to know that as we speak the *Nicholas* is sailing with orders for the commander of the Calais garrison, Sir William Bardolf. He is to march with all speed to secure the ford across the Somme estuary at Blanche Taque, the very same that my great grandfather used on his way to Crecy. I am seized with a desire to see those territories which are my inheritance. My trust is in God, and the French shall not stop my army or myself. We will go unhurt to Calais and if they attempt to prevent us we shall arrive victorious and triumphant."

At the very moment the English king stopped speaking, a loud clap of thunder announced the onset of the storm that had been threatening since the morning. It was almost as if Harry Plantagenet had laid down a challenge and the fates had answered in like manner.

CHAPTER FIVE

Meanwhile events were taking there course back in Suffolk. News of Richard's rescue of the Frostenden Lollard did not take long to reach Calveley Hall, and while Mowbray's array was marching to Southampton, Geoffrey Calveley decided to investigate the incident further. He had every right to do so for he had recently been appointed magistrate for that part of East Suffolk which included Frostenden. He determined that an indirect approach might be most effective, so on a sultry July evening he summoned his steward to his study.

"Titus, I have a task for you which will require you to lodge at Frostenden for a while." Titus Scrope was always happy to be sent on extended missions which allowed him to indulge his desires at his master's expense without the close accounting Geoffrey usually required.

"And what interests you at Frostenden?" asked Titus.

"Lollards."

"There are Lollards at Halesworth. That's a lot nearer."

"It is the Frostenden set that interests me," said Geoffrey, "and in particular I want to know why Cousin Richard was prepared to risk his liberty by protecting them."

"He only saved one. That does not make Richard a Lollard."

"I know, but my reports say he spoke to the Lollard by name. That means he must have had contact with him before."

Titus rubbed the stubble on his chin, "Interesting, I had not heard that. But why pursue your cousin now? He is on his way to France as is his master. He cannot harm you from there."

"Perhaps not, but you never know what war might bring. Remember Titus, the Earl of Suffolk, my master is also going to war. We do not know who will be promoted and who will disgrace themselves, who will live and who will die. If Richard distinguishes himself and finds favour with the king, I will need every weapon available to me for I feel in my bones that he suspects me of the destruction of his family."

"Unlikely," Titus demurred, "but if Richard has transgressed the Lollard laws you will, as a magistrate, be able to lock him up and throw away the key if needs be."

"Precisely Titus. If you come up with any hard evidence I shall be grateful." Geoffrey touched the steel cabinet where he kept his cash.

Titus grinned, "I can manufacture any evidence you like."

"No, it must be genuine. It may have to stand the test of open court. There are many Lollard sympathisers in Suffolk, some in the legal profession, who will expose unsatisfactory evidence."

"Well that might take a little longer and cost a little more. The Lollards are suspicious of outsiders since they were proscribed. It will take time to gain their confidence. I may have to be away for some weeks."

Geoffrey frowned, "Take as long as you need but do not spend too much. You have expensive tastes Titus."

"Money is for spending not hoarding."

"That," said Geoffrey pompously, "is where you and I differ. If I spent at the rate you do, I would not own two hundred and fifty acres of freehold and Calveley Hall."

"You inherited the house." Titus deliberately refrained from giving it Geoffrey's grand title.

"Maybe so, but it costs money to keep. Anyway I do not have to justify my fiscal affairs to you Scrope."

The steward shrugged, "I shall need at least ten pounds if you want the job done properly."

"Ten pounds!"

"Yes. Board, lodging, entertainment and contingencies."

"Entertainment? What entertainment?" asked Geoffrey suspiciously.

"Whatever is necessary to gain the confidence of the Lollards."

"Very well, but mark my words Titus, I shall expect some results for this money, and some change."

★ ★ ★

II

On the day King Harry's invasion fleet embarked for France, Titus Scrope booked into the Eagle Inn at Wrentham, a few miles north of Frostenden. He used the name Titus Roper and let it be known that he was looking for land in the area for his master in London. This gave him good reason to wander at will from village to village, and during the next few days he was able to discover the location of the Lollard community without making direct enquiries.

Wrentham was on the junction between the main highway to Yarmouth and the road to Southwold harbour. It was a favourite Lollard preaching point. The Lollards dared not announce their public meetings in advance for fear of being arrested, but Titus knew if he waited long enough they would eventually turn up. It only took a week.

Titus had just finished his lunch at the inn when about a dozen smart but simply attired people walked into Wrentham from the direction of Frostenden. The landlord looked through a window and brought another mug of ale to Titus, "Lollards," he whispered. "A pain in the arse but good for business."

"There is a woman amongst them," said Titus.

"That will be Mary Hoccleve. She is a fine preacher so they say though I've never attended one of her meetings."

Titus quickly swilled down his ale and wiped his sleeve across his mouth. "I think I'll go and listen. It might be entertaining."

"Be careful then Master Roper, Lollard meetings sometimes attract ruffians intent on trouble. Since Lollardy was made illegal, the roughnecks can cause a riot and claim the backing of the law."

Titus was not the only patron of the Eagle Inn to wander over to the crossroads where the Lollards were preparing for their meeting. Many of the audience were already the worse for ale and looking for some easy sport, though the sombre faced men who surrounded Mary seemed ready for trouble if it should come. The crowd had reached fifty or sixty in number when Mary was helped onto a small campaign table which the Lollards had brought with them. She was greeted with obscene comments and derisory cheers, but being an experienced preacher she took it all in her stride. As she looked down at the gathering while offering a silent prayer before starting, Titus got a good look at her for the first time; she was not what he had expected. Far from being one of the plain, old owls he had seen preaching in Halesworth market, this was a woman any man would be grateful to bed. He imagined running his fingers through her full, fair hair and handling the trim, shapely body. Yes, by God, any man would want her, and looking at the grim men who formed the protective cordon round the young preacher, he wondered which of them was hers. It did not occur to Titus that none of them were; all the young women he knew had a man somewhere whether they admitted it or not.

But Titus' lustful thoughts were tempered somewhat by the knowledge that he could not allow his carnal desires to interfere with the successful completion of his mission. On the other hand, who could tell what opportunities fate might bring if he managed to worm his way into the Lollard community. But how?

Although she was only small, Mary's voice was strong and deep for a woman. Most of the gathering kept quiet when she started to speak, but within seconds a slurring heckler who was standing in front beside Titus yelled, "What right 'ave you got to tell us what to believe!" Cheers of encouragement for their loudmouthed colleague came from various inebriated sections of the crowd but Mary, unlike most preachers who would try to ignore interruptions, answered him directly.

"I do not tell you what to believe friend. It is the church establishment that does that already. The priests and bishops place themselves between you and your God. Many of them are corrupt. Tell me friend, when did you last see a starving churchman or a bishop without a fat belly?" That struck a chord with the crowd, most of whom at one time or another had faced a winter without enough to eat. A murmur of approval told Titus that Mary had broken the ice. She quickly followed up her advantage before the heckler thought up some other inane remark.

"I do not say all churchmen are corrupt, far from it, but they are more concerned for their position and status than for your welfare, else they would preach Christ's words exactly as he spoke them, without putting distorted interpretations on them designed to mislead you. Friends, you would be right to wonder why they should want to do that. The answer is simple. Christ did not speak of priests and bishops apart from criticising the priests of the Hebrews. Certainly he never mentioned anything about a pope. His message was simple and direct and put in words that any man or woman can understand."

The heckler's eyes lit up and he shouted, "I can't understand bleeding 'ebrew." This was met with roars of laughter but Mary handled the situation calmly, "I cannot speak Hebrew either my friend but it does not matter. Nor is it necessary to understand Latin or Greek for now the Holy Bible can be read in English. The words are translated, not interpreted, exactly as Christ spoke them so what need is there now for bishops and priests when, at last, we can communicate directly with God." One of Mary's followers handed her a large, red bound book which he held as if it were made of the finest Egyptian alabaster. With some difficulty Mary held it out in both hands for the crowd to see, "Friends, this is an English bible, faithfully and accurately translated by the followers of the late John Wyclif of Oxford who – " She was interrupted by the heckler who, having failed to put her off her stride, lurched forward and grabbed the book. The sudden move took Mary's protectors by surprise, and before they could react the ruffian was already melting away into the crowd. The loss of such a precious object would devastate the Frostenden Lollards, but it also gave Titus an unexpected opportunity to further his cause. As the thief brushed past, delighted with himself for causing so much trouble, Titus felled him with a powerful blow to the side of his head. He bent down, retrieved the book from the unconscious rogue, and handed it back directly to Mary.

"Thank you friend," she said, her moist brown eyes looking into his. "You cannot know what good you have done this day. May I know your name?"

"Titus Roper."

"You will not find us ungrateful Master Roper, though we have little money. Do you live nearby?"

"No, I am on a business trip for my master in London. I am lodging at the Eagle Inn."

"Would you care to stay with us while you are here and save lodging expenses? We would be grateful for the opportunity to repay you in some way; that is unless you object to our community."

Titus could hardly believe his good fortune though he must not appear too enthusiastic. He said, "Mistress Hoccleve, your philosophy has some appeal to me," though not half as much as your body, he thought to himself, "but are not the Lollards proscribed?"

"We no longer call ourselves publicly by that name."

"Then I would be happy to lodge with you and indeed learn a little more of your principles." Mary smiled an open, unselfconscious smile which Titus had never before seen in attractive women of his acquaintance. He felt himself hardening.

Mary said, "I must resume preaching before I lose my audience. John Fletcher will call upon you this evening and bring you to us in time to share our supper. Will you be ready by then Master Roper?"

"Indeed I will."

And thus Mary Hocccleve unwittingly introduced the serpent into the bosom of her community.

* * *

III

Titus was welcomed like a homeric hero by the Frostenden Lollards. He was given a small cottage which had been vacated by one of the families so that he could have it to himself. The family seemed to regard his arrival as an honour rather than an inconvenience and happily squeezed into another dwelling occupied by relatives. Clean linen and a nightshirt had been left on the family bed for his use, and fresh herbs and flowers in earthenware pots were placed at strategic locations throughout the house to provide colour and scent. It was a great improvement on the smelly, noisy Eagle Inn.

While Titus was observing his new surroundings, a knock at the front door announced the arrival of pails of hot water carried by the three daughters of the house. They filled the tub in the washroom adjoining the kitchen; clearly Titus was expected to bathe before supper. Ah well, he thought as he began to unbutton his tunic, there's a price for everything.

Mary herself came to take him to the dining hall for the communal supper which was the meal the Lollards always ate together so that they all saw each other at least once a day. As Titus entered with Mary, everyone stood up and clapped, and even his hardened heart was taken aback by the warmth of the greeting. The three long dining tables were arranged in a U shape and Titus followed Mary to a place reserved for him beside her in the middle of the top table. After a short prayer, the meal was started.

Mary said, "The story of how you saved the bible has already circulated our community many times, and at each telling something gets added to it. I believe the current version says you laid low four huge ruffians whilst at the same time reciting the Lord's Prayer!"

Titus smiled, "That's how most heroic stories develop."

John Fletcher, who was sitting on Titus' right said, "The children already call you Mighty Titus!"

"Just Titus will do."

"And may we call you Titus, Master Roper?" asked Mary a little coquettishly.

"Certainly, I think first names are appropriate now. Tell me," continued Titus, intrigued by the awe in which the English bible was held by the Lollards, "what is your bible worth?"

"How do you mean, worth?" answered Mary a little nonplussed.

"How much could you sell it for?" Mary and John exchanged glances and Titus quickly realised he must not ask too many questions just yet.

"If you mean its value in coin, I cannot say," said Mary. "The only people we could sell it to would be followers of John Wyclif like ourselves if they did not already have one for, as you know, the established church condemns the English bible."

Trying not to appear too worldly, Titus said, "But its spiritual value must be great indeed."

John nodded, "Aye, we would give up everything before we gave up our English bible. There are only three in Suffolk and less than a hundred in all England." Now that is worth knowing thought Titus.

"And how is your business in Suffolk progressing?" asked Mary. Titus tore his mind away from bible selling and began to recount his well rehearsed cover story.

"Slowly at present. I am searching for land in this area for my master who is a wealthy mercer in London."

"Like the great Richard Whittington," interrupted John brightly.

"Just so. He desires to invest some of his wealth in land so that he can spend his twilight years away from the bustle of the city now that his son is old enough to run the business for him."

Mary enquired, "Where in London does your master live? My father works for the government in the new Westminster Palace. They may know each other." This caught Titus unawares. He dared not risk a straight lie so he confined himself to saying, "Alas Mary, I cannot say more. I am here in secret for my master does not wish his business associates to know of his intentions."

"We won't tell anyone," interjected John eagerly.

"Enough John," said Mary. "We should not press our guest on confidential matters. It is impolite."

A relieved Titus resumed his story, "I am the steward of the household. I manage the accounts and day to day domestic finance, but I was originally a steward on a country manor."

Mary's eyes widened, "That is most interesting. We have sore need of a steward. John does his best for us but he will admit that his strengths do not lie in administration and bookwork."

"That be so," agreed John. "I never seem to be able to get good prices for our produce in the market. I have even seen some of our goods sold on just after I've sold them for double the price I got moments before."

Titus nodded sagely, "There is much sharp practice in business as I have seen for myself many times, but after a while you develop an instinct which guides you through most of the pitfalls."

John shook his head sadly, "I do not have such skills."

"But I expect you do Titus," said Mary.

Titus shrugged, "I have some experience at least."

She smiled, "I am sure you are being too modest. Perhaps, if you have time, you might advise us on our few acres? What you have already done for us is beyond our ability to repay, but I hope you will forgive me asking yet another favour."

"Not at all. Tomorrow I will look at your land, your rotation sequences and so on, and see if I can offer any worthwhile comment. Next time John goes to market I will accompany him if I am still here, and together we might be able to push up the prices for your goods. Mary placed her hand on Titus' in a gesture of gratitude, unaware of the effect it had on him, and said, "The Lord brought you to us Titus Roper. While you are with us I feel all will be well. Is there any more I can do to compensate you in some way?"

"I would know more of your teachings Mary."

"Then I will come to you after supper and we can talk as long as you like."

If, a few days before, someone had told Titus Scrope that he would sit quietly through a two hour sermon delivered by a woman, he would have laughed himself hoarse, but that was precisely what he did when Mary came to his borrowed cottage after supper was finished. In truth he hardly heard a word she said, for while she was discoursing on the corruption of the church, the predestination of the chosen believers and their direct communion with God, he was observing the swelling in her bodice which hid her breasts, her narrowness of hip and above all, those deep brown eyes which looked at him so admiringly. It would have been the easiest thing in the world to place his powerful hand over her mouth, strip her and indulge his lust, many a woman had been raped by Titus Scrope, but instead he sat quietly wondering why he was treating her differently to other women. Certainly it was not out of loyalty to his master. Titus' manhood was as hard as burnished steel and Geoffrey Calveley's instructions were nowhere near the forefront of his mind. Eventually Titus decided his restraint was because he wanted this beautiful but unassuming woman to want him as much as he desired her. Just at that moment, to have Mary with her consent mattered more to him than anything else.

You're too old to go soft said Titus to himself reprovingly, but the words in his mind seemed thin and meaningless. Surely, at the age of forty six, he could not be falling in love. Or could he? Love was a blight that made strong men weak. Titus had always thought he was immune to its deadly effect. Time and time again he had seen men brought down by it. How he despised them! Yet upon reflection they had almost always found happiness. Manhood for happiness; was that to be the bargain? If so he was not yet ready to pay the price, but in the darkest recesses of his mind, where thoughts and hopes develop beyond the control of the conscious, he feared he soon would be.

Next morning Titus and John Fletcher toured the Lollard land together. It amounted to eighteen acres, barely enough to support an extended family, yet hard work and good husbandry enabled the Lollard community to live off it, albeit meagrely. The grain harvest had long been gathered in and it was time to plough again, but the fine weather was threatening to break. Time was of the essence.

"Why do you use oxen to draw your ploughs?" asked Titus as he watched two teams slowly working through the field west of the settlement. "They are slow and troublesome."

"That is true," agreed John, "but we have not been able to generate enough coin to purchase draught horses. The war has caused a great shortage of heavy horses. An animal of the right power would cost three or four pounds, perhaps more." Titus touched his money pouch. He still had more than eight pounds left.

"You really need more land John. If you could produce a good surplus and sell it for a fair price you would soon afford horses, which in turn would increase your productivity. Then you could acquire yet more land and build a bigger surplus and so on. That's the way estates develop."

"Two or three horses on our existing landholding might be enough to begin the development you have just described," said John.

"Very probably," acknowledged Titus, "but the first step is always the most difficult."

"Well we will just have to work harder and sell our produce better. I shall supervise the ploughing when you have finished your inspection Titus."

"Why wait. Let us start now. I can leave my work for a day."

"But you are a steward unused to manual labour."

Titus grinned, "I can plough with the best, you'll see."

After such a brave statement, Titus had no choice but to outperform his hosts. Although strong, he had not followed the plough for many years, and by the time work ended for the day his body was aching in every joint. But despite his aches and pains, he felt a simple sense of achievement such as he had not experienced since he was a boy. And by all the devils in hell he was hungry! As he lay panting beside his plough at the end of the final run for the day, John Fletcher approached carrying two large mugs of ale. He handed one to Titus saying, "You deserve this after your efforts. You must have ploughed two more runs than anyone else this afternoon. Be there nothing you cannot do well?" The compliment was not intended as flattery, so while his stock was still high with John Fletcher, Titus decided to nudge the conversation towards the true purpose of his visit.

"There is one thing you do well John that would terrify me."

"What may that be?"

"Speaking to a large crowd. I would never be brave enough to stand up before a mob of ruffians and preach the gospel."

John smiled, pleased that the man he so admired should think him brave. "I cannot take credit for that. When I stand up to preach I feel the Lord speaking through me. It be as if I am just his mouthpiece. He gives me the confidence to face the crowds."

"A pity he does not give you protection too."

John's brow furrowed and he put down his ale, "I do not understand you. God protects us all."

Titus pointed to John's heavily bandaged left arm and said, "Was it not you that was nearly killed by a mob of marshmen in Frostenden some weeks ago?"

"Ah, I see," smiled John as he understood what Titus meant. "On the contrary, that incident proves the power of the Lord's protection. It is true I suffered a broken arm and some cuts and bruises, but the Lord send Richard Calveley to Frostenden in time to save me. The hosts of Mammon scattered before the might of his sword."

"Whose sword? Calveley's or the Lord's?"

"On that day Titus they were one and the same."

Titus took another pull at his ale and pushed the conversation a little further, "Who is this shining knight who carries out the Lord's work?"

"I do not believe he be a knight, though such a brave man might well become one during the war against the French. He be a yeoman from Westhall."

"From what you say John, he sounds worthy of a knighthood. A veritable Saint George protecting strangers from evil."

"He's not a stranger. We met nearly a year ago when he came to visit Mary."

"Really, does he follow your faith then?"

"No, he came to have an oath of revenge solemnised because the friars at Dunwich refused to do it."

"I am not surprised. The church would not approve of such an oath. Does not revenge belong to the Lord?"

John looked troubled and nodded, "That be true but Richard had good cause. I think I would do the same under the circumstances." Titus, sensing he was on the verge of achieving his purpose, tried not to sound too eager, "What circumstances?" John scratched his head and paused for a moment. For an anxious second Titus thought his host could not or would not give him the information he sought. He was about to repeat the question when John swilled down the last of his ale and said, "I do not know much about it. You will have to ask Mary if you want to know more. All I can tell you is that Richard's wife and children were victims of a brutal murder carried out on the orders of his own cousin."

"His cousin!"

"Aye, you may well gasp Titus, but evil still stalks this fair land of ours."

"But why does Master Calveley not have his cousin arrested for murder? Surely the law should be allowed to take its course?"

"As you know, the law requires evidence. There is insufficient at present so I understand."

"Then how can Master Calveley be sure it was his cousin who ordered the murder?"

"Well he seemed very certain to me. Ask Mary, she may know."

"I will not do that John as it does not concern me directly, but I hope to meet this Richard Calveley some time. Will he return here after the war?"

"I cannot say. He has no reason to. I expect he will go back to Squire John Fastolf's Caistor Manor where he is the lieutenant. All he cares for now is his little daughter. Apart from revenge, his main purpose in life is to ensure she grows up to a lady's dowry."

"I thought you said his family was murdered."

"Except for his baby daughter. The murderers missed her."

"Does she too live at Caistor?" asked Titus, alarmed that in the event of Richard's death someone else had better claim to his landholding than Geoffrey.

"I do not know. I am sure she is well protected."

"That is all to the good," said Titus thoughtfully. "I would imagine her life would be in peril if Master Calveley's cousin found out about her."

"Then we should pray for her and Richard and invoke the Lord's protection against all who would do them harm."

A wry smile ghosted across Titus' lips as he said, "Amen to that."

* * *

IV

That night Titus lay between his linen sheets listening to the sounds of the night. Sleep would not come for he was troubled and confused. Something was happening inside him which he did not understand; the old certainties had been shaken. For as long as he could remember he had been a blackguard and revelled in it. Not once had he been troubled by conscience or thoughts of his eternal soul. Such was the concern of weak men and clerics. Life was for pleasure in whatever form it took and at anybody's expense except his own but now, after only two days' exposure to Mary Hoccleve and her quaint followers, he was beginning to have doubts.

Could it be that somewhere in his dark soul there was still a small part untainted by evil which the Lollards had uncovered? What was it that held him back from violating Mary and destroying her community from within? Certainly the universal admiration he received from them all must have something to do with it. Titus had not been admired before; feared yes, even respected by a few, and hated by many. But admired? Never! And it felt good! These Lollards accepted him at face value. They did not seek out his failings or criticise him because he was different from them, but Titus realised he regretted the fact he did not in truth measure up to their opinion of him. He could happily remain a while in this simple, honest community.

But there was a major hurdle to overcome. His relationship with Geoffrey Calveley must remain a secret, but then Geoffrey never travelled this way if he could help it. Titus could become steward to the Lollards without his master ever finding out where he had gone. But one man stood in his way, the only person who had direct knowledge of his involvement in rape, murder and arson; Richard Calveley. One more dark deed would have to be carried out before Titus had the security he needed. He would do what he could to protect the Lollards from Geoffrey, but Richard Calveley must die.

★ ★ ★

V

"I am leaving today to report back to my master," said Titus as he and Mary loaded his bags on to his pack pony the next morning.

"We shall miss you Titus."

"Will you miss me Mary?"

"Of course I will." The answer was open and honest but Titus read into it more than was intended.

"There is much I would tell you," he said, "for I have not always been the man you see now. I have done many things that shame me."

"So have I and so has everybody," replied Mary. "We are all sinners."

Not like me, thought Titus darkly. He wedged the last bag in place on the laden pony and said, "I should like to visit you again. Your way of life appeals to me greatly."

"And we still have need of a competent steward Titus."

He looked directly into Mary's eyes wanting to express his affection but the words would not come. Instead he spoke of the future.

"When I return I will tell you everything. If after that you are still willing to accept me, I shall stay and be your steward." Without waiting for a reply Titus Scrope tugged on the leading rein and began the journey home.

He soon reached Frostenden village, but before heading south he sought out the farrier who lived beside the village green. There he purchased two fine draught horses and ordered them to be taken to the Lollards with a note for Mary which read,

> *Mary, please accept these horses as*
> *a gift in return for the gift I have received*
> *from you.*
>
> *Titus Roper.*

CHAPTER SIX

On the sixth day of October the English army was ready to march. The king had tarried in Harfleur longer than he intended while some abortive negotiations with the French took place and now, in pouring rain, six thousand English warriors took the road to Calais, one hundred and fifty miles away. The army ought to have been able to cover this distance in about ten days and embark for England before the worst of the winter gales swept the Channel, but the success of King Harry's plan depended on the French remaining idle.

The Earl of Dorset was left in Harfleur with all the artillery and twelve hundred men to repair and defend the town. The rest of the army, travelling light, marched in the customary three divisions with the king in personal command of the centre. The English followed the coast road which would take them past Fecamp, Arques, Eu and on to the Blanche Taque ford where Lord William Bardolf should meet them for the last part of the march to Calais. Fastolf's men were assigned to the vanguard where Richard rode with Father Hugh.

The Franciscan, whose clerical buttocks were now hardened to the saddle, looked back at Harfleur's grey walls and said, "I never thought I would be sorry to leave that place."

Richard replied, "You surprise me Father. I thought you would have tired of handing out the last rites to so many men dying of the flux. At least the army's ill health will improve now we are on the march."

"Yes, but the men are worried. Look how fast they march even though the rain has reduced the road to a quagmire. Some say we are on a foolhardy errand."

"Who?"

"No-one in particular. It is just an undercurrent of murmuring which, as an officer, may not reach your ears Richard."

"We came here to fight the French. Apart from capturing Harfleur we have seen precious little of them. King Harry is offering battle which, if refused, will enhance his claim to the French throne in the eyes of the French as well as the English."

"But the men are weakened by the flux. What if the French do accept battle after all?"

Richard smiled, "Then you will be fortunate enough to see the majesty with which the English warrior fights. Just the sniff of battle will be the tonic our men need."

Richard's bold words began to sound hollow as the march progressed. The bad weather continued. Incessant, driving rain can sometimes dampen even the boldest spirits, and without the diversion of plunder thanks to the king's order to respect French non-combatants, the mood of the English deteriorated. But at least the pace did not slacken, and on the afternoon of the twelfth day of October the vanguard approached Eu, which marked the half way point to Calais. Inevitably the vanguard had become a little strung out and, having been unopposed for so long, complacent.

Sir Gilbert Umfraville, who commanded the vanguard, was half a mile ahead of the rest of his division with only his personal troop of two hundred men beside him, when they were met by a cannonade from the city walls. None of the English was hit but the garrison commander suddenly opened the gates of the town and a strong body of mounted men at arms burst forth taking Umfraville and his men by surprise. Because of the wet weather, the archers were marching with bows unstrung, and very soon the English were in trouble.

Sir Thomas Erpingham and Sir John Cornwall were leading the rest of the vanguard in support of their commander. There was no time to form squadrons for Umfraville was heavily outnumbered. Cornwall and Erpingham at once drew swords and waved their men onwards, spurring their horses into a steady canter which was the best pace they could muster in the sodden ground. The men at arms behind Richard and Father Hugh pushed forward and whether he liked it or not, the Franciscan was swept up in the charge. Cornwall bellowed the English battle cry and everyone, including Hugh, took it up.

"Saint George! Saint George!" It was enough to stir any man. Richard saw the fire in the cleric's eyes and managed to hand him his reserve weapon, a mace, for they were cantering knee to knee in a tight but unstructured formation.

"Take this Father," shouted Richard above the roar, "you might need it."

A wild eyed Hugh grabbed the mace and yelled, "Saint George! Hurrah!" Richard smiled inwardly. What on earth would Father Anselm say if he could see his protégé now; only the Lord knew.

It took little more than a minute to reach the vicious skirmish but the French commander, a seasoned, professional soldier unlike most of the French leaders, saw the odds no longer favoured him and quickly withdrew his men before the rest of the English vanguard caught up with him. He had done well. For every Frenchman, at least two Englishmen had fallen, which was a ratio the English neither expected nor could afford.

Unaware of the subtleties of military discipline, Hugh shouted, "They run! They run!" But Richard, surveying the dead and dying scattered either side of the road said, "Quiet Father. This was not a victory. There are at least fifty men who need your medical assistance and almost as many who require the last rites."

Before Hugh could dismount to begin his work someone shouted, "The king!" All eyes turned westward. King Harry, accompanied only by his standard bearer Sir John Codrington and his Welsh manservant Davy Gamme, was galloping fast towards them. He was not pleased.

Drawing rein close by Richard he demanded, "Umfraville! What is the meaning of this!"

Sir Gilbert, who had been unhorsed and wounded in the arm and neck replied, "The French surprised us Sire. Not all of them fear us as much as the dauphin."

The king's voice softened when he saw the extent of Umfraville's injuries. "So I see Sir Gilbert. I will get someone to attend to your wounds." He looked round and his brown eyes espied Hugh, "Aha my fiery Franciscan, I see you were well up with the action."

"Yes Sire."

"You have medical knowledge?"

"Yes Sire."

"That is well. Begin with Sir Gilbert here." Observing the mace which Hugh was still gripping, the king smiled, "Kill or cure I see. If I get wounded keep well away from me."

All those within earshot laughed dutifully except Umfraville. King Harry, now in a better mood, addressed all who could hear, "We will camp here tonight and take our revenge on Eu tomorrow. Sir John Cornwall and Sir Thomas Erpingham to me! We have matters to discuss."

During the evening the rain at last relented for a while and the army tried to dry itself out. In order to lighten the baggage train the tents had been left at Harfleur, so the English huddled round their camp fires as the clearing night sky brought with it a sharp drop in temperature. Food was also running low, and the combination of cold, hunger and the reverse outside the walls of Eu cast a pall of gloom over the army. Fastolf, Richard and Father Hugh were sitting quietly round their fire when Sir Thomas Erpingham arrived and sat down with them.

"I bring orders from the king," said the grizzled veteran. "Now that the French have shown signs of life, Harry would like confirmation that all is well with Lord Bardolf at the Blanche Taque crossing."

"It should be," answered Fastolf. "William Bardolf dwells at Dennington, not far from me. I know him well. If the king has ordered him to Blanche Taque, only the devil himself will stop him getting there."

Erpingham prodded the fire with a stick, "That is good to hear though we know there is at least one French army in Artois. At first light John, I would like you to march to Blanche Taque as fast as you can and send back a message that all is well, or not as the case may be."

"How far is it to the crossing?"

"About twenty miles."

Fastolf frowned, "Then we shall miss the assault on Eu."

Erpingham shook his head, "I doubt there will be one. The garrison commander has already offered to supply us with provisions for six days in exchange for leaving the town alone. I am sure we will accept the offer for there is nothing to be gained by assaulting the town, and the military skill the French showed this afternoon appealed to the chivalrous side of our king. Harry would prefer to allow a brave man to live."

"A charming if somewhat outdated concept," said Fastolf.

"It is with regret I have to agree with you John," sighed Erpingham. "I remember the twilight years of the third King Edward. I fought up and down the length and breadth of Aquitaine for the Black Prince against the Constable of France the great du Guesclin. We were not encumbered by such indiscriminate weapons as bombards, and the laws of chivalry were strictly adhered to most of the time though I have to admit, the nature of our war was less ambitious than this one. Then, all we wanted was to hold our French lands in full sovereignty. Now we want the whole country!"

"But then there was no King Harry," said Richard quietly.

"That is true," agreed Sir Thomas. "Our young lion will lead us to glory and we shall follow him to hell and back if needs be. That is where the French have always been unable to match us. Apart from du Guesclin, their leaders have been appalling. In my youth I was privileged to fight under the command of a great captain, Sir Hugh Calveley, a kinsman of yours Richard I believe."

"I am proud to bear the name," answered Richard, "but in truth Sir Hugh was a very distant kinsman."

"I also fought with your father in Poitou but I knew your Uncle Robert better."

"I knew neither well Sir Thomas," said Richard. "My father was taken by the plague when I was young and there was little love lost between him and his brother."

"That does not surprise me. Robert was a lesser man. He spent much of his energy chasing women, though on the battlefield he was as brave as any man. At least he quietened down for a while after he got married."

Richard said, "He gave up campaigning after he got married."

Sir Thomas seemed perplexed, "You must be mistaken Richard. Your uncle fought on for many years after his marriage."

"I am sorry to disagree Sir Thomas, but one of the conditions of the marriage contract was that Robert should give up campaigning, and from all accounts Maud made sure her husband stuck to the agreement."

Now Erpingham was even more confused, "Maud? I do not remember the wife's name, but it wasn't Maud."

There was silence while the old, grey knight gathered his thoughts, "When and where did this marriage take place?" he asked.

"I do not know the exact year," replied Richard, "but it was about 1380 in Woodbridge, Suffolk."

"Then the mystery deepens. The marriage I speak of was a good five years before that in Calais. I know because I was there."

"I never knew my uncle married twice."

"He may well not have in the eyes of God because his wife, his French wife that is, was certainly alive in 1380. She may still be."

Richard's eyes widened, "Then Uncle Robert married bigamously."

Fastolf, who had been listening with growing interest, put his hand on Richard's arm and said, "We may have just discovered a method by which you can take revenge upon your cousin. Sir Thomas, I have a most important question to ask which will have an impact on a quarrel between Richard and his Cousin Geoffrey, Robert's only child by Maud. Was there any issue from the Calais marriage? Does Richard have a French cousin?"

Erpingham thought for a moment before replying, "I am almost sure no children came from that marriage because Robert deserted his wife within a few months. The only way to be certain is to check the records in Calais."

"The marriage was bound to have been recorded by the officiating priest," said Father Hugh, "so that's the place to start. Which church was it Sir Thomas?"

"I do not remember, it was a long time ago, but there cannot be more than one or two churches in Calais. It should not take long to find out."

Richard's mind was in a whirl. This lucky revelation by Sir Thomas had at last given him some hope of avenging Ann and his sons. If the marriage with Maud was bigamous, then Geoffrey was a bastard. The disgrace would destroy Geoffrey's cherished attempts to scale the social hierarchy in Suffolk. He would be smitten where it hurt most; his pride. But Fastolf, with his legal knowledge as a magistrate, had seen further than this. He asked, "Richard, did your uncle leave a will?"

"Not as far as I know."

"Well if that is the case and there is no legal issue in France, you are very probably the rightful owner of Calveley Hall. When we get to Calais we must find time to confirm the date of the French marriage, obtain an affidavit from the church authority and if possible, trace Robert's first wife if she still lives. Armed with such information no court in England would dispute your right to your uncle's inheritance. It would seem, Richard, that thanks to Sir Thomas' memory, you have already achieved far more from this campaign than any plunder could provide."

Hugh sighed, "Thanks be to God."

"We must not assume too much just yet," cautioned Fastolf, "and most important of all we must keep this information to ourselves. If Richard's cousin were to hear of this before we are ready to move, he could make preparations, legal or otherwise, to thwart us. Remember he is in occupation of the property which gives him an advantage."

"You have my word John," said Sir Thomas.

"And mine," said Hugh.

But one man did not give his word. John Thorpe, the sergeant from Yorkshire, was lying quietly on his blanket behind a pile of firewood only ten yards away. He had overheard everything. Fate had dealt him a chance to make his own fortune and at the same time thwart Richard's ambitions. Thorpe was not the man to miss an opportunity like that.

⋆ ⋆ ⋆

II

"Are you sure this is the place?" said Fastolf. Richard looked at his map again and checked the points of reference, "It must be. You can clearly see the whitened path in the hillside where the chalk has been exposed by travellers approaching the ford, hence the name Blanche Taque, White Stain." The two men were standing on a bluff overlooking the Somme estuary which divided Picardy from Artois. The ebbtide revealed a broad swathe of mud about one hundred and fifty yards wide, in the middle of which the river wound its way in a narrow channel out to sea. There was no sign of Lord Bardolf.

Fastolf frowned, "I do not like the look of this Richard. William should have been here by now. What time do you think it is?"

Richard glanced up at the sun, which was just visible behind the broken cloud, and said, "About two hours after noon." Fastolf looked back at his company, now reduced to twenty nine out of forty because of the ravages of the flux; none of the missing eleven had been struck down by the French. He decided it would be unwise to split his small force even though the enemy had not been sighted since Eu, so they would all cross Blanche Taque together to find out why Lord Bardolf was absent. Perhaps he was simply waiting a little further upstream.

"Richard, fetch the men forward," said Fastolf. "We will cross while we can, scout a few miles ahead and return before the tide floods again."

The company cantered across the mudflats scattering wading birds and startled cockle fishermen as they splashed through the Somme, which was now only fetlock deep. They would need to recross before six o'clock to avoid being cut off from the rest of the army by the tide. On the far side the land rose gently away from them heralding the rolling countryside of Artois. Richard felt a desire to keep on galloping, for Calais was only sixty miles away, but the urge was quickly expunged by the sight that met them when they breasted a low hill a mile from the crossing point. A mixed force of about one hundred crossbow men and men at arms was resting and watering their horses in a small hamlet half a mile ahead. At first they took no notice of Fastolf's men, who had halted on the skyline above them, until a sharp eyed picket saw the red cross of Saint George on the surcoats of the English. He shouted a warning and in seconds the tranquil scene was transformed into a burst of frenetic activity as the French kicked over the cooking pots and prepared to ride out against the arrogant invaders from the north. Fastolf, unmoved, spoke quietly to Richard, "What a pity Father Hugh is not with us today, it looks as though we might have use for him."

Richard said, "Now we know why Lord Bardolf is not here."

Fastolf shook his head, "That company below us would not have been strong enough to thwart William. There is a larger force not far away I'll warrant."

"What about the crossing? Just a hundred men could hold up an army there."

"Indeed," agreed Fastolf. He turned to the nearest sergeant and said, "Take one man with you and ride like the wind back to Sir Thomas Erpingham. Tell him what you have seen and ask for the vanguard to be sent forward to Blanche Taque without delay. We will do what we can to hold the French but if we miss the tide the crossing is lost."

"Yes Squire John," replied Thorpe, but as the Yorkshireman turned his horse's head westwards he laughed to himself. He had his own game to play.

Fastolf ordered his men to advance to a low hedge lining a track which ran roughly parallel to the crest of the hill and a little below it. There they dismounted and the twenty two archers notched their arrows while the seven men at arms held the horses; Fastolf had no intention of coming to close quarters against odds of three to one. As he stood beside Richard watching the oncoming French he said, "We must hold them for three hours. If Sir Thomas is not at the crossing by then we shall have to leave. I've no wish to be cut off by the tide."

Richard looked at his map, "The vanguard should be at Cayeaux by now. Thorpe will reach them within the hour so three hours ought to be plenty."

At three hundred paces the French crossbow men dismounted. There were about forty of them. The men at arms remained on their horses and stayed just out of range of the English longbows while their comrades winched back their crossbows, placed their bolts and let fly a volley at extreme range. Some of the deadly bolts passed within a few feet of Fastolf's men, plunging into the soft ground just behind them. One eyed Henry Hawkswood gasped, "God's sacred balls! I never thought to see us outranged by the French."

"Genoese probably," said Fastolf. "They fight as mercenaries for the French and are reckoned to be the best crossbow men in the world."

Within a minute another volley arrived. One of the bolts passed through the stomach of a Wiltshire archer who fell to the ground screaming in pain, his dark lifeblood oozing through his fingers.

Hawkswood growled, "Bastards! May we not shoot back Squire John?"

Fastolf said, "I am sorry Henry but we must not provoke an attack. Every minute the French hold back brings the vanguard closer to us. You will have your revenge, I promise, but perhaps not today."

The hedge provided no protection against the fearsome crossbow bolts, and after more than half an hour of softening up, another two of Fastolf's men lay dead and one badly wounded. The normally bold English were unused to taking casualties without shooting back and failed to appreciate the subtlety of their commander's tactics. Fastolf was well aware of the strain on his men and when another archer fell screaming to the ground with a bolt through the groin he exploded, "God's teeth Richard! This is more than any man can stand! I'll soon have no company left. It's time we fought back. Give the order!"

Richard bellowed, "Archers advance fifty paces and shoot on my command!" The cheering English left the cover of the hedge and followed Richard down the slope, which was exactly what the French men at arms had been waiting for. Even as the longbow men reformed their ranks in the open ground, the horsemen charged.

"Remember the slope," said Richard quietly, "Aim low and take down the horses."

At two hundred yards the first volley went in and two or three horsemen were brought down. Years of discipline ingrained since childhood bore fruit as the next volley was loosed before the French had covered seventy yards. This time six saddles were emptied and the charge wavered slightly as the second rank had to pick its way through its unhorsed comrades. The third volley decided the issue. One arrow in three found a target bringing the charge to a shuddering halt. The French knew they must face two more volleys before closing with the English, yet already a quarter of their force had been brought down. The price was too high so they turned and galloped out of range.

Fastolf's men raised a cheer which was quickly cut short when a crossbow bolt killed another archer. Richard's next order was received with relish.

"Well done lads. Now show those crossbow men who is the master." The English let loose four flights of arrows before the cumbersome crossbows could reply. The penalty the Genoese paid for extra range was the need to use a two handed windlass to draw back their strings, and by the time they were ready to shoot again, six of them had been shot through by the heavy, ash battle arrows of the English. The Genoese soon followed the example of their mounted companions and fled out of range with cheers and hoots of derision from the English ringing in their ears. Determined not to lose the advantage, Richard ordered the men forward but Thomas Riches called across from his position on the flank, "Master Richard, look to your right." Two miles up the valley where a forest gave way to open countryside, a large body of horsemen had appeared. They were at least a thousand strong.

"Must have arrived while we were chasing off the French," said Thomas in his slow, unhurried Norfolk drawl.

"Lord Bardolf?" asked Hawkswood hopefully.

"Too many of them," answered Richard. "Let us return to Squire John."

Fastolf had seen the new arrivals. From the cover of the hedge the English watched nervously as more and more troops emerged from the forest and spilled into the valley below. Fastolf waited until the outriders of the French vanguard had joined up with the Genoese, then he turned to Richard and said, "It's time to go. We have done our duty here. How many do you think they are?"

"About five thousand so far but they are still coming out of the wood."

"I would say nearer six. At least we now know why William could not reach the crossing. Pray God Sir Thomas has!"

An unwelcome sight awaited Fastolf's men at Blanche Taque. Not only was there no sign of Sir Thomas and the vanguard, but where the mudflats had been there was now a broad expanse of water. The tide was coming in.

"Looks like we stayed too long," muttered one of the Norfolk archers. "What do we do now?"

"Get wet boy," said Thomas Riches. "What else."

Fastolf rubbed his chin thoughtfully, "Richard, how deep do you reckon it is?"

"The tide is running in fast Squire John. If we go now we might make it." Richard looked back as the pursuing French appeared barely a bowshot away and added, "There is no real choice anyway."

Fastolf spurred on his horse and plunged into the grey water closely followed by the rest of his company. Fortunately the tide had not long turned and the water was only stirrup deep until they reached the channel of the Somme.

We'll have to swim for it here lads!" shouted Fastolf. "Dismount and hang on to your horses necks; they'll get us through." This part of the crossing was particularly dangerous for the heavily armoured men at arms, one of whom lost his grip and quickly disappeared beneath the freezing cold water, but the rest of the company struggled across to the shallows on the far side of the estuary and led their horses to dry land on the west bank. The French, having gained control of Blanche Taque, did not need to risk pursuit across the river.

Fastolf looked at his wet, dispirited men and then glanced at the triumphant French on the east bank. "Seven good men lost to no purpose. In God's name what can have kept Sir Thomas. Surely he must have realised the gravity of our position?"

"Ask him yourself Squire John," answered Richard pointing to a group of horsemen who had just appeared from the direction of Cayeux. " It seems we have lost Blanche Taque by ten minutes."

* * *

III

Sir Thomas Erpingham knew trouble lay ahead. His vanguard was less than half a mile from the river crossing when they came across the body of an English archer lying in a ditch beside the road. The red hose of Castle Combe identified the dead man as one of Fastolf's men. Sir Thomas ordered the vanguard to gallop the last part of the journey to Blanche Taque, but when he saw Fastolf's bedraggled little force shivering on the west bank he knew he was already too late. The English were cut off from Calais by the Somme.

An angry Fastolf demanded, "Sir Thomas where were you? The crossing is lost." Erpingham wisely chose to ignore the ire in his distraught subordinate's voice and replied calmly, "Your messenger never reached us Squire John, else we should have been here sooner. His body lies across one of my pack horses."

"But I sent two messengers."

"We have seen nothing of the second." A quick inspection of the body revealed that the missing man was John Thorpe, and the general conclusion was he must have been murdered by the French peasantry, but instinct warned Richard that Thorpe was not a man who could so easily be killed.

When King Harry heard the news about Blanche Taque he remained calm, as was his practice in adversity, and called a Council of War in a farm house near the crossing which he made his temporary headquarters. This time only the divisional commanders York, Oxford, Cornwall and Erpingham were present along with Fastolf, who was asked to give his report on the unfortunate events of the afternoon. Umfraville was too ill to attend. All those present knew that whatever decision was made in the tiny farmhouse kitchen, which was barely big enough to accommodate the six big Englishmen, would determine the fate of the campaign.

After Fastolf concluded his report York, who was sitting at the crude wooden table with his head in his hands, groaned, "I said this march was madness before we left Harfleur. Now we are trapped. We cannot go forward and we do not have enough food to get back to Harfleur." Glancing at York's portly frame, the king said, "A little fasting will do you no harm cousin." There was an edge in his voice as he added, "Do you have any constructive suggestions?"

"Ask for terms. Offer to give back Harfleur in exchange for unhindered passage to Calais."

Erpingham demurred, "We lost too many men at Harfleur to hand it back so lightly My Lord. Let us march upstream until we find a crossing." Cornwall and Oxford nodded in agreement but the king cautioned them, "I should advise you My Lords that the division facing us is not the main French army. My scouts tell me that the banner of the Constable of France is not there. We must therefore conclude that another larger force is somewhere behind us, no doubt hoping to find us with our backs to the Somme and unable to cross. While I am confident God will grant victory to our just cause, fighting a battle on those terms is, shall we say, forcing his hand somewhat."

"Who then commands the army opposite us Sire?" asked Erpingham.

"Marshal Boucicaut, one of their better commanders. He will be less easy to outwit than most." Glaring at the Duke of York Harry continued, "As none of us can walk on water we will march rapidly upstream, as Sir Thomas suggests, until we find a way across. Then we will double back down the far bank and crush Boucicaut's army before the constable can reinforce him. But everything depends on speed. Tomorrow we will break camp before dawn and steal half a day's march on the French. Tell your men to be of good cheer. The French shall not stop us."

The plan did not work out as the council hoped because Boucicaut anticipated it. When dawn broke Erpingham and the vanguard were already approaching the outskirts of Abbeville but to their dismay, so were the French. Boucicaut was matching Harry stride for stride. Anxiety spread through all ranks in the English army for each step took them further away from safety and deeper into hostile territory. Every bridge was broken, every ford guarded. The English were marching for their lives.

They reached Hangest on the fifteenth day of October, Amiens on the sixteenth and Fouilly on the seventeenth, but still the French on the north bank of the Somme kept up with them. By now they were more than sixty miles from Blanche Taque and to make matters worse it started to rain again. But then an opportunity at last presented itself.

The vanguard was two miles east of Fouilly when it was attacked by a small force of French men at arms, which was easily driven off leaving a few prisoners in English hands. Some enthusiastic questioning by one of Erpingham's captains, which might not have been strictly within the ethics of chivalry, uncovered an accident of geography of great interest to King Harry. Upstream from Fouilly the Somme swings northwards in a great arc before returning to its original line at Voyennes fifty miles away, but on the English side of the river a small track ran straight across country to Voyennes cutting off the arc and reducing the distance to thirty five miles.

Harry did not hesitate. On the morning of the eighteenth day of October the English army left the line of the Somme and took the short cut to Voyennes reaching the town late on the nineteenth. The broken bridges which had previously prevented the English from crossing the Somme were equally effective in thwarting a French pursuit, so

Boucicaut was forced to remain on the north bank. At Voyennes the English found an unguarded ford and immediately began the crossing which was completed at dawn on the twentieth. The young Plantagenet lion had ridden his luck but at last his tired, hungry army could turn for home.

Boucicaut soon heard the English had slipped away from him, so he halted north of Peronne and awaited the arrival of the main French army commanded by Constable d'Alberet which marched into Amiens two days after the English had passed through. Hearing he had just missed the enemy, d'Alberet forded the Somme and united his forces with Boucicaut's on the twentieth day of October. The final act of the campaign was about to begin.

King Harry ordered his men to remain in camp on the twentieth in order to dry out after the Somme crossing and rest their weary, starving bodies for the march that lay ahead, but the revival of English spirits brought about by the successful river crossing was snuffed out as soon as the army reached Peronne. North of the town the sodden fields had been churned up by thousands upon thousands of hooves marking the passage of a huge mounted army, and now it dawned upon the English that far from dealing with Boucicaut's division alone, the united might of France stood between them and Calais.

The march continued with the well provisioned French foraging along the road to Calais a day ahead of the English, who were steadily getting weaker as they passed through the plundered countryside. King Harry's starving archers bore an additional burden for each had to carry a sharpened wooden stake which could be hammered into the ground for protection against a cavalry charge. But after three more days of marching north over the open chalk downs of Picardy, Constable d'Alberet decided the time was right to smite the invader.

Richard and Thomas Riches were scouting a mile ahead of the vanguard in driving rain which swept in from the west. It was late in the day and both men were soaked to the skin. They passed through the hamlet of Blangy, which might make a reasonable resting place for the night, so Richard said to his Norfolk sergeant, "We'll canter up to the crest of the next ridge and if all is well, fall back on Blangy to await the vanguard."

"I am not sure if my poor nag is able to canter Master Richard, but we'll do our best."

"Cheer up Thomas. Riding point has its advantages. At least we should find a dry billet for the night."

When Richard and Thomas reached the top of the ridge, all thoughts of billets, dry or otherwise, were forgotten. Ahead of them, covering the plain below in a blanket of steel, was the united power of France. A huge army was moving across their front from the east and, as the two awe struck Englishmen stared disbelievingly at their enemy, a break in the rain clouds allowed a shaft of sunlight to pierce the gloom and shine on the armoured host; it seemed that even God had changed his allegiance.

"Holy Jesus," gasped Thomas, "how many are there?"

"Quite enough to deal with us I should think," answered Richard. "Return to the vanguard as fast as you can and report what we have seen. I shall stay here and make an estimate of their numbers until the king arrives."

Within half an hour Harry and his commanders had joined Richard on the ridge.

"What is your estimate Master Calveley?" asked the king.

"About thirty thousand fighting men and almost as many camp followers Sire, but if you look to your right you will see yet more coming to join them."

Harry said, "Well now that the French have decided to face us, we must bring them to battle as soon as possible for as each day passes, so we get weaker." He turned to his standard bearer Sir John Codrington, "John, you have the map. What is that village ahead of us?"

Codrington peered at the damp vellum in the gathering gloom and replied, "Maisoncelles Sire."

"So, tonight we halt at Maisoncelles." The king addressed the rest of his commanders, "Bring your men forward rapidly. Tell them at last we have found the enemy. Glory and plunder lie ahead, for tomorrow a great battle will be fought." Richard turned his horse's head ready to rejoin his company, but Harry stopped him, "Wait Master Calveley, I would speak with you further." The king dismounted and bade Richard do likewise. Leaving his superb bay destrier and Richard's boney palfrey in the charge of Codrington, the king drew his simple Suffolk subject aside so none could hear them.

"I will talk plainly to you Master Calveley, but no-one must know of this conversation except your commander Squire John Fastolf."

"I understand Sire," replied Richard, overwhelmed at the honour being bestowed upon him.

"I am told you speak French?"

"Yes Sire."

"Good. I have a mission for you. Six to one are odds I do not favour, especially taking regard for the weakened state of our men. I would avoid battle if I can."

"But Sire, you just said –"

"Never mind what I just said. That was leadership. If the men do not believe in the cause and themselves they cannot win. I want you to go to the French camp this evening under a flag of truce and seek terms. I will come to your campfire tonight for their answer."

* * *

IV

An hour after dark Richard was led into the great tent of the French War Council. His blindfold was removed but as his eyes became accustomed to the light cast by twenty or more torches, he appreciated how shabby he must look compared to the three superbly caparisoned French lords sitting at the table facing him. He was not asked to sit down. An overweight, heavily moustached man wearing arms of France Modern quartered with Gules, who sat in the middle of the three spoke first, "I am the Constable d'Alberet. Your king does not see fit to send a knight of coat armour to speak with us?"

Richard replied politely, "Monseigneur, the Cross of Saint George is sufficient coat for any Englishman."

"But it will not protect you tomorrow," said a grey eyed, soldierly man on the constable's right who, from the coat of Argent and two headed eagle Gules, Richard recognised as Marshal Boucicaut.

"Monseigneur," said Richard, "Harry of England asked me to send you his compliments for the way you have led your men against him in this campaign." Boucicaut's stern face broke into a charming smile, but before he could reply, the third member of the council, the Duc d'Orleans who, as a prince of the blood wore the full royal arms of France Modern asked irritably, "Arry? Arry? Who is this Arry?"

The marshal answered, "It is a familiar name used by the English for their king because Henry claims all his warriors as personal friends."

"Pah! Ridiculous!" snorted d'Orleans.

"Ridiculous? Possibly. Effective, certainly," said Boucicaut, clearly a more thoughtful counsellor than d'Orleans.

Addressing Richard again the Constable d'Alberet asked, "Who are you?"

"My name is Richard Calveley, a lieutenant in Sir Thomas Erpingham's division."

"And what is your message?"

"Monseigneur, Harry of England intends to continue his march to Calais tomorrow. He does not seek battle, but if you try to stop him there will be much shedding of Christian blood. In return for a free passage to Calais, he will hand back Harfleur to you." The Duc d'Orleans replied angrily, "Hah! Your army is starving and weakened with disease; ours is well fed and healthy and many times the size of yours. You have invaded our land and taken Harfleur because your king lays an unjust claim to our throne. Will he give up that claim too?"

"No Monseigneur he will not."

"Then why should we let you pass." demanded d'Orleans.

"For your own good because if you try to stop us you will be beaten as your forefathers were at Crecy and Poitiers."

"Impudent commoner!" bellowed d'Orleans. "You strain our chivalry too much! Leave at once while you can."

"Not so fast Monseigneur," said Boucicaut. "You do not command here. We may require a day or two to discuss this proposal at a full War Council." The marshal was shrewdly putting the onus back on Harry for he knew, as well as Richard, the desperate plight of the English. If they waited, starvation would take its toll and weaken them still further. If they did not, then all Christendom would know who was responsible for the bloodletting to come. But Richard also gleaned something of value, for he could see at first hand how divided the French command was. The Duc d'Orleans was stupid and impetuous, Marshal Boucicaut was a wise leader but Constable d'Alberet was too weak or too lazy to control his squabbling subordinates.

"Monseigneur," said Richard, deliberately addressing the marshal instead of the constable in the hopes of adding to the divisions in the French camp, "our king will not wait for an answer for he will march tomorrow come what may."

"Then tell him to commend his spirit to God for he will not see the sunset," said d'Orleans.

"I will do as you say Monseigneur," answered Richard.

King Harry came to the orchard where Fastolf's company was stationed, an hour before midnight to hear Richard's report. The king, leaning on an apple tree, seemed unmoved by the failure of the French to accept his terms, but when Richard told him of the apparent dissension in their command he was well pleased. Gazing at the French campfires lighting up the northern sky he said, "How typical of the French. Yet again it will be their undoing. At Poitiers their commanders actually rode into battle still arguing! Tomorrow I must not give them time to agree amongst them themselves; we will take the initiative."

Fastolf said, "The men are ready Sire. The sooner the better."

"Aye Squire John but I wish they all had at least one good meal in their bellies before the fight."

"We will eat well tomorrow night Sire," said Richard, now perfectly at ease in the king's company. Harry smiled, always happy when he had something to give, "Squire John, I am mindful of the service you have given in this campaign and I am pleased to acknowledge it in kind. You shall become my lieutenant in command at Harfleur with a fine house and land to match your new status. Any reward you choose to give men in your own command, who have served with distinction, will be financed out of the royal exchequer. No doubt Master Calveley here will be one of them." Fastolf was briefly lost for words. The campaign had still to reach its climax yet he had already achieved far more than he could have hoped for.

"Sire," he said, "you do me great honour. As for Richard, he has a legal battle coming up in Suffolk concerning title to property. I had intended to pay his legal costs. It might seem a dull reward but lawyers do not come cheap."

The king laughed, "God's teeth! Squire John, that was rash. Three quarters of the ransoms from this campaign will end up in lawyers' pockets. Nonetheless send the bills to the treasury. I shall instruct my chamberlain to pay them in full. Now I had better get on with my rounds. Standing here is costing me far too much. Sleep well and may God protect you tomorrow."

Richard lay under the dripping hedge listening to the rain hissing in the fire. Apart from the occasional challenge from a sentry, all was quiet in the English camp. What a contrast to the French! From the laughter and revelry coming from their lines it sounded as if the battle had already been won. Sporadic bursts of cheering marked the arrival of yet more reinforcements for the lily banner and, despite King Harry's confidence Richard, like the rest of the English, went to sleep thinking this was his last night on earth.

CHAPTER SEVEN

Geoffrey Calveley sat down to a dinner of roast fowl. The smell of the brown crispy skin and honey sauce caressed his palate, which had already been prepared by a few glasses of good Aquitaine clairet. It was the last day of October. The tidings from France were encouraging so far as Geoffrey was concerned for it was said that the hot blooded, young English king had plunged into the French interior with inadequate forces. With luck that might hasten the demise of Cousin Richard too. When Titus had returned from Frostenden bearing news that Richard knew who was responsible for the murder of his family, Geoffrey had been thrown into abject terror, but now it seemed that the blight on his life would be removed by the French.

Outside the rain, which had been falling for most of the month, continued to soak the already drenched land, but the large fire in Geoffrey's hall kept him well insulated against the wet autumn weather. He had been surprised when Titus told him the Lollards were not involved with Richard, but now his cousin was apparently lost in France it no longer mattered anyway. But since the visit to Frostenden Geoffrey had noticed a change in his steward. It was difficult to put into words, yet as he watched Titus pouring himself another glass of wine, he felt that somehow his steward had lost his cutting edge. Perhaps it was age. In due course Geoffrey knew he would have to obtain the services of a younger man but Titus would be awkward to replace; he knew too much.

The fowl was less than half eaten when a servant entered the hall. He was understandably nervous for the master hated to be disturbed at meal times.

"Begging your pardon sir," whined the servant, "there is a man called Thorpe asking to see you."

"Tell him to come back tomorrow," snapped Geoffrey. "Only blackguards and charlatans are out at this time of night."

"He says he has information of great value to you sir." The word value gave Geoffrey pause for thought. He put down his chicken leg, "See what he wants Titus."

A few minutes later Titus returned looking serious, "I think you'd better see him. He has just returned from France." With a sense of foreboding, Geoffrey wiped his mouth on his sleeve and said, "Bring him here then."

John Thorpe was nothing if not resourceful. Disposing of the unsuspecting Wiltshireman who accompanied him across the ford at Blanche Taque had been easy. Five nights hard riding brought him back to Harfleur where he quickly found a cog due to sail for Ipswich. The proceeds from the sale of his horse and the few coins plundered from the murdered Wiltshire archer ensured Thorpe had more than enough money to pay for his passage. He had been walking all day and was spattered from head to foot in mud, but he was strong and his aching legs were soon forgotten as he was ushered into Geoffrey Calveley's home.

The impact of his news was all that Thorpe had hoped for. The colour drained from Geoffrey's face until it was as white as the knuckles on his hands, which were gripping the oak dining table as if his life depended on it. His mouth opened and closed like a beached fish, but no words would come so Titus took the initiative.

"Are you saying my master is a bastard?"

"Exactly," replied Thorpe with a triumphant gleam in his eyes which Titus did not much care for, "I have described the conversation precisely as I heard it. Sir Thomas Erpingham, Squire John Fastolf, the

Franciscan and Richard are the only people aware of the truth apart from yourselves and," he added with a malevolent smile, "me of course."

"And the proof?" enquired Titus.

"They are confident it will be found in Calais," answered Thorpe.

"If they get that far of course," said Geoffrey. It was as much a question as a statement.

Thorpe shrugged, "When I discharged myself the army was in a precarious position but I expect they'll muddle through somehow."

"Then everything is lost," groaned Geoffrey. "Me, a bastard! How could my father have done this to me!"

"All is not necessarily lost," said Titus. "Your cousin can be disposed of before he does any damage."

"But not Fastolf and Erpingham," interjected Thorpe. Titus glared at the large Yorkshireman standing by the fire, his wet clothes steaming, with growing distaste. He had not liked the last Yorkshireman he met either. That had been John Smith of Beverley whom Titus had bribed to drug Richard's drink on that fateful day of the land auction in Beccles a year before. At least Smith had kept his side of the bargain but Titus decided he would not trust Thorpe as far as he could throw him. He tried to reassure his master, "If your cousin disappears, men like Erpingham and Fastolf will soon forget about a minor title dispute that does not affect them directly. They have more important things to think about."

"And the Franciscan?" said Geoffrey.

"His grey robes will be no protection against a sharp blade."

Geoffrey, slightly encouraged, recovered himself a little and spoke to Thorpe, "And what's in this for you? I do not suppose you came here just for my wellbeing. How much do you want?" Thorpe did not answer immediately. He was enjoying himself. He slowly scanned Geoffrey's large, expensively furnished hall and let his eyes rest on the food. "I have eaten nothing today."

Geoffrey's appetite had gone. He pointed to an empty seat at his table and within seconds Thorpe was demolishing the remains of the fowl and helping himself to Geoffrey's clairet. The food was soon eaten, but as the Yorkshireman reached towards the fruit bowl Titus, who could barely restrain his irritation, moved it out of range and growled, "Well, what is it you want?"

"Patience," said Thorpe, spraying the steward's tunic with masticated fowl. Geoffrey placed the fruit bowl back in Thorpe's reach, and only after the Yorkshireman had munched his way through two large apples did he lean back in his chair as if he owned the place, and speak his mind, "I could not help noticing as I passed through your land Master Calveley, the dilapidated state of your cottages and the poor maintenance around your boundaries. Your broken fences positively encourage trespassers."

"No-one dares to trespass here," said Titus menacingly. Thorpe continued as if Titus had not spoken, "If you were to spend a small amount on cottage repairs you could double the rent to your tenants and recover the cost in less than a year."

"What do you know of rent!" demanded Titus, who had been telling his parsimonious master the same thing for years.

"Let him finish," said Geoffrey. "Anything that increases income should be considered."

"Exactly," agreed Thorpe knowledgeably. "It strikes me Master Calveley that you could use the services of a good steward." That was too much for Titus. He jumped to his feet and bellowed, "You dare criticise me you northern yokel!" The Yorkshireman was unimpressed by the outburst. He took another gulp of wine and smiled, "I take it you are the steward here then. You should be honoured to dine in your master's company."

"Sit down Titus," said Geoffrey, intrigued at the confrontation between two outright villains. Speaking to Thorpe he asked, "You have experience of stewardship?"

"Oh yes," lied Thorpe, "I spent many years on Sir Richard Strelly's estate in Nottinghamshire. Estates up north tend to be much larger than down here."

"They would wouldn't they," sneered Titus.

Geoffrey asked, "And what age are you Master Thorpe?"

"Twenty eight." That's the best part of twenty years younger than Titus thought Geoffrey. How strange that only a little while ago I was wondering how I should go about replacing him. It's almost as if fate is telling me what to do.

Ever the opportunist, Geoffrey decided to exploit this unexpected development. At the very least it would keep his ageing steward on his toes. He tossed two gold coins on the table, "As you see Master Thorpe, I already have a steward but I am sure a place can be found for you in my household. Take this money as a commencement of employment bonus. We can discuss detailed terms and conditions tomorrow." He almost added, "When we're alone," but seeing the look on Titus' face thought better of it.

Becoming all respectful Thorpe replied, "Thank you sir. You can count on me for any service, any service at all if you take my meaning."

"That I do Master Thorpe," acknowledged Geoffrey. "Now I will arrange temporary quarters for you before making more permanent arrangements tomorrow. Is there anything else you need?"

"Nothing that cannot wait until tomorrow thank you sir."

After the servant had taken Thorpe away Geoffrey asked, "Well Titus, what do you think?"

"If he's had experience of stewardship then I'm a Turk's arse."

"Constructive comment only if you please."

Titus shook his head, "Thorpe's bad news. He has no respect. We do not need him."

"I thought you may take that view," said Geoffrey affably, "but we cannot allow him to wander through the countryside at will armed with the knowledge he has. If I paid him off he would soon be back for more." Titus had not thought of that. He had allowed his temper to take control. Now he realised his master had acted wisely and was ashamed of his own uncharacteristic impetuosity. A menacing tone added a chill to Titus' voice, "So you see our bluff Yorkshireman as a possible problem."

Geoffrey shrugged, "He might be, he might not. He might make an excellent steward but if he weren't here I would not have to make a choice between you and a younger man would I?"

After dinner, Titus retired to his quarters and Geoffrey sat alone in front of the log fire. He was pleased with himself. Setting Titus and Thorpe at each other's throats was a masterpiece. If Titus was victorious, a potential source of blackmail would be removed, and if Thorpe should triumph a new steward would replace an ageing one who was beginning to lose his touch. More important still, the winner should be more than capable of disposing of Cousin Richard before too much damage was done. The title to Calveley Hall would remain exactly where it was.

★ ★ ★

II

Had Thorpe arrived just a week later, he might have become steward of Calveley Hall without peril, for Titus had plans of his own but these were not yet far enough advanced to allow Titus to abandon his links with Geoffrey. His stay with the Lollards had blunted Titus' appetite for murder but eliminating John Thorpe would be a pleasure. It would not, however, be easy. The Yorkshireman was young and strong and had the confidence of one who knew how to handle himself in a fight. Guile would be needed to dispose of this victim. It was time for Titus to call in a debt.

It was ten minutes after ten o'clock at night. The rain had stopped and a half moon was making sporadic appearances through breaks in the cloud. A cloaked and hooded Titus Scrope stood in the dark yard beside a hay cart at the back of Calveley Hall looking balefully at the small outhouse attached to the kitchens which had been allocated to Thorpe for his first night in Geoffrey's household. Next to him was another, shorter figure which shivered with cold.

Titus whispered, "Now Annie, you know what to do?"

"Of course," replied the smaller figure, "you've told me hundreds of times. I'm to tell him I've been sent with Master Calveley's compliments and then, when he's asleep, I place a candle in the window."

Drawing from beneath his cloak a pitcher of wine Titus said, "This will help him sleep. Make sure he drinks it but take no more than a sip or two yourself."

"Drugged is it?"

"Enough to knock out a horse."

"What about my money?"

"I'll give it to you afterwards."

"And my William's debt to you?"

"I said I'd forget it didn't I," said Titus, irritated by the persistent questioning. "Your William can keep my ten shillings if you do your job well. Now get in there!"

An hour passed, then another. God's sacred arse, he's making a pig of himself thought Titus as he fingered the point of the sharpened dagger strapped to his boot, but just as he was beginning to wonder if something had gone wrong, the candle appeared in Thorpe's window. Titus silently crossed the yard like a hooded ghost and pushed open the heavy wooden door. Inside a naked Thorpe lay across the bed, face down. Annie was getting dressed, and in the flickering candle light, Titus could see deep scratch marks down her back.

"Everything all right?" he whispered.

"Sweet Jesus he's a brute. I thought he'd never finish. I earned my money tonight." Titus watched her trying to fit her large breasts inside her tight gambeson and began to feel the urge himself. But first he must dispose of Thorpe. He handed Annie a shilling and said, "Take his legs while I lift him to the hay cart, then forget everything that's happened here tonight. You've done well Annie. I'll see your William keeps out of trouble."

Thorpe was a heavy man and it was hard work moving him, but Annie was strong for her size, far more use than her hopeless husband thought Titus, and after a deal of straining and heaving they managed to load the supine Yorkshireman onto the cart. Annie, her job done, departed for home while Titus began to push the cart down the rutted path to the cess pit, his favourite place for dumping corpses. No-one ever felt inclined to search for missing persons there. This particular murder was going well. He would slit Thorpe's throat at the cess pit to minimise the mess, clear up the Yorkshireman's quarters and claim he must have left during the night for reasons of his own. All so simple! Geoffrey might not believe him but that did not matter provided there was no evidence to prove otherwise.

The path steepened as it approached the old gravel pit, which was now used for dumping the household effluent. The stench which greeted Titus from below made his stomach heave but he was not sick, he had done this too often for that. He had to brake hard to stop the laden cart running away down the slope, and by the time he reached the edge of the pond of ordure the backs of his legs were aching. But soon all would be over. A quick slit with the dagger and John Thorpe would slide into stinking oblivion.

First it was necessary to weight Thorpe's body to make sure it would sink. Titus had stowed in the well of the cart an old millstone and a length of hemp for this purpose but in the dark it was difficult to see where things were. He soon found the millstone, but while he was searching under Thorpe's legs for the hemp rope, he was suddenly gripped round the neck from behind by what felt like steel tipped claws.

"Thought you'd got rid of me Scrope didn't you," rasped Thorpe as he tightened his grip, but Titus could not answer; his eyes were almost popping out of their sockets. He vainly clutched at the Yorkshireman's hands but Thorpe was much too strong.

"Tables have turned now Scrope eh," snarled Thorpe, who was still not completely free of the drug's effects. He could not yet move his legs; they felt leaden, but fear and elation, that heady combination a close brush with death often brings, gave his hands extra strength. Titus knew time was running out for him. His senses were beginning to fade. He desperately felt for his right boot but his back was being arched over the cart. He could only just reach. Stretching his arm to the utmost, his fingers gripped the dagger handle. The moon momentarily glinted on the thin blade of death.

"You'll die in shit Scrope where you belong you bast -."

Thorpe's gloat of triumph was cut short as Titus stabbed backwards into his right arm. The grip of steel slackened and Titus tore himself away gasping for breath. This time there was no delay. He launched a frenzied attack on the big Yorkshireman, stabbing wildly wherever he could pierce his victim's guard. Thorpe vainly tried to protect himself but he was still helpless from the waist down. Eventually, like a wounded Castilian fighting bull, his reactions slowed as his lifeblood ebbed away. Titus moved behind him and grabbing a handful of hair, pulled the large head back exposing the vulnerable throat. With a whoop of victory the steward of Calveley Hall secured his position as he drew the edge of his blade across Thorpe's jugular vein. The air vents quickly filled with blood, the massive body coughed, twitched for a few seconds and was still.

Titus dropped his reddened blade and slumped to the ground resting his back against one of the hay cart wheels. His clothes were drenched in Thorpe's blood. It was everywhere; he could even taste it. He would have to dump his garments in the cess pit along with Thorpe. Breathing heavily he muttered, "Christ that was close! You're getting too old for this sort of thing Titus Scrope, too old." Clambering unsteadily to his feet he removed his tunic and hose and tied them to the millstone. Then, attaching the millstone to Thorpe's leg he tilted the cart towards the cess pit. The body slid into the pool of ordure and was quickly sucked down into the stinking ooze.

"Yes you arrogant bastard," whispered Titus. "To hell with you. You'll be followed by another before too long."

* * *

III

"I do not have much time Master Roper. Tell me what you want then be about your business." Sir Hubert Manyng, master of the manor of Frostenden, was a short, stout, red faced man of forty. Although a knight of the shire, he had always managed to avoid such knightly duties as serving his king in war, preferring instead to concentrate on civil advancement in his local community. As well as an important landholder, he was a Justice of the Peace and likely soon to be a Member of Parliament. Titus, standing in the manor house hallway, looked at the pompous little man unable to keep the contempt out of his eyes, but his voice did not betray his true feelings.

"I am indeed most grateful to you Sir Hubert for sparing me some of your valuable time, for I have a proposition that should interest your good self."

Mollified by Titus' humility, and totally oblivious to the sarcasm lacing every word, Sir Hubert said, "Pray continue Master Roper."

"It concerns land Sir Hubert."

"Are you buying or selling?"

"Buying Sir Hubert."

"None of my land is for sale."

Ignoring the last remark Titus said, "I have for many years admired the field at the southern end of your landholding."

"The eight acre field beside the forest where the Lollards abide?"

"The very same Sir Hubert." Manyng had always considered that to be the least productive area in his estate, but it would not do to let this commoner know it.

"Well, what about it Master Roper?"

"I would buy it from you Sir Hubert."

Manyng raised his eyebrows in disdain, "I told you Roper, none of my estate is for sale. By God, you'll be asking for the hand of my daughter next!"

"Two pounds per acre sir," said Titus quietly. That was double the true value as well he knew. Some of the bluster went out of Manyng's voice. His small, blue eyes narrowed appraisingly at the prospect of easy money and he pointed to one of the chairs that lined the walls of his hallway.

"Sit down Roper and tell me why you want this land."

Titus did as he was bid, "For the Lollards sir. They need more land and your field would be a natural extension to the land they already hold."

Manyng's eyebrows knitted together, "But the Lollards are proscribed."

"You would be dealing with me, not them," said Titus. "I will sublet to them on an informal basis. They are indeed a strange community, but they work hard and are good for business. They produce goods they cannot sell at full value so I intend to be their agent. I shall sell their surplus at a fair market rate and keep a commission. There is nothing illegal in that and no doubt some of the commission could find its way into your coffers Sir Hubert."

"How much commission if I decide to sell?"

Titus knew his fish was hooked, "Ten per cent."

"Twenty five," countered Manyng.

"Twenty."

"That sounds fair Master Roper. Now what about the rent for my land? You know you ask a lot of me to part with some of my estate. It goes against all the instincts of a knight." You wouldn't recognise a knightly instinct if it got up and bit you, thought Titus.

"I would hold the land free of rent," he said, "so I will offer another pound per acre to the purchase price."

"Indeed," acknowledged Manyg, trying to keep his voice calm. Roper could have little idea of the value of land to offer so much for it. "So you will pay me three pounds an acre, that is twenty four pounds in all, plus twenty per cent of the commission you make on the sale of Lollard goods."

"Precisely Sir Hubert."

"Then you have a deal Master Roper. Come back in a week with the money and I will have my notary prepare the documents."

"I have the money with me and would wait here until the documents are ready."

"But that is not convenient Master Roper."

"There are other landholders Sir Hubert." Manyng, though annoyed by Roper's insistence, would not let pride come before profit, "Very well Roper. I shall send for my notary at once."

By the time Titus left Manyng's manor house the watery, autumn sun was low in the west. He was well pleased. True, he had overpaid the pompous little knight but that did not matter for on this fourth day of November, he had secured his wedding gift for Mary Hoccleve. He no longer felt any doubt. If she were to hesitate when he asked her to marry him, such a fine gift would surely tilt the balance his way. He could not remember such happiness. His life was about to change. He would leave his dark past behind and start afresh with Mary and these quaint Lollards, who admired him so much. Titus Scrope would soon be consigned to history and be replaced by Titus Roper, the Lollard steward. The only cloud on the horizon was Richard Calveley. He would have to be dealt with before Titus could finally join the Lollards.

Clutching the title to Manyng's eight acres, Titus followed the forest path that led to the Lollard settlement. He would offer marriage to Mary this very day then go back to Calveley Hall and await Richard's return with the army. As he walked purposefully along the path in the shade of the great oaks and elms, he noticed fresh hoof prints in the soft earth. Titus knew the Lollards discouraged visitors to their secluded community. He strode out more quickly, for his well honed instincts warned him that trouble lay ahead.

CHAPTER EIGHT

Richard slept fitfully in the damp Maisoncelles orchard. The rain fell intermittently throughout the night and when he was woken at first light by Father Hugh, his gambeson was drenched.

"Come on Richard," said the Franciscan, "the game's afoot. Everyone else is already up." Richard stretched his cold, wet limbs. He was tired, hungry and ached all over. The last thing he felt like was a battle.

Hugh placed a soft, wrinkled apple in his hand. "I managed to salvage some unpicked apples from the orchard. They have seen better days but at least it's food."

"Thank you Father. Will you help me armour up?" Richard got wearily to his feet and looked about him. He knew, if he survived, he would always remember this day, the smell of the damp wood ash, the long shadows cast by the dawn sun which had, for a while, broken through the rain clouds, and above all the silence. Military camps were usually noisy, bustling places but on this day, the twenty fifth day of October, Saint Crispin's day, apart from the rasp of weapons being sharpened and the occasional bark from a scavenging dog, the English prepared for battle in silence. There was nothing to be said, for all that must be said had been said; they knew their duty and none felt like talking with the prospect of almost certain death so close.

While Hugh was buckling the straps down the side of Richard's cuirass, a half hearted cheer from the direction of Maisoncelles village announced the presence of the king. Richard looked over the hedge, which had sheltered him during the night, and saw Harry and his council cantering forward along the Calais road to inspect the dispositions of the French. Above them fluttered the Plantagenet banner, the three lions of England quartered with the three lilies of France Modern. It looked superb in the gold sunlight of dawn, but while his heart told him the royal banner could never be brought down by the French, Richard's mind dictated otherwise.

He turned to Hugh and said quietly, "I must make arrangements in case I fall today for I have left no formal will. Will you see my instructions are carried out Father?"

"Of course."

"They are very simple. Now that I have the finance available for my legal costs, I wish you to ensure my daughter Joan comes into her full inheritance when she reaches maturity."

"It shall be done."

"Also I would like you to visit Mary Hoccleve, the Lollard, and tell her I intended to become better acquainted with her. To Mary I bequeath one tenth of the ransom monies owing to me after this campaign to do with as she will. Finally Dunwich Priory shall also have one tenth of my ransom monies in acknowledgement of all that you and Father Anselm have done for me. Joan shall have the rest."

"I pray I do not have to implement your instructions," said Hugh, "but if the worst should happen I will see to everything. And thank you for the bequest to Dunwich." He finished buckling the last strap on Richard's armour and passed him the muddy, stained, off white surcoat with the faded red cross of Saint George.

"Well Richard, how do you feel?"

"Cold, wet and very frightened."

"God will grant Harry victory today."

"He is an Englishman I suppose."

Hugh did not appreciate the flippant nature of the comment and answered thoughtfully, "I have often wondered about that. Although it cannot be proved theologically, I think you are probably right. After all, who would choose to be anything other than English?"

Richard looked in the direction of the French and said, "I can think of a fair number less than a mile from here."

There was no food left, so no time was needed for breakfast and by seven o'clock the English were ready to move. Sir Thomas Erpingham had been given the task of drawing up the army in battle formation astride the Calais road just north of Maisoncelles. The men at arms, now less than a thousand strong, were organised into three divisions, the left commanded by Sir Thomas Camoys a garter knight, the right under the Duke of York and the centre under the direct command of the king. Some of the archers were wedged into the gaps between the divisions, but most were concentrated on the flanks where they were drawn forward slightly thus giving the entire English line a concave frontage.

The flanks were protected by two forests, Agincourt on the left and Tramecourt on the right, which restricted the width of the killing ground to three quarters of a mile. Fastolf's little force was split for the first time in the campaign. His archers were somewhere out on the left while he, Richard and his four surviving men at arms stood in the front rank of the king's division. Father Hugh remained in Maisoncelles with the baggage, sick and other clerics, but the king could only afford to allocate thirty archers for their protection. The French, who were in no great hurry, formed up more slowly than the English, and as they massed between the two forests half a mile from the English position, Fastolf said to Richard, "This battlefield favours us. You would have thought we had chosen the ground rather than the French. With both our flanks protected by the woods, they will not be able to exploit their huge superiority in numbers."

Richard looked along the thin line of dismounted English men at arms. "We are only four ranks deep with no reserve. It is difficult to see how we can hold the French when they close with us."

"Hopefully Henry Hawkswood, Tom Riches and their five thousand incorrigible archer comrades will stop it coming to that. The ground is ploughed and sodden, far too muddy for effective cavalry manoevring. One charge and the soil will cut up like a quagmire. The archers ought to be able to keep them at bay."

As if to confirm Fastolf's view, King Harry emerged from the English ranks to give a battle speech. As he cantered towards the right flank, his destrier kicked up huge clods of soil, spattering the men in the front rank with mud and leaving deep hoof prints in the ground which filled with water almost as soon as they were made. The king addressed the Duke of York's division and the archers on the right for five minutes and was given a rousing cheer when he finished. Then he cantered back to the centre and drew rein almost in front of Richard, smiling broadly as if he was about to enjoy a day at the hunt. He sat his horse with his back to the French, affecting an attitude of complete disdain concerning what they might or might not be doing. His voice was not especially powerful, but its clarity and unusual metallic tone, enabled him to be heard quite easily by all the men in the centre of the army.

It was not so much a speech as a friendly chat. Whatever the circumstances, Harry was always able to make those around him feel they were his personal friends without losing that quality of remote magnificence so essential to a warrior monarch. His brown eyes seemed to look at them as individuals, his easygoing battlefield humour shared by all. The king's unshakable confidence and total conviction of the justice of his cause transmitted itself to his men like a potent drug which quickly drove out doubt and the possibility of failure. Was not God the final arbiter of all things? He would ensure justice prevailed as he had done before when the great King Edward destroyed an equally large French army not far away at Crecy, three generations ago. Superiority of numbers meant nothing then, nor would it now. God's will would prevail whatever the odds, but lest he had provided too cheerful a picture Harry ended by warning his archers, "Remember my noble lads, you masters of ash and yew, the French have promised to cut off the string fingers of any archer they capture so that he may never draw bow again. But fear not. Fight hard and ere this night falls you will be burdened with honour, glory and such plunder as will be beyond your wildest dreams!" The men at arms and archers cheered their young king as he spurred his horse towards the left flank to deliver his speech for a third time, leaving behind him warriors eager for the fray with the fierce light of battle in their eyes.

Harry returned from the left flank shortly after eight o'clock, took up his position again in the centre division and waited for the French attack. The French had formed themselves into three huge divisions, one behind the other, which were crammed into the open space between Agincourt and Tramecourt woods, infantry in the centre and cavalry on the flanks. In the first division the infantry consisted entirely of dismounted men at arms and knights, many of whom were of noble birth. With typical Gallic disorganisation, each thought he should personally lead the attack. More and more warriors jostled themselves forwards into the front line until the Genoese crossbowmen, who were supposed to soften up the English with clouds of armour piercing bolts, were bundled out of the way and spent the battle standing uselessly in the rear. Soon, nearly ten thousand armoured men had packed themselves into the first division impatiently waiting for the order to advance. It did not come.

The two armies stood facing each other for some hours, separated by three bowshots of open farmland. Perhaps the sight of the silent English line had given the French pause for thought, or maybe the counsel of a cooler mind like Marshal Boucicaut was beginning to prevail in the French command for, if nothing happened, it was the starving English who would have to make the first move or collapse where they stood. King Harry was well aware of this, and when he saw some of the French sit down to begin their midday meal, he decided to wait no longer. The stentorian voice rang out, "Marshal of the Archers!"

"Yes Sire," replied Sir Thomas Erpingham, who had been appointed to command the archers on that fateful day.

"The French seem reluctant to fight us do they not?"

"That they do Sire."

"Then take us to them!"

The grey haired veteran, visor up, cantered to the front of the army and stationed himself at the head of the centre division. Richard, dry mouthed and frightened now that the moment of truth had arrived at last, watched Sir Thomas as he bellowed, "Prepare to advance!" The old knight held his marshal's baton aloft so those out of earshot on the wings could see the order. Every warrior knelt down, kissed the ground and took a fragment of soil into his mouth representing the earth to which he would eventually return. Then grasping their weapons, the English stood up and waited for Sir Thomas' next order.

"Advance banners in the name of Jesus, Mary and Saint George!" He pointed to the French with his baton and at once the trumpets blew and the drums began to pound out the pace of the advance. A mighty roar went up from six thousand English throats, "Saint George! Saint George!" Suddenly Richard's anxiety seemed to leave him. Shouting the name of England's patron saint along with all his comrades, and the fact that he was moving instead of waiting, released the tension which had made his limbs feel stiff. Confidence pulsed through his veins as if he had drunk a bottle of wine; the fire of battle was in him. No memories of England crossed his mind, no thoughts of Joan, Ann or Mary. At this moment all he lived for was to kill Frenchmen.

The French reaction to the advance of the ragged English was surprise. Most of the knights and men at arms in the first division quickly got to their feet, but some of the bolder souls refused to allow the northern leopards to interrupt their meal and remained seated, confident that such a small force would not, in the end, provoke an attack from the might of France.

When the English had crossed the small track linking Agincourt and Tramecourt, they were about two hundred paces from the French. Sir Thomas gave the signal to halt. He redressed the ranks as if on parade in front of Westminster Palace and returned to his place beside the king to report all was ready. Meanwhile the Genoese crossbowmen, who should have been shooting their terrible bolts into the ranks of the English, were idling their time away in the rear.

The English archers hammered their sharpened wooden stakes into the soft earth to provide an impenetrable hedge of points against the enemy cavalry. Then, mindful of the French threat to cut off their string fingers, the archers taunted their opponents by waving their fore and middle fingers in the shape of a V, defying the French to come and get them.

Just as the sun re-emerged from behind a bank of cloud, King Harry of England gave the order to shoot.

* * *

II

A shadow passed across the watery sun as five thousand three foot, armour piercing, ash arrows landed amongst the French first division. The result was chaos. Where, seconds before, Richard had been watching a motionless mass of armoured men, now there was utter confusion. Even though the English had been in full view, the French seemed to have been caught unawares, refusing to believe that the smaller force would attack the larger. Hundreds fell. Some came reeling out of the ranks screaming, clutching goose feathered shafts which had buried themselves deep in their bodies. Others simply slumped forward, killed outright but unable to fall because of the press of men either side of them. There seemed to be no leadership, or perhaps a vital link in the chain of command had been broken for the French made no attempt to move and waited like lambs tethered for the slaughter as the next volley of arrows arrived creating yet more terror.

After the third volley came a response. Richard looked across to the French right where a column of cavalry began a forward move. There were about a thousand of them. The great warhorses sank fetlock deep into the sodden, ploughed soil, and with their armoured masters weighing heavily on them they could only move at a trot. On good ground the French would have charged at a fast canter giving the archers the opportunity to fire off two, or at most three volleys before closing with them, but in the cloying soil the horsemen were already in disarray before they had covered half the gap separating the two armies. But the honour of France was at stake. The painfully slow charge continued. Richard looked on with mixed emotions. Each superbly fitted out knight must have been worth at least five hundred pounds, yet they were being bowled over by the sixpenny archers of England.

He said, "This is not war, it's slaughter."

Fastolf was unmoved, "Slaughter is part of war Richard."

"But our archers are using those knights as target practice. It does not seem quite right."

"I wonder if you will feel such sympathy in a few minutes," said Fastolf, pointing to the first French division. "The cavalry was only a preliminary to the main attack. Here comes the infantry."

A few of the brave horsemen managed to ride through the arrow storm only to be impaled on the wooden stakes protecting the archers. None reached the English men at arms, who stood open mouthed watching the chaotic scene unfold before them. The cavalry had not quite finished its part in the battle. In their haste to escape the terrible English arrows, the survivors turned tail and smashed through the ranks of their own advancing infantry causing further confusion amongst the French. Riderless horses, some badly wounded, galloped back and forth in panic seeking escape from their terror. The English opened their ranks when necessary to let the frenzied animals pass through, but the French were unable to do so because of another development unforeseen by their commanders.

Because everyone wanted to be in the place of honour in the front line, there were no gaps in the first division, no room to deploy. Instead a solid mass of men had been squeezed into the space between the two forests lining the sides of the battlefield. The French command had failed to realise that this space narrowed towards the English position so that for every step forward the first division took, the more it became compressed. As they struggled onward in their heavy armour, shields held high against the English arrows, the French began to find their arms increasingly pinned to their sides. Some were even lifted off their feet as pressure from behind pushed them on. The state of the ground compounded their difficulties for the cavalry had turned the already muddy field into a morass.

By the time the French closed with the English line they were exhausted and almost helpless. The sideways compression became unbearable as they were funnelled into the gaps between the wooden stakes protecting the archers, and those that fell wounded by the deadly arrows were trampled to muddy asphyxiation beneath the feet of their comrades. Richard, like many of King Harry's men at arms, had abandoned his sword in favour of a mace, which would be far more effective against heavily armoured men. Some of the English had left their shields with the baggage so they could wield two handed halberds, mauls or fearsome war hammers. Richard tightened his grip on his shield, raised his mace and braced himself. At the last second he noticed the banner leading the French against him was Boucicaut's.

The impact was almost unstoppable. Richard's shield was rammed hard up against his cuirass. He nearly lost his footing when a stocky knight thrust at him with a shortened pike. The Frenchman was unable to strike a second blow because the pressure from behind pushed him within range of Richard's mace. The mace swept downwards smashing the skull inside the French helmet.

Now there was no time for fear. The clamour of battle, screams of pain, howls of triumph and above all the clash of metal on metal as steel weapons hammered on armour made thinking almost impossible. Each man fought on gut instinct leavened with whatever discipline and experience he had. With plenty of elbow room the English could wield their weapons freely. Many of the French were pushed forwards unable to raise their arms to defend themselves because of the press, and were slaughtered where they stood.

The English line buckled but did not break. Soon a wall of dead and dying Frenchmen began to build up at the point of contact between the two armies, but as fast as the English killed them, more French filled the gaps. Sometimes isolated pockets of French knights would push on into the English ranks, almost breaking the line but Harry's men stood firm.

After a while everything became blurred, each warrior absorbed in his personal world of life and death, kill or be killed, the sheer animal lust for survival. Richard found himself using the edge of his shield just as much as the mace for a weapon; whenever a Frenchman came in range he struck with whatever was nearest. But despite the damage he was inflicting, he was still being pushed steadily back by the sheer weight of the attack. Fastolf was fighting hard on his right but the man on his left crumpled under a mighty blow from a French battle axe. The gap was quickly filled from behind and despite the pressure to his front, Richard had time to recognise the arms of England quartered with France Modern. He was fighting side by side with his king!

The French axeman swung again. King Harry raised his shield to parry the blow but the axe glanced to one side, neatly severing one of the fleurons which decorated the golden crown surmounting the king's helmet. Undaunted, the king dispatched his opponent with a powerful upward sword thrust which penetrated the protective mail under the Frenchman's armpit.

Grey and red lumps of brain spattered across Richard's already bloodied surcoat as Fastolf's mace clove in the skull of yet another helpless son of France. But the Norfolk squire was beginning to tire. He stepped back to avoid a halberd thrust and stumbled over a corpse which had almost been buried in the mud. With a cry of triumph, a French knight wriggled free of his tightly packed countrymen and stood over Fastolf, axe raised for the killer blow. Richard swung his mace over his fallen master's head, forehand to the right, and struck the exultant French knight a frontal blow to the helmet, knocking him back senseless into his own ranks. He used the brief respite to help the dazed Fastolf to his feet and dragged him back through the English ranks to where the wounded were gathering.

Lifting his visor he panted, "I think we have earned ourselves a short rest Squire John. Are you all right?"

"I think so," gasped Fastolf, removing his helmet and wiping his sweaty brow. "I struck my head when I fell but my vision is beginning to clear now. So is my mind. Richard. I owe you the greatest debt any man can owe; my life. John Fastolf never forgets a credit or a debt. I shall pay you somehow." Richard was about to dismiss the incident as something any Christian would do, but checked himself. A grateful Fastolf might be very useful. Instead he simply said, "Thank you Squire John. Let us rest a minute or two until you are recovered before returning to the fray. My arms feel leaden."

The second French division had by now pushed up behind the first, stretching the English line to the utmost, but many of the archers, seeing their men at arms hard pressed, put down their bows and joined the hand to hand fighting wielding their two handed mauls. Others weaved their way through the hedges of sharpened wooden stakes and attacked the flanks of the exhausted French, moving in hunting packs and killing almost at will with little danger to themselves. When Richard and Fastolf rejoined the fighting the wall of dead was shoulder high in places. Some of the archers were literally walking along the top of the heaped corpses swinging downwards with their mauls crushing the skulls of the compressed French who could only watch and pray as their nemesis approached.

But those few French knights and men at arms who had room to fight properly gave a good account of themselves. A huge, black bearded man at arms stepped forward and swung at Richard with a two handed axe. Too tired by now to leap out of the way, Richard took the full force of the strike on his shield. The power of the blow knocked him off his feet and he fell headlong into the bloody mud and slime. Landing on his back he was able to cover himself with his shield ready for the next blow from the axe. It never came. The Frenchman, also in the last stages of exhaustion, was poleaxed by an English man at arms in the second rank, but the massive, armoured body fell forward and crumpled on top of Richard pinning him in the quagmire. Everything went dark, the din of battle suddenly became muted. Cold slime began to ooze into Richard's visor slit; he was drowning in mud. Surely he could not, he must not die this way. Panic lent him extra strength. He kicked and thrashed, all the time sinking deeper, but just as the liquified mud started to obstruct his breathing, he managed to heave the dead weight above him far enough to one side to wriggle free. A knight wearing the livery of Lord Mowbray helped him to his feet and he found himself in the rear rank a few paces off the fighting. Taking the opportunity to remove his helmet, he cleared the mud from his air passages while he rested for two or three minutes. Then, having stared death in the face and lived, he pushed forward to the front rank again, confident he was destined to survive this terrible day.

Four paces to Richard's right, the young Earl of Suffolk was killed by a halberd thrust. Marshal Boucicaut himself was captured but only after he became isolated from his countrymen fighting three English knights. The leader of the French second division, the Duc d'Alencon, somehow managed to wriggle his way through the press to confront the Duke of Gloucester, whom he wounded before being struck down himself by an English battle axe. The Duke of York fell wounded but, less fortunate than Richard, was crushed underfoot and drowned in the churned up morass.

An hour after the first volley of arrows, Richard felt the ferocity of the conflict beginning to ease. No-one could fight with such intensity for much longer. The French survivors, shocked and exhausted, slowly retired across a battlefield littered with dead and dying men and horses towards the third division which had not yet been committed to the fight. The soldiers in this division were generally of lesser quality than the first two, and when they saw the destruction of their comrades they began to melt away from the battle despite the best efforts of their commanders, the Comte de Merle and the Sieur de Fauquembourges.

In their way the English were almost as shocked as the French, numbed with exhaustion and hardly daring to believe the battle was over. While the knights and men at arms removed their helmets and rested, the more lightly armed archers began to roam the battlefield, sorting out the wounded and prisoners worthy of ransom, and finishing off the rest with their needle sharp misericords. Soon more than four thousand disarmed prisoners had been gathered in the rear of the English line, guarded by a thousand archers.

A blood soaked Fastolf looked at the magnificent array of French chivalry assembled behind them and said, "God's teeth! There's enough ransom gathered here today to pay for the campaign many times over."

"How much do you think?" asked Richard as he tried to wipe away some dried blood on his face from a wound he could not remember getting.

"I cannot say," beamed Fastolf, "but for certain there is enough to make us all rich men!" He spoke too soon.

★ ★ ★

III

Merle and Fauquembourges were proud warriors and could not accept that the flower of French chivalry had been beaten. Riding amongst their demoralised countrymen they gathered together about a thousand men at arms, some from the fast disappearing third division, the remainder from the boldest survivors of the other two who were prepared to try again. In themselves they posed no threat to the English, but some of the fleeing French were passing through Tramecourt wood while a maverick band had come down the small track from Agincourt to Maisoncelles and started to plunder the scantily defended English baggage train.

Surrounded by so much enemy activity, King Harry could not take the risk that victory might escape him even at this late stage. He had read of battles where such things had happened. A weaker man might have baulked at what must be done but Harry of England was utterly ruthless when he had to be. Knowing he had too few men to guard the prisoners and face another attack, he gave orders that all the French captives should be killed and the battle line reformed. The order was greeted with gasps of horror. Even the hardened English soldiers found such a task unpalatable, partly because of the loss of ransom money but mostly because few had a taste for cold blooded murder. Harry could not afford to wait while his men overcame their finer feelings. He threatened any who disobeyed with death and sent his personal bodyguard of archers to begin the grisly work. Fastolf, who had as great a sense of duty as any man, muttered, "Pray God the killing ends soon. I've had enough for one day."

"Amen to that," said Richard, turning his eyes away from the butchery which was taking place behind them. "Are we expected to join in the murdering?"

Fastolf replied, "The order is for everyone but I shall not hurry to obey. This has taken the sweetness of victory away." Richard had experienced no sweetness even before the dreadful order and now, as he heard the screams of terror and cries for mercy coming from the prisoners, he was overwhelmed with shame, shame not just for the murders now taking place, but for the entire loss of Christian life that day. How could one man's quarrel, even a man as illustrious as Harry of England, justify the carnage at Agincourt?

Richard had experienced a foretaste of this feeling of guilt after his first encounter with the French near Bolbec but it had not lasted long. He decided that it was probably an aversion to such one sided contests rather than to war itself. He was certain of one thing however; he would do no more killing that day whatever the king ordered.

Richard and Fastolf were spared the butchery as were fifteen hundred of the more valuable prisoners, because Merle and Fauquembourges launched their attack before the killing was complete. Leaving five hundred archers to guard the survivors, the king ordered the rest of the English to reform the line at once. The men at arms were not needed and, with the benefit of hindsight, it was clear that the killing of so many captives had been unnecessary. Fauquembourges, whose bravery had indirectly led to the massacre of his countrymen, lay dead in the Agincourt mud, crushed when his wounded horse fell on top of him. The rest of his men, those who still could, fled the field.

King Harry ordered a general advance in the wake of the fleeing French. The time was two hours after noon.

★ ★ ★

IV

The plunder in the French camp was bountiful. The hungry English searched first for food; most had not eaten properly for many days. Fortunately the French had been in the middle of cooking the midday meal when the battle started, so there was more than enough to satisfy the voracious English appetites. In one of the kitchen tents Richard found a complete side of beef cooked and ready to serve. He put down his mace and shield, removed his helmet and sliced off a large chunk with his dagger. It was the best beef he ever tasted.

His appetite was satisfied surprisingly quickly for his stomach had become accustomed to meagre rations and could not accommodate a sudden influx of food. Many of the English made themselves sick by overeating, others found caches of wine with similar results. Cutting off another piece of beef for later, Richard gathered his arms again and slowly walked alone to the edge of Tramecourt wood. There he was greeted by the incredible sight of the remnants of the French army fleeing across the open plains of Picardy. There were still thousands of them. As he watched the rout in the pale afternoon sun, he concluded that just as King Harry had predicted, God must have wanted the English to win. There could be no other explanation for such an unlikely, yet so comprehensive a victory. The English were tired and with the lure of fine loot in the French camp, no effort was made to pursue the beaten enemy. All felt they had done enough for one day.

Richard was about to return to see what he could find in the way of booty when a sudden shuffling noise in the forest edge startled him. It seemed to be coming from a place where a narrow footpath emerged from the tree line. Gripping his mace and shield tightly, he carefully approached the path and peered into the dark forest eaves. It would be a bitter irony indeed to become a casualty after the battle was over. He need not have worried. Two large brown eyes peered back at him. They belonged to a huge, pure black destrier, quite the finest warhorse Richard had ever seen. The high backed saddle was still in place and the reins hung loosely around the forelimbs. An arrow projected from the blue and white emblazoned saddlecloth just in front of the stirrup leather. The rider probably lay dead somewhere on the battlefield and Richard, who always had a way with horses, determined he should be the new master of the noble beast.

Carefully, he gathered up the reins and reassuringly stroked the frightened creature before examining the injury caused by the arrow. The lozenge shaped tip had penetrated the front edge of the saddle which reduced the impact before it struck the flesh. There was no need to remove it immediately so Richard gave his prize a friendly pat on the neck, gently tugged the reins and walked him slowly back to the battlefield, all thoughts of plunder forgotten. He would employ Father Hugh's medical skills to remove the arrow before attempting to ride his new steed.

"We were attacked twice during the battle," said Hugh as he placed a moss poultice on the destrier's wound, "once at the beginning and once near the end. That's how I got this lump on my head."

Richard, pleased that nothing serious had befallen his clerical comrade smiled, "I assume you resorted to pugnacity instead of prayer?"

"Well I could hardly stand by and let the French help themselves to the few provisions we had left."

"I suppose not," agreed Richard.

Hugh wiped his hands and admired his handiwork, "Your beast will make a full recovery Richard which is more than I can say for some of our lads. Have we any idea what the losses were?"

"Hawkswood and most of our men came through unscathed. Thomas Riches took a head wound but he'll be all right."

"And the French?"

"No-one really knows yet. My guess would be about nine thousand dead but we will know more when the burials have taken place."

"Sweet Jesus!" gasped Hugh, "so many."

Richard muttered, "It was terrible. I hope never to take part in a battle like that again."

The Franciscan crossed himself and asked, "What happens now? Do we march on Paris?"

"I doubt it. It is late in the year and we are laden with plunder."

"You do not appear to be overburdened with French loot," said Hugh.

Richard stroked the destrier's nose, "This is my plunder. I have enough ransom money owing to me without the need to look for more. Now I must find Squire John, he may know what the king plans to do next."

Richard left his new horse in Hugh's care and walked back towards the killing ground. On his way he had to pass the French captives, most of whom were sitting or lying on the muddy ground in a state of severe shock. One of them, sitting a little apart from the others with his head in his hands, seemed familiar. Richard walked up to him and tapped him on the shoulder. He instantly remembered the open, honest face.

"Sieur de Freuchin! What are you doing here?" The young French knight was momentarily confused, but when recognition dawned he burst into tears, "Mother of God, now I am condemned for certain!"

Richard sat down beside him and said, "I take it you refer to your broken parole which you gave us at Harfleur."

The disconsolate French knight nodded, "Yes. I could not resist joining the muster for the great battle. How could I have known it would end this way? Now death will be my reward for that is the price of breaking parole."

Richard lowered his voice, "Listen Mon Sieur, there has been quite enough death for one day. Those of us to whom you owe ransom would be ill served by your execution. We would lose our money; I assume you still intend to pay us?"

A glimmer of hope entered de Freuchin's eyes, "But of course. What exactly are you saying?"

Richard looked around to make sure he could not be overheard, "I shall get you away from here Mon Sieur before you are identified. It will be dark by the time the muster of prisoners is taken. Make sure you are as near last as possible without drawing attention to yourself. I will come to you at sunset. Stand as close to Tramecourt woods as your guards will allow."

"Very well," said the grateful Frenchman. "I regret I do not remember your name."

"Richard Calveley, Lieutenant of Caistor Manor." As he got up to leave Richard added, "Make sure your armour is unbuckled. You will have to leave it with me."

The burial parties were still hard at work when Richard returned to the prisoners. While Father Hugh engaged the nearest sentry in conversation Richard, wearing the helmet, brigandine and white surcoat he had taken from a dead archer, hurried to de Freuchin. There was not much time; most of the prisoners had already been identified and their parole terms agreed.

"Quickly Mon Sieur," whispered Richard, "take my clothes and give me your armour." Though still dull eyed with shock and exhaustion, the nearest French captives soon understood what was happening and unobtrusively formed a cordon round the two men to screen them from the guards. De Freuchin was much the same height as Richard though less well muscled, so apart from some tightness around the limbs, which could easily be accommodated by adjusting the buckles, the French knight's armour was a good fit. The brigandine hung loosely on de Freuchin's slim frame but the cross of Saint George emblazoned on his white surcoat made him look every inch an Englishman.

"How can I ever repay you?" said the grateful knight. In a single day, first Squire John and now de Freuchin feel in my debt thought Richard. I shall never forget Saint Crispin's day.

"We English have won a victory," he said "but I feel in my bones that this war has a long way to run yet. Now walk boldly towards Maisoncelles, no-one will challenge you dressed as you are, and when the chance comes, slip into Tramecourt wood." The young Frenchman embraced Richard, much to the startled Englishman's embarrassment, and walked quickly in the direction of Maisoncelles.

Just as Richard was about to rejoin Hugh, a grey haired French knight touched his arm and whispered, "Thank you Mon Sieur. God bless you for your action this day."

Richard looked into the old knight's faded blue eyes, which seemed to carry the same ancient wisdom as Father Anselm's. "Mon Sieur," he replied, "you are the enemy but I cannot hate you."

"And you English may fight like lions but you will never conquer France."

CHAPTER NINE

"Give this letter to Millicent and tell her I will show her Harfleur when the war is won," said Fastolf as he handed Richard a rolled and sealed parchment. It was the day after the battle and Lord Thomas Camoys had been ordered to take the advance guard of two hundred men, all of whom were mounted, to Calais. From there the news of Agincourt would be sent to England so that preparations could be made for the king's triumphant return. Fastolf had allocated Richard, Father Hugh and four of his lightly wounded archers to Camoys' troop while he and the remaining twelve of his original company stayed with the king. Richard slid Fastolf's letter into his belt, mounted his horse and said, "You have no idea when you will be coming home Squire John?"

"In a year perhaps. Harfleur must be refortified and the war carried further into Normandy. I shall take ship to Harfleur from Calais confident in the knowledge that my lieutenant will be in charge at Caistor. One more thing Richard," added Fastolf. "As my lieutenant you hold my authority but be advised by Millicent. I have heard it said that our estates run particularly smoothly when I am away."

Richard smiled, "I do not doubt it Squire John. I shall heed her advice."

"And lastly, I give you my permission to use my retainers to assist your claim against your cousin should you have need of more direct support than a writ, but they are not to be used to help Lollards."

"I understand."

"Write to me of your progress, especially of what you unearth in Calais concerning your uncle's first marriage."

"I will. God protect you Squire John."

Lord Camoys' troop, laden with plunder, left the army and headed north along the Calais road. Richard, out of loyalty, still wore his father's armour and rode the faithful palfrey which had served him so well in the campaign. The Sieur de Freuchin's armour was packed on the black destrier which Richard held on a leading rein. Despite the agreement that all plunder taken by Fastolf's company should go into a communal pot, the squire had turned a blind eye to the value of the destrier which would fetch ten pounds in any auction in England. De Freuchin's armour was another matter and Fastolf's expert eye had valued it at forty pounds, which would be deducted from Richard's share of the campaign loot and ransom monies.

As Camoys led his troop out of the English camp, Richard noticed with some satisfaction that Marshal Boucicaut's banner was amongst the captured French; at least he had survived the battle unlike so many other French commanders. Once his ransom was paid he would probably replace the Constable d'Alberet, who had been killed leading his men in the first attack.

There was no sign of the enemy, but on the second day out from Agincourt ten miles south of Ardres, an outrider came galloping back to report a large body of men blocking the Calais road. Lord Camoys instructed his men to deploy into battle order while he and his bodyguard went ahead for a closer look, but the alert was soon over because the new force turned out to be three hundred hobelars from the Calais garrison who had been shadowing the French. The two forces united and rode north, entering Calais in the early evening with the news of the great victory. The burghers, who valued the occupation because of the cross channel trade it brought, welcomed the tidings and the bells of the Church of Our Lady were rang in celebration.

Calais was a strange town. It had been under English rule for nearly seventy years and was the entrepot for the flourishing trade and commerce that went on between England and continental Europe. During this time it had become partly anglicized largely due to successive monarchs' policy of transplanting into it as many English people as possible. Calais held the important wool staple of England, and the well known mercer merchant, Richard Whittington, had been its mayor on two occasions.

Lord Camoys' troop and the hobelars dismounted at the barracks outside the town walls where the Lieutenant of Calais came out to greet them. Lord Bardolf was one of the handsomest knights Richard ever saw. Tall, clean shaven and with a smile that would charm the birds off the trees, he was the very image of Richard's mental picture of Sir Lancelot. His reputation as a warrior was unsurpassed too, and like his old friend Camoys, he had been chosen as a garter knight.

The two commanders shook hands and Camoys gently taunted his friend.

"Where were you William? We delayed the battle as long as we could for you!"

"God's holy balls Tom, I tried to get there but the Frenchies had us penned in like a stopper in a bottle."

"We guessed as much at Blanche Taque. I have much to tell you but before I forget, Sir Thomas Erpingham begs a favour. One of his men at arms needs to look through the parish records on an important personal matter." Turning round and addressing Richard for the first time Lord Thomas said, "Step forward Master Calveley and explain your requirements to Lord Bardolf." Richard, caught unawares at this unexpected assistance from such exalted knights, found himself tongue tied until Bardolf, who was also in his late twenties, smiled, "Take your time Master Calveley. Who is your commander?"

"Squire John Fastolf of Caistor Manor."

"I know John well," said Bardolf.

Camoys added, "Fastolf distinguished himself in the campaign, his knighthood cannot be long in coming."

"That is well," replied Bardolf. "Now Master Calveley, what do you require of me?"

Within half an hour Richard, accompanied by Father Hugh, was walking through the narrow streets of Calais towards the Church of Our Lady carrying a letter written personally by Lord Bardolf instructing the parish priest, Father John Chapman, to give his full co-operation. 'You will need this letter,' Bardolf had said, 'for Father Chapman is an ill tempered sort, a frustrated bishop I shouldn't wonder!'

It felt odd walking through a French town that was so English. The names above the colourful shop fronts were mostly English as were the merchants who sat outside the taverns watching the stallholders packing their wares for the evening, but the language in the streets was definitely French. Richard sensed an undercurrent of hostility from the common folk which seventy years of English rule had done nothing to overcome. How long then would it take to win the hearts of the rest of the country?

Richard and Hugh stopped for a moment in front of the church to look at the imposing rather than beautiful façade. The words 'Church of Our Lady' had been painted on a stone plinth beside the entrance but underneath the paint, carved into the stone, the words 'L'Eglise de Notre Dame' could still be seen. For Richard, that summed up the superficial nature of the English occupation.

The bell ringing had stopped and all was quiet as Richard and Hugh entered the deserted church. A few candles cast a little light in the side altars but the evening gloom was unbroken in the nave.

"Hardly encourages the faithful does it?" said Hugh. His words echoed around the church interrupting the oppressive atmosphere. "Come on Richard, let us root out this Father Chapman who seems to care so little for his parishioners. Even our little priory church at Dunwich is never completely empty." The Franciscan seemed intent on taking the initiative now they were in ecclesiastical territory, and Richard was happy to follow on behind. Hugh took Lord Bardolf's letter from Richard and strode down the nave to the transept where a heavy, wooden door in the south wall marked the entrance to the presbytry. He knocked loudly and when the door was not opened within thirty seconds, he knocked again even more loudly. This time there was an immediate response. The door swung back to reveal a small, neat sparrow of a man clad in black clerical garb who, to judge from the napkin in his left hand, had been in the middle of his evening meal. His right eyebrow arched when he saw Hugh's muddy, grey Franciscan habit, for no love was lost between the established church hierarchy and the independent orders of friars.

"Well," said the parish priest, "what is it that is so urgent you must needs try to smash down my presbytry door?"

"Work of a parish nature," replied Hugh with equal hostility, "which, from the looks of the deserted state of your church, may be somewhat unusual for you."

"I do not have to stand here being insulted by a beggardly Franciscan. Be off with you to your thieves and lepers!" But before Father Chapman could close his door, Hugh placed a booted foot in the way and thrust Lord Bardolf's letter under his nose saying, "Read this priest." After quickly scanning Bardolf's orders Father Chapman knew he would have to submit.

"You had better come in," he muttered.

"Thank you Father," said Richard, trying to ease the strain between the two priests, which was mortally embarrassing for one who had been brought up to respect the clerical estate. "Perhaps you would like to finish your meal before assisting us?"

"It does not matter," said Father Chapman coldly as he stood aside to let them enter.

The contrast between the gloomy church and the light, cheerful presbytry was remarkable. A part eaten fowl, bowls of fruit and a goblet of clear, red wine adorned the dining table. The chairs which lined the table had padded, finely upholstered seats, and a friendly pine log fire crackled merrily in a well designed recess which kept the smoke out of the room. With a grumpy, backhand flick Father Chapman indicated that they should sit down while he moved his food from the table to a window ledge ready for a servant to collect; clearly he had no intention of offering sustenance to his visitors.

Hugh paused before sitting and pointedly looked round the well furnished room, "I see our church looks after its own in Calais," he said scornfully, but Father Chapman ignored the criticism and addressed Richard, "Lord Bardolf's letter says you wish to refer to the marriage register. What date?"

"I am not sure, but the marriage I am searching for took place some time between 1374 and 1376."

"What! Three years!" expostulated Father Chapman. "That will take all night!"

"I assume the records are kept in annual volumes," said Hugh, "so we can take a year each and thus reduce the commitment of your valuable time to a minimum."

The Calais priest entered an adjoining room and, five minutes later, returned carrying three calf bound ledgers, the records of marriages in the town between 1374 and 1376. He dumped them on the table sending clouds of dust into the air, then picking up the top one asked, "What are we looking for?"

Richard answered, "The date of the marriage of my uncle, Robert Calveley, and the name of the lady he married." Most people would have at least asked why, but Father Chapman wanted his ordeal to end as soon as possible, so without more ado he picked up the ledger for 1375 and began leafing through the yellowed pages.

The lists were not quite as long as Father Chapman had made out but some of the entries were barely literate, much to Hugh's audible disgust. The Franciscan's ill humour improved somewhat after an hour or so when Father Chapman said quietly, "I think this is it. Robert de Calveley took the hand of Blanche only daughter of Philippe d'Ardres on the sixteenth day of May 1375, witnessed by Jean de Fresdin and John Calveley of Dunwich in the county of …." His voice died away and his eyes widened.

"What is it?" Asked Richard as he hurried round the table to look at the entry with Hugh.

"Blanche Calveley," said Father Chapman, "I should have recognised the name. She still lives."

"A witness!" exclaimed Hugh. "Just what we need."

The Calais priest shook his head, "Not so fast. We must consider before taking precipitate action. Blanche Calveley resides in the convent attached to this church. She took her vows saying her husband had been killed in battle shortly after their marriage. Would that be true?"

Richard sighed, "Regrettably not but I see no good reason why we should bring back bad memories for her if you, Father Chapman, would write out and seal an affidavit which might be used in court to assist the litigation of a property claim. The affidavit will need to describe this entry in the register word for word and the date of course. Then in the event of a dispute the presiding magistrate would be prepared to come to Calais for verification if necessary."

Father Chapman, eager to conclude the visit agreed. "There will be no difficulty doing what you ask. Come back in the morning at nine o'clock to collect the document."

Richard said, "One more thing, the most important question of all. Do you know if there was any issue from Blanche's marriage?"

Father Chapman rubbed his chin, "I think not, but only Blanche herself can answer that with certainty. Now that we know the date of the marriage I shall check the register of births up till the day she entered the convent. If there is nothing, I beseech you to leave her in peace."

"That sounds fair," acknowledged Richard. "We will return tomorrow."

* * *

II

Next morning Father Chapman confirmed there was no entry in the register of births so Richard, Hugh and Fastolf's four wounded archers, one of whom was Thomas Riches, embarked on a small cog destined for Yarmouth. A favourable southwesterly hurried the vessel northwards but a day out from Yarmouth Roads the wind shifted to the easterly quadrant, cutting the rate of progress and dropping the temperature sharply. By the time Yarmouth came into view off the port bow, the cog's rigging was white with frost and the mariners had donned their heavy winter clothing.

Richard stood on the port beam admiring the pilot's skill as he navigated his vessel into the narrow harbour entrance. After many months of wearing armour day in and day out, the freedom of donning normal clothes once more was exhilarating. The cog slowly threaded its way on the flood tide towards its berth and a warm feeling of wellbeing flushed through Richard as he watched the quaint portside houses pass by. He was returning to England a hero of the greatest victory ever to grace English arms, with plunder, ransom money and the promise of royal patronage in his dispute with Cousin Geoffrey. His master was indebted to him for saving his life and he had got through the campaign with barely a scratch. And today, to cap it all, England was greeting him with one of those wonderful, still winter mornings when the sun shines from a cloudless sky, lighting up the frost crystals like multi-coloured jewels festooning the landscape, or in Yarmouth's case, the townscape.

One of the mariners tossed a rope to a docker who welcomed him home with a coarse reference to his lonely, lustful wife, but the simple jest resurrected dark, brooding thoughts which were never far from Richard's mind. To dispossess Geoffrey of Calveley Hall would be satisfying but inadequate recompense for the murder of Ann and the boys. He was still no nearer determining how he was going to avenge them fully without breaking the law of the land and becoming a criminal himself. And even if he could somehow settle the score with Geoffrey through a conviction for murder, there still remained Titus Scrope. He would have been Geoffrey's instrument, the actual perpetrator of the murders. He must die by Richard's own hand whatever the consequences.

He pulled his heavy, fur lined cape tightly round himself and tried to clear his mind. There was still Mary Hoccleve, what must he do about her? When he thought of Mary the anger in his soul disappeared;

he determined to visit her as soon as possible but what would he say then? There were many important decisions that would soon have to be made but Richard decided that for the rest of today at least, he would put them to the back of his mind and relish his homecoming. A voice behind him said, "The third of November is my birthday. Most auspicious for our return to Merry England."

Richard turned round, "Congratulations Father Hugh. Had I known I would have bought you a present."

"Quite unnecessary Richard," said the Franciscan. "What do you propose to do now we are back?"

Richard answered, "First we must go to Caistor Manor and report to Millicent Fastolf. She will want to know everything we can remember about the campaign. Then tomorrow we shall visit Calveley Hall and give my cousin notice to quit, and after that I will return you safe and well to Dunwich Priory." The usual brightness suddenly left Hugh's face. He looked at his feet and said quietly, "So soon?"

"I would have thought you were more than ready for a rest, and I would like to spend some time with Joan or else my little daughter will grow up a stranger to me."

"Of course," said Hugh, "you must see Joan as soon as possible. It's just that the confines of the priory will take some getting used to after all we have been through together. I thought there might be more work to do yet." Richard looked at the unhappy Franciscan who had become his closest friend. Poor Hugh; his vocation had never been particularly strong and maybe now it no longer existed at all. War, particularly war crowned with glory, has a strange effect on men. During the campaign all the talk is of going home to family and loved ones, of the idyllic life that awaits the conquering heroes, but when the campaign is over and the fellowship at an end, the separation of comrades who have faced death together and have developed a trust proven in battle is a difficult moment. The return to domesticity after the excitement of war is a contrast that sharpens with time as the discomforts of campaigning are forgotten and only the good times remembered.

It was at this moment that Richard finally realised he too could never again be satisfied with the life of a farmer. He had developed a taste for war and knew it would not be too long before he rejoined the struggle against the French. He now understood why his father had spent so much time away from home, but the desire for a warrior's life did not reduce Richard's hunger for land; that was in every Englishman's blood. He would have to find a good steward to manage Calveley Hall during his prolonged absences until Joan was old enough to take over the management as Millicent did so effectively for Squire John. If Joan took after her mother she would become a fine steward in her own right with a dowry worthy of a knight. But in contrast to the busy times that lay ahead for Richard, all Father Hugh could look forward to was a friar's cell.

Richard tried to cheer up his sad friend, "Come now Father Hugh, you have done enough for one campaign. At least you are part of a preaching order, not a contemplative one. You are not restricted to the confines of the priory."

"True," agreed Hugh with a shrug.

"There will be more campaigning. Perhaps Father Anselm might be persuaded to release you again."

Hugh shook his head, "I doubt it. He will expect me to concentrate on my pastoral duties."

"Do not be too sure about that," said Richard. "Father Anselm is an astute man. He will know how best you can serve God."

Even as he spoke, Richard had no idea just how astute Anselm really was, for Richard himself was unwittingly about to play out the part the wise old Franciscan had set for him in the overall scheme of things.

* * *

III

Millicent Fastolf greeted Richard, Hugh and the four walking wounded with a celebratory banquet to which the entire manor was invited. She eagerly devoured all the news from France and, after reading Fastolf's letter, professed herself ever indebted to Richard for saving her husband's life at Agincourt.

The next day Richard departed for Calveley Hall to serve notice on Cousin Geoffrey and, although he was not wearing armour, he took the precaution of bringing two of Fastolf's men with him as well as Father Hugh. One of these was Thomas Riches, who still wore a bandage on his headwound, the other was a certain Will Potter, another Norfolk archer. He had sustained a blow in the mouth from a French mace which had removed most of his front teeth.

They left Caistor Manor rather later than intended due to the merriment of the night before, especially on the part of Father Hugh who was determined to make the most of his last night of freedom. As they cantered along the road south, Richard spoke to Thomas who was riding at his side, "I regret taking you and Will away from home again so soon but it will only be for one night."

Thomas replied, "That's all right Master Richard. From what I hear it would not be safe for you to enter your cousin's property unprotected." He turned to Will Potter, who was riding behind them, with a pale faced Father Hugh, "We don't mind do we Will?"

Potter smiled a broad, toothless grin, "Yew be doing me a favour booy. Oi forgot what an ugly old rooster moi good wife be."

Thomas laughed, "Then you're well matched."

"Aye, but at least oi knows she won't be pestered while oi be away."

"Wives are like warriors," answered Thomas philosophically, "the ugliest are often the best."

Three hours after noon they approached Frostenden village. Richard had intended to ride straight to Calveley Hall but the desire to see Mary again diverted him from his main purpose. He drew rein and spoke to the others, "If you care to wait at the village tavern for an hour, I will rejoin you then."

Thomas said, "If you are minded to visit the Lollards I have no objection to coming with you."

"Nor I," said Hugh. "They are fellow Christians not infidels. We shall all come with you."

Riding through Frostenden forest they were not challenged though Richard knew they would be being watched. Bare headed, unarmoured, and wearing just a leather jerkin, hose and boots, he would be easy to recognise, but had he planned this visit properly he would have ridden his new destrier and worn the Sieur de Freuchin's armour to impress Mary as the returning hero. But on second thoughts, Richard decided his attire was appropriate, for accoutrements of war were unlikely to impress any Lollards, particularly Mary. When they entered the clearing that housed the Lollard community everything was just as Richard remembered, which was in itself cause for satisfaction, for so often fond memories add much gloss to the truth. John Fletcher, who was giving his garden an autumn dig, saw him first, "Richard! Welcome back." He came running over but suddenly stopped, looking past Richard's shoulder, "Tom, you old rascal! So the French found you too hot to handle."

"They did indeed," laughed Thomas Riches, "though one of them managed to fetch me a fine blow on the pate before I dispatched him to the next world." Richard watched in amazement as the Norfolk sergeant dismounted and embraced John Fletcher.

By way of explanation Thomas said, "John Fletcher and I are kinsmen, Master Richard, which is why I wanted to accompany you here."

"Why did you not say?"

"It does no good to announce you are related to a Lollard. Had John not been here today I would have said nothing." A voice Richard remembered well called out, "Richard! Richard!" It was Mary. She tried to walk the fifty yards from her house to him but before half way she was running. He dismounted and for a blissful moment he thought she would run straight into his arms. But that would have been unseemly so she stopped herself a pace away and looked up into his eyes. John Fletcher looked at them both and smiled. His wife had often said that Mary needed a good man. Preaching was all very well, but it was not right for a woman to be without earthly love. The trouble was that no-one in the Lollard community could envisage any man being good enough for their Mary, but now that was all set to change even though neither Richard nor Mary fully realised what was happening to them yet. John Fletcher did, and it pleased him.

"Come with me," he whispered to Richard's companions, "those two need to be alone."

"We prayed for you," said Mary as she and Richard walked slowly towards her house.

"Did you pray for me?"

"Especially me."

"Thank you Mary. Your prayers were answered for even in the thick of the fighting I received hardly a scratch. I thought of you many times."

"But why?"

"I dare not say yet." Her brown eyes seemed to understand what was in his heart but she too was uncertain.

"Is the war over?" she asked. "This morning we heard there was a great victory."

"It has only just started. There will be much more campaigning before our king wears the French crown."

"You will go back?"

Richard lowered his eyes knowing his answer would disappoint her. "Yes."

"But why? Surely you have done your duty now. Cannot others take over the warrior's mantle?"

"Mary, you must understand that you see before you a Richard Calveley who is changed from the man you once knew. I now understand I was born to be a warrior like my father, not a farmer. I will remain a warrior while there is breath in my body and wars to fight, though even wars have their quiet times. I am truly sorry to disappoint you but I wanted to see you once more. I presume you now wish me to leave."

She answered huskily, "I want you to stay as long as you are minded to."

"Why?"

"Like you Richard, I dare not say." Suddenly the embers of hope flared up in Richard's heart. Now anything seemed possible, for Mary had not sent him away even though he represented a way of life abhorrent to her, or so he had thought. But before more could be said, a sudden movement at the entrance to the clearing made both of them turn and look back. Mary sensed Richard's body taughten and saw his hand instinctively feel for his dagger. His face darkened and his eyes flashed green fire, "Scrope you bastard! What in God's name are you doing here!"

Titus had seen Richard a second earlier, but that brief moment told him much, like the falling away of the scales of a blind man. His worldly mind immediately understood the terrible truth. The way Richard and Mary were looking into each other's eyes, the closeness with which they stood, the general attitude of their bodies revealed to experienced eyes their fondness for each other. He had been duped! All along she had felt nothing for him. Titus Scrope had been fooled by a woman! What an idiot he had been. But self recrimination quickly gave way to the far more basic instinct of self preservation, for Richard was advancing upon him with murder in his eyes. Titus knew he would be no match for him in open combat. Dropping the title deeds to Sir Hubert Manyng's land, he turned and ran.

CHAPTER TEN

"Where in hell have you been? I've been searching for you everywhere!" Geoffrey Calveley's anger was in part caused by a notion, fortunately wrong, that Titus Scrope had deserted him. "I had a visitor while you were away on your jaunt. My cousin! Fresh back from Agincourt. You were supposed to stop him even reaching here." Titus was unmoved by his master's tirade. The small study where he was sitting had been well warmed by the open fire against the chill autumn night, but nothing could melt the cold that sat in Titus' heart like a lump of black ice. He had returned to Calveley Hall by a cross country route to avoid another encounter with Richard. All the old notions he had espoused before meeting Mary had come flooding back. He was the old Titus Scrope again; he should never have broken trust with himself and allowed another human being to hurt him. Previously he had been content but now he was humiliated, a new emotion for Titus and an unwelcome one. In truth he admitted that Mary had not actually encouraged him to believe there could be love between them, but it had never occurred to Titus that she might love another. And of all people his arch enemy! Where there had been love before, there was now raging bitterness in Titus' heart. In order to recover his self respect he had to hit back.

"When did your cousin get here?" he asked quietly. Geoffrey, red faced and frightened, was pacing up and down his study in near panic.

"Two hours before you did," he replied petulantly. "Does it matter? The point is that he should not have got here at all."

Years of experience had taught Titus that the only way to handle his master in a crisis was to be firm. He raised his voice a little, "Sit down Geoffrey and listen to me."

"Do not speak to your master like that," said Geoffrey, but he sat down all the same.

"Murdering Richard now would avail you nothing except a certain degree of satisfaction," continued Titus. "While on my jaunt as you call it, I did some research which clearly points out the direction we must take. First of all I found out that Richard's daughter Joan still lives."

"What!" exploded Geoffrey. "How can that be?"

"We could not find her when we disposed of the rest of Richard's family and there was no time to carry out a thorough search. I had always assumed she perished in the flames when we set fire to the farm house but clearly I was wrong."

Geoffrey moaned, "This gets worse. Where is she?"

"I do not know but the first place I would search would be Dunwich Priory. Richard seems to have a strong connection with the Franciscans, but the fact is that if you kill Richard, all his rights and titles will simply revert to his daughter. What happened when he came here?"

"He confirmed John Thorpe's story and gave me three months to quit Calveley Hall. He had an affidavit signed by a Calais priest which I am sure will stand the test of court. There was nothing I could do because he was accompanied by two formidable looking archers and a Franciscan."

Titus paused for a moment. Once he committed himself to the course of action he had in mind, Richard would be destroyed but there would be no hope for Mary either. Even now he felt pangs of regret as he launched a series of events whose consequences would soon develop beyond his control.

He said, "I have a plan which will not only finish your cousin but will attaint his family as well. That means Richard's daughter will have no claim to Calveley Manor and you will hold it with full legal title. Murder will not be necessary. The law will murder for us."

★ ★ ★

II

While Geoffrey and Titus were plotting at Calveley Hall, Richard was at Dunwich Priory in the congenial company of Father Anselm. They were having a late supper together while the other friars toasted the return of Father Hugh. Thomas Riches and Will Potter shared in the celebrations leaving Richard free to spend some time alone with the old prior. Much had happened since Richard last shared a meal with Anselm in the priory guest house, and the Franciscan's heart warmed as he sat and listened to his old student's continuous chatter. Last time, in the aftermath of his family's destruction, Richard had spoken little but now Anselm could hardly get a word in, and he began to hope there was more to Richard's happiness than a glorious campaign in France.

To Richard this day was even more important than Agincourt, for despite the untimely arrival of Titus Scrope at Frostenden, enough had passed between Mary and himself to reveal their mutual affection for each other. It was certainly stronger than mere friendship. More might have been said but Richard's anger when he saw Titus had shocked the Lollards, who were unused to such displays of ire in their peaceful community. Soon however he would return and tell Mary of his feelings for her in the proper fashion.

"How did your cousin react when you served notice on him?" asked Anselm as he poured them both a large goblet of after dinner clairet.

"He took it remarkably calmly," said Richard. "I confess I was surprised. There was none of the bluster I expected. At first I put it down to the fact that his live-in assassin, Titus Scrope, was not present, but on second thoughts Geoffrey may already have heard about the death of his patron, the young Earl of Suffolk, at Agincourt. For the moment Cousin Geoffrey is without a protector."

"Could it be that your cousin had foreknowledge? Perhaps your news concerning his illegitimacy was already known to him."

"I do not see how. Other than me, only Sir Thomas Erpingham, Squire John and Father Hugh knew."

Anselm raised a sceptical eyebrow, "Richard, it does not do to underestimate your enemy. Consider. If he had expected you to serve notice on him he may already have a plan in place to foil you. Even as we speak a counterattack may be on its way."

Richard shrugged, "I think it unlikely Father but I shall be careful."

The old Franciscan nodded his approval and tossed another log onto the crackling fire. "Tell me," he asked, "what are your plans for Calveley Hall?"

Richard took a long drink from his goblet, relishing the warm, fragrant wine. Thinking of Mary he answered, "I do have plans but they are not clearly formulated as yet because some things depend on factors not entirely in my control. Of one thing at least I am certain. I must spend more time with Joan. She did not recognise me when I arrived this evening. I cannot allow her to grow up thinking of her father as a stranger, so as soon as Calveley Hall is vacated I shall move in and relieve you of the duty of looking after her for me."

"It is no duty," replied Anselm wistfully. "We have all grown fond of her here. She has brought life to the priory. Does that mean your campaigning days are over now Richard?"

"No, I shall need a good steward to run the hall and the adjoining land while I am away. Toiling behind the plough is not for me any more."

"Just like your father," smiled Anselm. "Do you have anyone in particular in mind for the job?"

Richard shifted uncomfortably. "Well yes, but I am forced to request yet another favour from you because I would like Father Hugh to be my steward. There are good reasons. I have no doubt he would make an excellent steward and there is no man I would trust more to look after my home. And I fear for Hugh because I know he does not look forward to returning to the sheltered life of the priory after what he has seen and done in France. If you had seen him with the light of battle in his eyes you would perhaps find it easier to understand what I mean."

Anselm gazed into the fire and pondered for a while. When he spoke there was an air of resignation in his voice, "Do not priests sometimes make excellent warriors? Look at the fighting orders of the Knights Templar and the Knights Hospitaller."

"That is true Father but we are talking of Franciscans in Dunwich Priory, not warrior monks in Jerusalem. I am sure Hugh would have been in the vanguard in the struggle against the infidel, but Jerusalem has long been lost to us, the Templars have been destroyed and the Hospitallers are confined to an offshore island."

Anselm nodded, "Of course you are right Richard, but it is difficult for an old priest set in his ways to accept the permanent absence of one of his charges. But I know I must bow to the inevitable. I too was worried about the strength of Hugh's vocation long before he went to France. That is why I allowed him to go with you. I have never lost a priest, but I realise the only way I can keep Hugh is to give him as much liberty as possible consistent with his vows. Have you spoken to him on this matter?"

"No Father," said Richard.

"Then you shall have Hugh as your steward. I will talk to him in the morning."

"Thank you Father. I am aware of the Franciscan vows but Hugh's service must be rewarded, so apart from his living expenses I shall pay a salary each month to your priory, if that is in order."

"It is, and if your cousin resorts to law to fight your claim, Hugh may be of use in that regard. He was a lawyer's clerk in Yarmouth for two years before donning the habit of Saint Francis. Hopefully that will satiate his desire for combat."

Richard smiled, "Let us hope so."

Anselm's brow furrowed, "There is one more thing that troubles me Richard. You say you will be taking Joan to Calveley Hall, yet you could be away for years at a time campaigning for the king. Hugh has many qualities, but being a substitute parent is not one of them."

Richard did not want to tempt fate by anticipating too much, but having looked after Joan for more than a year Anselm had a right to know she would be well cared for. Richard replied, "If all goes well there will be a woman in Calveley Hall to look after Joan."

"In what capacity? A housekeeper?"

"My wife."

Anselm's eyes twinkled as he asked, "Does this concern a certain Lollard preacher perhaps?"

"How did you know?"

"Just a shrewd guess my boy. I am truly pleased and wish you both long life and happiness but," a shadow seemed to pass across the Franciscan's face, "there is something I must caution you about. Since you have been away the Archbishop of Canterbury has stepped up the persecution of the Lollards. In this he has the full support of the crown for King Henry, even before he came to the throne, has always been a fervent supporter of the church. Anything or anyone who threatens it is likely to incur his wrath."

"Apart from that fool Oldcastle, the Lollards have threatened no-one except the well fed bishops in the church hierarchy," said Richard.

"You do not have to be a Lollard to acknowledge there is too much wealth amongst the prelacy," agreed Anselm. "It stands in stark contrast to the hard lives of most of the laity. I trust Richard you have not become a Lollard?"

"You can admire a cause without wishing to be part of it Father. I have no appetite for Lollardy. I remain a committed but critical Roman Catholic."

"Then you are no different from me and the rest of the preaching orders. If the church hierarchy does not change its ways, then one day the state will intervene and reform the clergy with or without its consent."

"But since Oldcastle's rebellion the influence of the Lollards has declined," said Richard. "Surely no-one could perceive of them as a threat to the church now?"

"Perhaps," acknowledged Anselm. "I do not speak of tomorrow, but of three or four generations hence. One success the Lollards have achieved, which cannot be undone, is to open the eyes of influential people as to how little of the massive church establishment is truly supported by the scriptures. Things that have long been regarded as cornerstones of faith are of man-made, not scriptural origin."

"Even the papacy?" asked Richard mischeviously, but Anselm was not amused.

"Be careful of what you say even in jest. You could find yourself in peril if you were accidentally overheard, for persecutions always give troublemakers and opportunists their chance."

"I shall follow your advice Father, as ever."

As he lay in bed in the priory guesthouse waiting for sleep to come, Richard knew he would have to persuade Mary to temper her public preaching until the persecutions ceased. He resolved to return to Caistor Manor for a few days to help Millicent Fastolf with some outstanding estate matters, then he would visit Mary again. Instinct told him to hurry.

But although Richard moved quickly, Geoffrey moved more quickly still.

* * *

III

Retribution struck while Richard was still at Caistor Manor. It was the morning of the seventh day of November. The clear, frosty weather had given way to a continuous, sullen rain which blew in with a chill northeasterly wind. Richard's work for Millicent at Caistor Manor was almost complete for the time being, which would leave him free to visit Frostenden for a few days. If all went well he would then ask Mary to marry him. Richard and Millicent Fastolf sat by the cheerful fire in the large manorial hall working out the cropping patters for the following year.

"I would like to try something different this time on the low meadow," said Millicent, whose knowledge of estate matters never ceased to surprise Richard. "Since we drained it last year," she continued, "it ought to take a crop of barley, and decades of grazing should have put the soil in good heart. What do you think?" Before Richard could reply, the heavy hall door swung open and William, the old manservant, entered. Ignoring Richard as usual, whose presence at the manor he had never fully accepted, William addressed Millicent, "Beg pardon for interrupting My Lady, but Tom Riches is outside. He says he brings important news."

Thomas Riches was in an agitated state when he entered the hall, but he waited until William left before speaking. "Master Richard, I came as soon as I heard. The Lollards at Frostenden, they have been arrested."

"What! All of them?"

"Yes Master Richard. The sheriff's men came yesterday with a warrant and took them all into custody."

"What was the charge?"

"Heresy." Richard's heart sank. Father Anselm's worries had proven to be justified, but surely even the old Franciscan had not expected the persecution to reach Frostenden so soon. Or perhaps there was more to it than that.

Richard asked, "Who brought the charge Thomas?"

"I do not know. Is there aught we can do?"

"Where are the Lollards now?"

"The sheriff came from Beccles so I assume that is where they went."

Millicent put her hand on Richard's arm and said, "I can finish sorting the cropping patterns. You go to Beccles and find out how we can help. Take plenty of silver. Gaolers are notoriously open to bribes."

"May I come too?" pleaded Thomas. "My cousin is amongst those arrested."

"I should welcome your support Thomas," said Richard, "but I do not think it wise that two of Squire John's men are seen bringing succour to Lollards. We must consider his position in the county."

"Stuff and nonsense!" snorted Millicent. "If Tom wishes to go then he should go. I shall look after John's reputation, have no fear of that."

It was nearly dusk when Richard and Thomas steered their mounts carefully across the wet cobbles in Beccles market square where, more than a year ago, the fateful land auction which changed Richard's life had taken place. It was still raining and the shopkeepers were packing up early because business was so thin. The gaol, a seamy single storey building made of large, roughly hewn flints and lime mortar, was located just east of the square at the top end of a narrow street that led down to the marshes which flanked the River Waveney.

Richard dismounted, unlatched the massive, iron studded door and entered the dark interior followed by Thomas. The stench was stomach churning, and as both men stopped to allow their eyes to become accustomed to the gloom, a voice low to their right said, "Can I 'elp you gentlemen?" The voice belonged to a bald, unshaven man who was sitting at a table, upon which was a candle and a ring of large, iron keys. He stood up to reveal a short, hugely fat figure clad incongruously in a poor fitting but expensive leather tunic and grubby linen hose. Clearly, working in such surroundings had its compensations.

Richard addressed the troll-like gaoler. "I understand you have here a group of people from Frostenden." The gaoler frowned and sucked his gums as if he was having difficulty recalling such an event in his busy schedule. He looked at a ledger, though Richard doubted he could read, and said, "Came in yesterday?" Richard nodded. The gaoler shut the ledger and shrugged, "Only one of them's 'ere. A pretty little flower though I expect 'er petals 'ave faded a bit by now."

"Where are the rest of them?" asked Richard.

"Who wants to know?" Richard placed a silver shilling on the table and the gaoler smiled a yellow toothed grin, "Ah, I see you understand turnkey language. That'll save a lot of time. The gaol is already well attended so there was no room for the Frostenden lot. They're camped out in the marshes under guard."

Thomas exploded, "What! In this weather! They'll die of ague!" The gaoler slowly turned his vivid blue eyes on Thomas Riches, then looked back at Richard, "Keep your dog under control in 'ere."

Thomas stepped menacingly forward but Richard put a hand on his shoulder and said, "Leave it Tom, there are more important matters. Get down to the marshes and see if you can persuade the guards to move their charges to the common land; it's drier there. Then wait for me at the White Boar." Placing a leather money pouch in Thomas' hand Richard added, "This should make the guards wish to co-operate."

When Thomas had gone Richard spoke to the gaoler again, "The Frostenden prisoner you hold here. Her name is Mary Hoccleve?"

"Might be."

"What arrangements have been made for her confinement?"

"Same as for everyone else. This ain't no city prison you know. Just one large cell the other side of that door." The gaoler pointed over his shoulder to a black, iron door behind him. Richard shuddered as he imagined what the conditions must be like inside and said, "So Mistress Hoccleve is sharing the same quarters as vagrants and common felons."

The gaoler, sensing a potential deal sighed, "That's about the size of it."

"I would like to make alternative arrangements for Mistress Hoccleve. She is a gentlewoman."

"Impossible. She's my charge and it's my responsibility to see she don't slip away before she comes to court." Richard felt inside his other leather pouch and rattled the coins, "You must realise that Mistress Hoccleve is an honourable woman. If she gives you her parole and I pay you well, might it not be possible to improve her accommodation?"

"Mebbe. It depends don't it."

"Six pence each day until she is released." The gaoler could see the desperation in Richard's eyes and knew there was a good bargain to be had. He said, "I suppose she could lodge in the chapter house in Saint Peter's monastery near the saltings. The abbot sometimes takes in important prisoners on my behalf. His cells are secure enough, but he'll want paying too which won't leave me with much will it."

"What is your price then?"

"A shilling a day."

Richard had no choice and placed seven more silver coins on the gaoler's table. "There's enough for a week. I will come back and pay you in advance each week, and if Mistress Hoccleve is pleased with her treatment there will be a bonus for you when she is released."

The prospect of such easy money engendered a new spirit of co-operation in the gaoler. He quickly pocketed the money and said, "I will go and make the arrangements now. I expect you'd like to speak to Mistress Hoccleve alone so I'll fetch her into my office and you can talk while I'm gone. You won't mind me locking the outer door will you?"

Mary looked pale and shaken but her eyes lit up when she saw Richard standing waiting for her. As soon as the gaoler had gone Richard gathered her into his arms. She did not resist and nestled against his chest, safe within his protective strength. For Richard their appalling surroundings were fleetingly forgotten during this first moment of physical contact between them. True, she was in a state of extreme vulnerability, but that alone could not account for the tightness with which she held on to him.

"Mary," he whispered, "there is so much I wish to say." She responded by squeezing his waist yet more tightly. He gently stroked her long, fair hair, "Mary, there is little time. We must plan what to do."

Without slackening her hold on him she said softly, "A moment longer." They stood in each other's arms, neither speaking for a while. It seemed ridiculous that anyone could be happy in such dreadful conditions, but now that the last uncertainties of doubt were gone, their brief moment of bliss transcended the grim walls of Beccles gaol. At last they prised themselves apart and Mary, her voice rough with emotion whispered, "How bitter to discover each other too late."

"It is not too late," said Richard.

"The charge is heresy my dear. You know the penalty don't you?"

Richard tried to sound more confident than he felt, "We are a long way from that and heresy is notoriously difficult to prove if you do not confess. Say nothing to anyone except me. I will get a good counsel to advise us. Meanwhile I have made arrangements to get you out of this hell hole pending the court hearing."

Mary sighed, "I thank the blessed Lord for you Richard Calveley." Then looking down at her clothes she said, "I must look dreadful. Could you have some of my things sent to me?"

"You will always be beautiful to me Mary, and as for your wardrobe I will attend to it in person."

She vainly tried to brush the grime from her dress and said, "In the oak chest beside my bed you will find a torn piece of white cloth with the edge of a red cross on it. You may recognise it for it was part of the surcoat you tore off to make a sling for John Fletcher when you saved him from the marshmen. It brought me comfort while you were in France; I would like it with me now."

Richard smiled, "You thought of me even then? I wish I had known"

"I am a preacher. How could I have said anything?" He spontaneously took her into his arms again, but the heavy trudge of the returning gaoler cut short the embrace. Richard lowered his voice to a whisper, "Quickly now, who brought this charge against you?"

"I have thought about that but I cannot even guess."

"Very well, I will find out from the town clerk, then we should have some idea of what this is all about."

As the lock in the gaol door began to turn, Mary suddenly said, "Richard, I'm frightened."

"Do not be my dear, I shall let no harm befall you. Upon that you have my word."

The town clerk's office lay in a small, whitewashed building which adjoined the moot hall in the market square. Although Beccles had no town charter, it was still large enough to afford a full time clerk and hold quarter sessions attended by the local magistrate. Outside the office door a poster proclaimed the date of the next quarter session which was to be the fifteenth of November, only eight days away. At least Mary would not have long to wait. Richard went inside and found the clerk, a small, ruddy faced man putting on his cloak ready to leave. They knew each other from occasional meetings at the White Boar on market days.

"Hello Richard," said the clerk, "you caught me just in time. What can I do for you?"

"The Lollards who were arrested yesterday; may I see the charge sheet?"

"I don't see why not. A bad business that. Live and let live I say. Why anyone should want to see people burned at the stake is beyond me. Here you are." The clerk handed over a sheet of parchment and added, "You will not like it."

The seal at the bottom of the warrant should not have surprised Richard, but it still came as an unpleasant shock. It belonged to Geoffrey who had used his power as a magistrate in the coastal area to order the arrests.

Richard muttered, "The bastard."

"Your cousin I believe?" said the clerk apologetically.

"Regrettably so. Thank you for your help. This has given me much to consider."

As Richard left, the clerk called after him, "At least the quarter session magistrate is Sir John Satterley. He is a fair minded man."

CHAPTER ELEVEN

Sir John Satterley sat at his desk in the high raftered, Beccles moot hall looking at the crowd assembled on the public benches. Heresy always attracted the morbid, especially when a woman was involved. To his left sat the accused, Mary Hoccleve and John Fletcher, who had been identified as the leaders of the 'heretical nest' by the accuser, Geoffrey Calveley. Sir John looked at the self satisfied accuser on his right and tried to keep the contempt he felt out of his face, for he must not only be impartial, but seen to be impartial. Still, he could not help disliking the new magistrate from Holton who had started to style himself, Squire Geoffrey.

Between the participants and the public benches stood a cordon of sheriff's men to discourage the outbursts of disorder which frequently accompanied legal hearings. Richard had arrived well before the commencing hour of ten o'clock and planted himself in the middle of the front bench, from where he could see all that took place. He was now beginning to comprehend the extent to which his cousin had outflanked him. It almost seemed that Geoffrey had been forewarned as Father Anselm had feared; Richard's claim to Calveley Hall would come to nothing if he became attainted with Lollardy. By attacking Mary, Geoffrey was forcing Richard to commit himself openly to her cause. The fact that Richard was helping her out of personal regard would carry little weight with a church court. Yet how could Geoffrey have known that his cousin would rush to Mary's aid, for the first true words of affection were only uttered after her arrest? Neither Richard nor Mary could know that they were facing but the first gusts of Titus Scrope's storm of revenge.

The bells of Saint Michael's church tolled ten o'clock so Sir John nodded to the town clerk who sat midway between the accuser and the accused. The clerk stood up and his call for silence was quickly obeyed because everyone was eager to hear the proceedings.

"This is not a trial. It is an inquiry," said Sir John Satterly in a surprisingly powerful voice for his slight frame. "I am here in my capacity as the King's Justice to investigate the evidence against the two defendants and their followers and to decide whether or not they should be committed for trial under The Burning of Heretics Act passed by Parliament in the Year of Our Lord 1401." He paused for a moment and stroked his short, black beard as if in some doubt about what he was going to say next, but then he continued, "Should this matter go to trial it will be heard in a church court, and the severity of the punishment if a guilty verdict is given is well known to you all. I shall therefore expect a high standard of good, hard evidence if this case is to go further." He glared at Geoffrey and added, "I trust I make myself clear." The bland expression Geoffrey had studiously maintained since his arrival remained unaltered.

Addressing the town clerk Sir John said, "I understand the total number arrested is forty four. Where are the other forty two, under house arrest?"

The clerk cleared his throat, "On Beccles common under guard."

"Have they been provided with tents?"

"No sir."

Sir John's brow furrowed ominously, "Where is the sheriff?"

"He is unable to attend the inquiry," replied the clerk nervously. "He has duties elsewhere."

"Then I shall see him when he returns. These people have as yet no evidence of wrong-doing against them other than an accusation by one man. But they have been rounded up and penned in like cattle. I will not have it. If they must remain in custody after this inquiry they shall return to Frostenden under house arrest."

Richard smiled ironically. While he took heart from Sir John's strong sense of justice, he wondered what the Beccles magistrate would say if he knew the rest of the sorry tale. When Richard had returned to Frostenden to collect the things Mary asked for, he found the Lollard settlement ransacked. Every house had been broken into and plundered, the stock of animals driven off and the winter stores taken. Even if the Lollards were permitted to return home they would probably starve this winter. Whether the damage had been done by the local villagers or the sheriff's men made little difference to the final outcome for, innocent or not, the Lollard community at Frostenden was finished. Richard did however manage to recover a few things for Mary, which had been overlooked by the plunderers, including the torn piece of his white surcoat. As he looked at her sitting beside John Fletcher, he could see she was holding it to her breast as if she could somehow draw strength from it to face her ordeal.

Sir John addressed the defendants, "While this is not a trial you must nonetheless answer my questions as if you have taken the oath. Now you are accused of heresy. Are you guilty or innocent?"

John Fletcher answered, "Sir, Mistress Hoccleve has been deputed to answer the inquiry's questions on behalf of us all."

"Very well." Sir John's voice softened as he continued, "Mistress Hoccleve, I await your reply."

"Innocent sir." The answer was given in the strong, ringing voice Mary used when preaching. It was fortunate that the charge was heresy and not Lollardy, for Lollardy was too specific to be a matter of opinion.

"Enter innocent in the record," said Sir John, "The burden of evidence now lies with the accuser. Bring forward your first witness Master Calveley." Despite his best efforts, he could not help but emphasise the word 'Master' when he spoke to the self styled Squire Geoffrey.

Ignoring the slight, Geoffrey replied, "I call Michael Brooks." A large, black haired man got to his feet and slowly walked from the back of the hall to the witness stand beside the clerk. He stood facing the magistrate, side on to the public benches grinning broadly as if he was at a Sunday fair. Someone at the back shouted, "Go on Michael!" Brooks turned and waved; he had obviously spent some time in the White Boar before coming to the inquiry. Sir John pointed to the man who had yelled his support for the witness, "Remove that man at once and anyone else who tries to interrupt these proceedings." Then turning his attention to Brooks he said coldly, "Brooks, you will have respect for this inquiry or you will be arrested for contempt. The choice is yours." Apart from some scuffling at the back of the hall where Brooks' supporter was being ejected, the entire assembly remained silent. Sir John's authority was absolute.

Although he did not recognise the name, Richard, who seldom forgot a face, realised he had seen Brooks before, when he had intervened to save John Fletcher from being beaten to death on Frostenden village green. That was back in the summer but Richard could clearly recall the snarling face of the mob leader whom he felled with his sword pommel before rescuing John. If Brooks typified the standard of Geoffrey's witnesses, there was indeed room for hope.

"Well Brooks, what have you to say to the inquiry?" demanded Sir John.

Brooks cleared his throat and tried to gather his wits, "I live on the edge of the marshes near Frostenden and I often go to the village to sell thatching reeds. On many occasions have I seen the two accused preaching heresy on the village green."

"Can you remember the dates and times?"

"Yes sir. I have with me a list written in writing which tells whether it was morning or afternoon and what day of the month it was."

"Good," said Sir John, apparently impressed by the marshman's detailed recall, "hand the list to the clerk. Did you write it yourself?"

"No sir, I spoke the words to a friend who wrote them for me."

"How do you know your friend wrote what you spoke?" Brooks looked blank so Sir John ordered the clerk to read the list out loud for Brooks to approve. When the clerk finished, Sir John resumed the investigation, "Were those the correct days and times?"

The marshman replied pompously with pre-rehearsed words that could not have been his, "That be a true and accurate record."

"Good, then we make progress. Now Brooks, what sort of heresy did the accused speak?" The witness looked uncomfortable. He glanced towards Geoffrey for guidance, but Geoffrey stared steadfastly at a point on the floor in front of him; the marshman was on his own. He stammered, "Well, it was heretical talk sir."

"Yes, so you said Brooks, but what sort of heretical talk? For example did they speak of worshipping Mohammed?"

"Who?"

"Come along man. You say it was heresy so you must have some idea of what that means." Brooks was in trouble. He looked round the hall as if searching for inspiration, but just when Sir John was on the verge of standing him down, the marshman's face lit up, "It was Lollard heresy, that was it, definitely!"

"Excellent Brooks, now give me an example of the Lollard heresy you had the misfortune to hear."

The witness scratched his head and replied thoughtfully, "Well I remember the woman saying all bishops are fat." The sniggers which echoed round the hall were stifled as soon as Sir John looked up, but this time he issued no reprimand. He continued, "I dare say most bishops are fat. To say so may be considered disrespectful, it is hardly heresy. Anything else?"

"She said we should give money to the poor before the church."

Sir John threw down his quill in exasperation, "Giving alms to the poor is central to the ethos of Christianity. Stand down Brooks, you are a waste of time." As the marshman stumbled back to his place, Sir John spoke menacingly to Geoffrey, "I hope your other witnesses do better than that Master Calveley, or I shall be looking to you for payment for this inquiry."

Three more witnesses were cross questioned by Sir John and none of them could provide evidence which stood up to his incisive interrogation. It was now past eleven o'clock and Geoffrey realised he was losing. He would have to use the final damning evidence which he had hoped to save for the church court.

As the fourth witness returned to his place humiliated, Geoffrey stood up and said, "Sir John, I have only one more person I wish to call."

"Thank the holy saints for that. I have never before seen such a pitiful selection of scoundrels for witnesses. You and I shall have words after this Master Calveley."

"I doubt that will be necessary sir. I call Titus Scrope."

Richard's confidence, which had been gradually strengthening during the farcical proceedings, was suddenly shaken again. Titus knew enough about the Lollards to be an effective witness, but would Sir John accept the hearsay evidence of one man as sufficient grounds for a trial? Titus, who had been observing the inquiry from the back of the hall, walked forward carrying something large and heavy under his arm. A grey cloth obscured it from view but Richard guessed it boded ill.

As he took his place, the steward of Calveley Hall looked directly at Richard, an expression of triumph writ large across his face, but when he began to speak his voice did not exude the euphoria of victory. This did not sound like the Titus Scrope Richard had grown to know and hate. It was as if the victor was suffering almost as much as the vanquished.

Titus spent the next half hour describing his dealings with the Lollards in the lucid, deadpan manner favoured by advocates. At no time did he look directly at Mary or John Fletcher; instead he confined his field of view to Sir John and occasionally the town clerk. At the end of the account, Sir John acknowledged the quality of the witness with yet another barbed remark at Geoffrey's expense, "Thank you Master Scrope. You have provided the inquiry with an illuminating record. What a shame you were not called first so we could have been spared the antics of the first four witnesses. You are however aware that the two accused have entered pleas which do not tally with your assessment. I must therefore weigh your words against theirs." Titus seemed to be fighting a battle within himself and remained silent for a few moments.

When at last he spoke again, it was almost in a whisper, "Sir John, I have brought material evidence which will support my statement." He withdrew the grey cloth to reveal the Lollard Bible, the most treasured possession of the Frostenden community. John Fletcher stood up and angrily demanded, "Where did you get that?"

Sir John snapped, "Sit down Master Fletcher. If you wish to speak I will call you in the proper manner. Continue Master Scrope."

Titus took a deep breath, "This is the Holy Bible translated into English by the followers of the late John Wyclif. I recovered it from the house of one of the accused. If you look inside the front cover you will see a note of dedication."

He handed the book to Sir John who opened the book and read aloud, "To Mistress Mary Hoccleve with greatest respect from John Fox Mayor of Northampton. May this work inspire you in the instruction of others so that the true followers of Christ come to know him directly."

Until now Sir John had done his utmost, within the law, to prevent the charge from going to trial, but in the light of this new evidence he knew he was beaten. He handed the book to the clerk and sighed, "I shall need to retain this book. John Fox was a well known Lollard. Mistress Hoccleve, have you anything to say which might have a bearing on this inquiry?" Mary shook her head, "No sir."

"Master Fletcher?"

"No sir."

Sir John raised his voice so that all in the moot hall could hear, "The finding of this inquiry is that there is insufficient evidence against John Fletcher and the other forty two accused to take this matter to trial. They are free to go. As for Mary Hoccleve, I find that there is a case to be answered. Consequently, she will be taken from Beccles to Norwich to be tried in the church court. The charge will be heresy."

John Fletcher stood up. "Nay Sir John, this be not fair," but before he could incriminate himself Mary whispered, "Quiet John. You will not help me by getting yourself into trouble. The others will look to you for leadership now."

Richard attempted to break through the cordon of sheriff's men to comfort Mary, but there were too many of them. She was taken away under close escort.

When Richard turned back to look for Geoffrey and Titus to vent his anger, both had slipped away by a side door.

★ ★ ★

II

Richard and Father Hugh stopped to look at the spectacular view below them. Ahead, shrouded in morning mist, was Norwich, the second greatest city in the realm. From their vantage point on Mousehold Heath, Richard and Hugh could see thousands of smoking chimneys which turned the mist into a pall of smog gathering in a great, grey cloud over the city. The homely picture was deceptive for Norwich had a violent history. Indeed one of its mayors had been murdered during the great peasant uprising of a generation ago only yards from where Richard and Hugh now sat their horses. The expensive flint and mortar curtain wall which surrounded the city was more than an extravagant afterthought. Dominating the skyline was the cathedral. Completed more than two hundred years before, the cathedral was a great source of pride for the citizens. It was in its precincts that Mary would face her nemesis later that morning, and Richard was determined to be there. Father Anselm had readily allowed Hugh to accompany him for this was church business, and Hugh's knowledge of the clerical estate might be of service.

"I used to love coming to Norwich," said Richard. "Ann and I would come here once or twice a year. We always parted with more money than we intended, but the bustle and excitement of the city encouraged spending."

Hugh, impressed by the sheer size of the place answered, "This is my first visit. Would that the circumstances were different so I could appreciate it more."

"When all this is over we shall return and I shall show you round on market day, but for now we must go straight to the cathedral. The trial starts at nine o'clock."

The two men walked their horses across the Yare bridge and arrived at the cathedral's northeast gate which had just been opened for the day. Beside it sat a beggar and Richard placed a penny in his filthy, claw-like hand. He noticed beneath the dirt that the man bore a deep scar across his forehead which stretched from the hairline to an empty eye socket.

"That is a sword cut unless I am very much mistaken," said Richard. "How did you come by it?"

The beggar, who Richard judged to be in his late fifties, replied in a hoarse whisper, "In France young sir, fighting for the king."

"Who was your commander?"

"A doughty warrior sir whose name alone struck fear into the French. He was Sir Hugh Calveley."

Richard looked at Hugh, "Is that not a remarkable coincidence? Surely it is a good omen for today. Perhaps the Bishop of Norwich will be merciful."

"Let us hope so," said Hugh.

Richard turned to the beggar. My name also is Calveley. You fought for a kinsman of mine. It is not right that a man who has risked his life for England should end up as you. Take these, they are all I have with me at present." He pressed two gold coins into the beggar's hand and added, "I had more fortune in the French wars than you, but now almost all I hold dear depends on the mercy of the bishop." For the first time the beggar looked directly at Richard. One eye of brightest blue shone starkly against the dark background of the grimy face and Richard could see that this wreck of a creature had once been a finely featured man.

Hugh asked, "What misfortune brought you to this?" The blue eye flickered a sidelong glance at Hugh but quickly returned to Richard, who began to feel uncomfortable before the unwavering stare.

"It was the plague sir," said the beggar, answering the question as if Richard had asked it. "It took my wife and very nearly me, though why I should have been spared instead of her I never understood. I know of no-one else who has survived the plague. Afterwards people thought I was bewitched and shunned me for fear I might bring misfortune upon them. Since then I have lived on whatever charity has been afforded me. In return for your generosity I wish I could give you comfort, but

I must tell you to expect no mercy from the Bishop of Norwich. He is harder than steel and colder than ice."

Richard asked, "How do you know this?"

"It was he who expelled me from Norwich when I asked permission to bury my wife in Saint Andrew's churchyard. Trust to the strength of your arm young sir and expect nothing from this bishop."

★ ★ ★

III

Richard Courtenay, Bishop of Norwich, tapped his jewel encrusted fingers impatiently on the desk as he looked at the sallow faced clerics who were to constitute his jury. They sat like so many sheep staring at him while they waited in the cathedral library until it was time to enter the chapter house where Mary would be tried. What the bishop took to be muted, unquestioning, irritating acceptance of all he said was, in fact, abject fear, for Richard Courtenay cut a formidable figure in Norfolk society. This trial had to go well because Courtenay was as ambitious as any soldier or statesman. His sights were firmly set on the see of Canterbury no less, and the burning of a Lollard would clearly demonstrate to the crown the fervour of his support for the king's personal crusade against heresy.

"I expect loyalty from you all," he warned, grey eyes flashing either side of his hawk-like nose. "No dissembling or weakness. Heresy is like wildfire; it must be snuffed out before it catches hold or we will all be swept away."

Robert Burnham, Dean of Norwich, was less cowed than the rest and asked, "Suppose this Mary Hoccleve is innocent?"

"Pah!" snapped the bishop. "You have read the record of the Beccles magistrate's inquiry. It is obvious to any man of reason that she and the rest of her sect are subversive Lollards. They would all be here today on trial but for Satterley's lenience."

Undaunted Burnham continued, "But what if the witnesses are as incompetent as before?"

"There will be no witnesses. My interrogation alone will provide you with more than enough evidence."

Courtenay's voice suddenly softened into a menacing purr, "Robert, it sounds to me as if you want this heretic to go free. I am forced to wonder why." The dean's show of spirit abruptly ended. He bowed his head and said no more. This jury would not stand in the way of the bishop's ambition.

Sitting beside Father Hugh on one of the ornately carved oak benches in the chapter house, Richard looked up at the vaulted ceiling with the beggar's words of warning still ringing in his ears. Surely no bishop could be as heartless as the beggar suggested? Mercy was a virtue encouraged by the church, and even Courtenay's heart must soften when he saw Mary, pale faced and small, standing alone between the two stern, black cloaked Benedictines from the monastery within the cathedral precinct. Maybe the beggar's wits had become addled or his memory faulty, but when Richard saw Courtenay sweep in ahead of his jury like a dark angel leading his lesser devils, he knew the beggar had not been mistaken. This bishop was not one of those plump, red cheeked caricatures of popular scorn, but a lean, cadaverous figure with the eyes and bearing of that most fearsome of God's creatures, the religious fanatic.

Unlike the Beccles moot hall, the cathedral chapter house was almost empty of onlookers for the hearing. The trial of an obscure Suffolk woman held no appeal for the citizens of Norwich, or perhaps they just preferred to keep well away from their formidable bishop. Courtenay settled himself at his desk like a great bird of prey on its nest, while his jurors took their places on the front bench reserved for them. Richard and Hugh sat behind the jurors with about fifteen other observers, mostly clerics. Courtenay was about to begin the proceedings when he caught sight of Hugh's grey habit.

"I see we have one of our mendicant friars with us today," he sneered. "I suppose we should be honoured."

Hugh stood up and replied boldly, "Not so My Lord Bishop. I am here to see justice is done." The cringing gasps from the Norwich priests whispered round the spacious chapter house, but Hugh was unafraid for he did not take discipline from the established church hierarchy. Courtenay was well aware of his powerlessness over the preaching orders and chose the route of scorn instead of fear to subdue the insolent Franciscan.

"If ever I need legal advice from itinerant Franciscans I shall confine myself to a house for the insane. Sit down friar, you remain here on sufferance." While admiring Hugh's spirit, Richard did not want Mary's remote chance of mercy reduced still further.

He whispered, "Do not goad him Father. Mary is in enough trouble already."

"Sorry, I could not help it. It is men like Courtenay who positively encourage heresy."

The bishop opened the trial as if giving a sermon to a packed cathedral congregation on a Sunday, for he knew the record of his words would be read by the Archbishop of Canterbury himself. For about ten minutes he harangued the court on the dangers of heresy and how it behoved every true catholic to carry out his duty by reporting anyone, even in his own family, who espoused heretical causes. Pausing briefly to allow the impact of his words to have their full effect, and to let the recorder catch up with him, Courtenay turned his predatory eyes on to Mary.

"Tell me mistress, you are a Lollard are you not?"

Mary's voice sounded thin and frail as she answered, "I am a true and devout Christian My Lord."

"Nevertheless, you are a Lollard."

"I have never called myself that."

"Do not bandy words with me Mistress Hoccleve. You are not dealing with an ignorant country magistrate now. I say you are a Lollard and a leader of a group of Lollards. You have a bible written in English, is that not so?"

"It is so My Lord."

"Then what does that signify?"

"It signifies I read the bible in English. I also read it in Latin and Greek as no doubt you do."

The bishop's eyebrows knitted ominously together, "You will have respect if you hope for mercy from this court."

Mary, who was a match for anyone in open debate replied, "Why should I hope for mercy when I am innocent My Lord?"

"The possession of an English Bible dedicated to you personally by the Lollard Mayor of Northampton is sufficient proof of your guilt. Six years ago the great Thomas Arundel, Archbishop of Canterbury, banned the possession and reading of the English Bible. Do you believe in the infallibility of the Pope?"

Mary paused and said, "God made no man infallible."

"Aha!" crowed the bishop, "another Lollard heresy." Turning to his jury he said, "This woman has condemned herself out of her own mouth. I see no need to permit the trial to continue further. Denying the Pope and reading English bibles are characteristics of the followers of John Wyclif."

Subservient nods from the jury told Mary of the certainty of conviction, yet her fear was temporarily displaced by anger by this arrogant, rabble rousing prelate. She spoke quietly but more firmly now.

"May I speak My Lord?" Courtenay nodded and she continued, "My Lord, it is arrogant and un-Christian men like yourself who provide the fertile ground in which heresy, as you call it, can grow. When was the last time, if ever, you visited a poor family or gave solace to a beggar? You and your pale skinned kind have lost touch with the common people who, whether you like it or not, constitute the majority of your flock. Did not Jesus Christ spend his time with the poor and needy, and was it not the Pharisees who had him put to death? You My Lord are a Pharisee. You preach Christianity but you do not practice it. What I have done is to try and tend the poor folk, the folk you in your great palace have forgotten."

Richard wanted to stand up and cheer, for Mary had put into words the feelings of many ordinary English men and women, but instead he waited anxiously for Courtenay's retribution. When it came it was not the frontal blast Richard had expected, but the subtle attack of the ambitious statesman who knows his own skills are on trial. The bishop's mannered restraint was not matched by the fire in his eyes. His voice remained calm, but only just. "Mistress Hoccleve, this court has permitted you to give full vent to your outrageous heretical views. Let it not be said that the church has not allowed you a fair hearing. Despite the personal slander you have heaped upon all the dedicated priests who serve their parishes faithfully and unselfishly, I intend to show mercy. You have condemned yourself many times over. If, as I expect, the jury finds you guilty, the sentence is unequivocal. You will be burned under the 1401 Act De Heretico Comburendo. However it remains in my power to offer you the chance to recant, but I am mindful that many recanted heretics revert to their old ways, therefore I give you the chance to prove your sincerity by naming your fellow Lollards, whom the Beccles magistrate so incompetently allowed to walk free."

Mary spurned the offer contemptuously, "My Lord, you will not use me to further your own ambition. I shall name no-one."

Mary looked across the chapter house to Richard. It was a poignant moment for them both. She had just ensured a terrible death for herself as the price of retaining her honour and self respect. Their newly discovered awareness of each other would now be unable to flower, yet Richard was proud of the way Mary had conducted herself during this mockery of a trial. They remained locked in a spiritual embrace as each juror gave his predictable verdict, drawing inner strength from each other for the dark days to come.

"Would it be too much to ask you to pay attention mistress?" The venomous voice of the bishop cut into the powerful channel of energy which locked Richard's and Mary's eyes upon each another. "This does, after all, affect your future somewhat. You have just been found guilty of heresy. I therefore have no alternative but to sentence you to death by burning, to be carried out in the town of Beccles in Suffolk as a warning to those who may be considering espousing causes similar to your own. As for the date, now let me see." Courtenay thumbed through the ecclesiastical diary on his desk as if arranging a church outing.

"I shall need a day or two to get the sentence confirmed by the civil authorities which takes us to Friday. But that is a working day and not ideal for a large crowd. Next Sunday would be excellent. That is December the 8th, the feast of the Immaculate Conception. I suggest mistress, if you can find it in your black heart to pray, you offer your soul to the Blessed Virgin for it will be on her day you shall face the final judgement. Have you aught else to say before I conclude these proceedings?"

"Only this My Lord bishop," answered Mary, now speaking with the strength and defiance of one who knows she is lost. "I shall indeed pray, not for myself but for you. You will need intercession from the Blessed Virgin far more than I when your time comes."

"Take her away!" snapped the bishop, "while my patience lasts." Richard was left thinking hard upon what the beggar had said, 'Trust to the strength of your arm and expect nothing from this bishop.'

Richard Courtenay never succeeded to the see of Canterbury.

★ ★ ★

IV

I cannot let 'er stay elsewhere sir, not now she's been convicted," said the Beccles gaoler, "but I've emptied the gaol of all the other felons so she's at least got a bit o' privacy." It was the Friday before the execution and Richard had hoped to move Mary to the more comfortable surroundings of the monastery of Saint Peter for her last two days on this earth, but the gaoler dared not co-operate this time. It was not that he was unsympathetic, far from it, but prisoners under sentence of death had to be held under close arrest.

"I understand," said Richard. "I have here a shilling for you to buy Mistress Hoccleve some decent provisions to ease her last days."

The gaoler pushed the shilling away, "It's a bad business this, a bad business. I will not take your money sir. I've enough left over from what you gave me before to see all 'er needs are met. She's special ain't she. She don't bear no grudge, no grudge at all."

Richard smiled, "You're right, she is special and I thank you for your understanding. May I have a few minutes with her?"

"O' course. I'll make myself scarce and when you're ready to leave, call me."

The gaoler unlocked the door to Mary's cell then went outside, leaving Richard to swing open the cell door. Mary was sitting reading a small bible in the light cast from the single, barred window above her, looking remarkably well considering the circumstances.

She glanced up and spoke in a calm, relaxed voice, "Richard, you came."

"Of course. Did you think I would not?" Mary put down her bible and walked tentatively towards him, but brushing inhibition aside he strode into the cell and took her into his arms. She did not resist but nor did she respond. He stepped back disappointed, but she understood and said, "It is all right my dear. You must forgive my inadequate reaction. Now that I have accepted my fate and commended my soul to God, I feel a serenity I have never experienced before. When death is certain and paradise only a short time away, terror soon flees one's mind. In such a state of calm the earthly senses become muted." To Richard she seemed strangely distant, as if she had already begun to disassociate her spirit from her body in anticipation of the terrible ordeal that awaited her. To give her hope of life would only serve to destroy the serenity Mary had achieved, yet Richard had already determined he could not stand idly by and let her die. But to give her hope and then to fail her would be the cruelest blow of all; he would have to leave her in ignorance of his intentions.

"Is the gaoler looking after you properly?" he asked.

Mary nodded, "Poor man. He cannot do enough for me. He seems to think my death is his fault."

"He has become a great admirer of yours."

"How is John Fletcher? Is he giving leadership to the others?" Richard could not tell Mary that the Frostenden community had been scattered to the four winds, so he simply said, "He is coping well enough though it is difficult for him."

"John has great moral strength. He will manage. Remember me to him and say I shall pray for them all. I welcome the chance to intercede directly for them and to meet your Ann again. We shall have much to talk about."

Richard looked directly into Mary's deep, brown eyes and said the words at last, "I loved Ann but now I love you Mary. With my heart, my soul and every fibre in my body I love you. I bless the light that shines upon you. It is important that you know before …." His voice trailed away.

And now she came close to him again and held him tightly as she had done before. "Richard," she murmured, "this is not helping me." She looked up at him and before she could look away again he kissed her lips, gently at first, but then with steadily increasing passion. She responded with equal fervour as the ingrained bonds of restraint were finally broken, and for the first time in her life she began to understand that man and woman are designed to be together, not divided by man made religious convention.

At last, they separated and Richard whispered, "That was no preacher's kiss."

"And this is no preacher," she answered, as she kissed him again with the ferocity only newly discovered love can bring.

After many minutes they separated once more and Mary said softly, "Why is it that I have only understood this now, just as I must leave such wonders behind?"

Richard shrugged, "I cannot answer that but I am glad it happened. It will strengthen our memory of each other."

"I too am glad Richard, though I am not sure how it will affect my resolve to face what must come."

He smiled and kissed her softly on the forehead, "Well my resolve is greatly strengthened. I will see you again before the time comes."

"When?"

"I am not sure but do not be surprised if it is when you least expect it. Now I must leave, there are things to do."

"I do not understand."

"You will Mary, you will."

CHAPTER TWELVE

Sunday the eighth day of December the feast day of the Immaculate Conception, dawned cloudless and still. Another freezing night had dusted Beccles market square with a fine, white frost which still lay thick in the north facing shadows. Unusually for a Sunday morning, there was considerable bustle in the square because most of the shopkeepers, with an eye to good business, had decided to open for the day. Mary Bradby, the owner of the White Boar Tavern, was not one of them. She stood outside the closed tavern door looking contemptuously at the busy scene in front of her.

"Not open yet Mary?" called the baker who was setting out his stall in front of the shop next door. "The crowds will soon be here wanting to quench their thirst."

"My tavern stays closed today," sniffed Mary Bradby. "The gloaters can quench their thirst somewhere else. Mary Hoccleve's fate is an affront to all women."

The baker shook his head and muttered under his breath, "Women! Who will ever understand them!"

One man in Beccles who would have agreed with Mary Bradby was the gaoler. In his simple way he now understood that law and justice are not always the same thing. He knew that he was about to witness a gross injustice so he decided to do what he could to make his prisoner's last few hours a little easier. Out of respect he knocked on the cell door before opening it and asked, "Is there anything you want this morning Mistress Hoccleve?"

She looked at a bundle beside her and said, "Yes Michael there is. I would look my best to meet my maker, but before I put on this gown Richard brought me I would like to bathe." The gaoler scratched his bald pate and pondered on this unusual last request.

"Well I suppose the nuns at Saint Peters might oblige. I will make the arrangements. You shall 'ave your bath."

By midmorning crowds of onlookers had filled most of the square. It could have been market day. Jugglers and tumblers amused small knots of spectators and one jongleur had already composed a song called 'The Ballad of Bad Mary'. The more morbid stood behind a cordon of sheriff's men, who ringed the wooden stake in the centre of the square, watching the black clothed executioner carrying out his preparations. Burnings were a relatively new form of execution in England and frequently went wrong, usually through the use of too much green wood. When this happened the victim usually ended up being partly scorched and smoked like a kipper, and the final death blow would have to come from a dagger instead of the flames. Fortunately there was little difficulty in finding enough properly dried out wood at this time of year, so the executioner went about his work confident there would be no repetition of his last sputtering effort in Ipswich.

The most notable absentee was Sir John Satterley, who refused to witness a form of execution he abhorred, so in his stead the magistrate from Holton, Geoffrey Calveley, took the seat in the middle of the small platform which had been erected to separate the town notables from the rest of the milling crowd. It was now past eleven o'clock and the execution was scheduled to commence at noon. From his elevated position Geoffrey looked round for Titus, but his steward was nowhere to be seen. He'll turn up, thought Geoffrey, old Scrope wouldn't miss this for the world. He's probably satisfying his lust with a doxy while he's waiting. I'll keep a seat for him.

At half past eleven a hush of anticipation began to settle on the crowd as they strained for a glimpse of the victim who would soon appear from the direction of the town gaol. The gaoler, now barely able to hold back the tears, opened Mary's cell door for the last time. She looked beautiful. Her white gown, tied into her narrow waist by an embroidered, red leather belt, and her long, fair hair which fell in golden waves around her shoulders, gave her the appearance in the gaoler's dewy eyes of an apparition from heaven. She smiled at him and said, "Thank you for what you have done for me Michael. I never expected to find such kindness in a place like this." Her brow furrowed slightly, "Has he not come?"

"Master Calveley?"

"Yes, he said he would visit me again before the end."

"Something beyond 'is control must 'ave stopped 'im else h'ed 'ave bin 'ere by now, I'm sure of it."

"What could have happened?"

The gaoler cleared his throat, "We must be moving now if yer don't mind. I know you are prepared but I should warn yer there's a large crowd out there. I shall stay with yer as long as I can if that's all right."

Mary took a deep breath. "It is Michael. Let us go." She had hoped to draw strength from Richard's presence but as she stepped out of the dark gaol into the bright daylight, she suddenly felt alone. This was a journey she would have to complete on her own, but with Richard at her side she could have faced what was to come with greater fortitude.

The narrow lane which led from the gaol to the square had been kept clear of onlookers, and as she walked slowly between her sheriff's escort, Mary began to fear her nerve might fail her. She looked up at the clear, blue winter sky wishing it was all over. It was not death but dying that terrified her.

They entered the square opposite Saint Michael's church. A roar went up as the white clad figure appeared. The crowd surged forward threatening to engulf the solemn procession in a tide of morbid curiosity. The escort fought back the noisy press to little effect at first, and Mary halted wondering whether she would be crushed instead of burned.

"It's all right, I'm still 'ere," growled the gaoler from behind her. Had it not been for that one supportive voice she would have been unable to continue unaided, but eventually the sheriff's men managed to force a passage through the crowd, and the slow walk resumed. Mary looked up and for the first time saw the place of execution. Her legs almost gave way and again she had to stop, gathering the last of her willpower for the final few paces. Suddenly a man broke through the escort and stood in front of her. It was Titus Scrope. Anguish lined his face, his voice shook with desperation, "Mary! Mary! I did not mean this to happen. How could I have known you would not recant!"

"Do not reproach yourself Titus," said Mary. "I did not realise what was happening to you. I bear some responsibility for showing you too much innocent friendship. Only now do I understand your agony." One of the sheriff's men tried to pull Titus away but he shook him off as a lion might a jackal.

"I dare not ask your forgiveness Mary."

"You already have it. I shall remember you as Titus Roper not Titus Scrope for I believe you have at last found the real Titus deep inside yourself. It was my good fortune to be the means by which you discovered your true nature Titus Roper." As he was pulled away by three men from the escort, he heard her last words, "I shall pray for you Titus."

A grating, hateful voice boomed from the platform of notables, "Scrope! What in God's name are you doing! Get up here at once!" It was Geoffrey Calveley. Titus did not acknowledge the summons; his mind was in turmoil. If only she had spurned him, scorned him or at the very least vented anger upon him. But instead she had forgiven and accepted some of the blame upon herself. That only made his guilt harder to bear. He knew he could not live with it. Ignoring his master, Titus pushed his way through the seething crowd until he reached the north side of the square where a small track led down to the River Waveney. The last person to see him was Mary Bradby who was hanging some linen out to dry at the back of the White Boar. She never forgot Titus' ghastly pallor and wide, expressionless eyes. He looked like a living corpse as he shambled, staggered almost, towards the river which here ran dark, treacherous and deep.

Titus Scrope's body was never found.

★ ★ ★

II

Back in the market square Mary's nemesis was almost upon her. The strange interruption by Titus had, if anything, settled her nerves a little, and she approached the black masked executioner without further hesitation. He held out a gloved hand into which she pressed a coin to show she bore no personal enmity to a man who was only doing his duty. The gaoler, now weeping openly, bade her farewell. He had intended to return to his gaol before the execution began but Mary said, "Stay Michael if you please. I would fain have a friend nearby this day."

Michael found a place at the front of the crowd and watched as Mary, accompanied by the executioner, began to climb the heaped faggots, brushwood and kindling which were piled up around the wooden stake. At the top she stood with her back to the stake while the executioner tied her waist and feet to it, but he left her arms free so she could receive the last rites with her hands in the position of prayer.

"Chew on this," he whispered as he pushed a small piece of root into her hand. "It dulls the senses." As soon as the executioner returned to the smoking brazier, which he would use to light the brushwood torches gathered in a heap beside him, the pale faced parish priest, John Attegate, clambered up the pyre to administer the last rites. His voice was unsteady. "Are you ready for the great sacrament of Extreme Unction my child?"

"I do not believe in the sacraments Father," said Mary. "That is why I am here."

The priest, who was probably younger than Mary, was appalled "But surely you must understand that your soul cannot enter the kingdom of heaven without being properly shriven and prepared?"

"I have already prepared myself Father. Leave me now and do not worry. You have tried to do your duty." The priest quickly disappeared into the crowd and now, at last, Mary was truly alone. She chewed hard on the root the executioner had given her and looked at the hundreds of white faces staring up at her. The largest congregation I've ever had, she thought with bitter irony. Apart from a dog barking in the distance and the ominous crackling of the brazier, there was complete silence as the crowd waited for the noon toll of Saint Michael's church bell. It could not be long coming.

The heavy, brooding silence was suddenly broken. There was a disturbance at the far end of the square. For a split second Mary wondered if the executioner's root was playing tricks with her mind, but a female scream from the direction of the Ipswich road was real enough. A moment later the market stall which blocked the southern entrance to the square was overturned, scattering assorted pies and hams everywhere. In its place, like a vision from Viking Valhalla, was a knight mounted on a huge, black steed. His face was hidden by a tilting helm, the sun reflected red gold on his burnished plate armour, and upon his white surcoat, emblazoned as if in blood, was a large, red cross.

A man shouted, "God preserve us! It's Saint George!" The knight spurred his charger forward, clearing the terrified crowd with the flat of his sword. Metal shod hooves rang out on the cobbles sending sparks flying in all directions. Even the sheriff's men backed away as the unidentified warrior forced his way towards the lone, white figure bound to the pyre.

Geoffrey, who had already guessed what was happening, shouted, "Stop him!" One of the bolder men in the escort stood in the way of the knight, but a mighty sweep from the red and white shield threw him back against the platform leg which snapped under the blow. The town notables, including Geoffrey and the sheriff, were pitched unceremoniously into the crowd as the platform collapsed, increasing the confusion for now there was no-one to give orders.

Mary was perplexed by the startling appearance of the formidable warrior, and as he drew closer she was even a little afraid. Then she saw the surcoat was torn. She touched the missing piece, which was even now secreted inside her gown against her breast; he had come for her after all.

Richard stood up in his stirrups, leaned over the firewood and cut Mary's bonds with his sword. Now came the most dangerous part of the rescue. He sheathed his sword, gripped Mary's red belt in his mailed hand and hauled her up and over the front of his saddle like a sack of flour. Turning his horse he drew his sword again, but an enterprising sergeant in the sheriff's escort had gathered together a group of pikemen who blocked the escape. No horse would charge a mass of sharp pike points, so Richard began to look round in vain for an alternative way out. He never found out about the vital, unexpected contribution to his plan made by Michael, the Beccles gaoler, nor fortunately for Michael did anyone else.

Michael knew almost as soon as Geoffrey who the gallant knight was, but unlike Geoffrey he hoped the rescue would succeed. He even found himself cheering when Richard lifted Mary into his saddle. But the initial shock was beginning to fade, and with the pikemen cutting off the route to safety it began to seem to Michael as if the bold rescue attempt would falter. Quickly looking round he saw that the executioner had melted away into the safety of the crowd leaving him briefly alone beside the burning brazier. Taking careful aim, the gaoler gave the brazier a surreptitious but firm kick. The glowing casket tipped over, spilling red hot coals across the feet of the sheriff's pikemen. Before there had been order, now there was mayhem. The sheriff's men dropped their pikes and scattered, hopping and dancing like madmen under a full moon. To Richard it seemed like the parting of the Red Sea. He spurred his horse into the gap that had miraculously opened before him. No-one in the crowd attempted to block the path of this re-incarnation of Saint George, and in less than half a minute he had disappeared from view down the Ipswich road.

The burly, red bearded sheriff soon extracted himself from the mass of flailing arms and legs caused by the collapse of the platform, and started to try and restore some order. Michael, grinning from ear to ear, quietly returned to his gaol. As the disappointed crowd began to disperse, an angry Geoffrey tapped the sheriff on the shoulder and demanded, "What are you going to do now?"

"I shall organise a pursuit," replied the sheriff, "just as soon as I can get enough mounted men together."

"How many?"

"A dozen or so."

"That will not be enough."

Irritated by this questioning of his professional judgement, the sheriff said, "Master Calveley, I do not tell you your duties as a magistrate, so refrain from telling me mine."

"But I am confident I know where your quarry is headed."

The sheriff's attitude mellowed, "You know who that knight was?"

"He is no knight, he is my cousin, Richard Calveley."

"But he wore no identifying device."

"Under the circumstances would you? My dear sheriff, we were about to burn his woman. I suggest you send half your men in pursuit towards Ipswich, but if my guess is right, you will do well to send the other half on the direct road to Caistor Manor. My cousin is Fastolf's lieutenant."

The sheriff looked uncertain, "But Squire John Fastolf is a well known power in Norfolk and a magistrate. Surely he would not allow sanctuary to a criminal?"

Geoffrey put a reassuring hand on the sheriff's shoulder. "Fastolf is still in France."

* * *

III

Richard finally drew rein as he approached the Crossbow Inn, four miles south of Beccles, but instead of halting outside the inn, he turned off the road into the oak forest behind it. Fifty paces into the forest, in a small clearing where a woodman's cottage had once been, Thomas Riches was waiting. He had with him some clothing and two spare horses, one of which was the faithful grey palfrey that had borne Richard throughout the campaign in France.

"God's teeth Master Richard! I never thought you would really do it!" said Thomas as Richard and Mary entered the clearing. Mary slid from the great, black destrier and collapsed semi-conscious onto the frost hardened soil.

Richard removed his helmet and dismounted, "It was a close thing Tom. Put my cloak round her, she must be freezing."

"You were not recognised?" asked Thomas as he wrapped Mary's limp body in Richard's fur lined cloak.

"No, though certain people may hazard an accurate guess if they were there. Hopefully the direction of my escape will put them off the scent for a while. I never thought I would be using de Freuchin's armour so soon."

Thomas started to unbuckle Richard's leg straps and sighed, "It seems a shame to dump such valuable armour. There cannot be a better suit in all England."

"Do not be tempted Tom. You must dump it where it will never be found. Once you have removed the whitewash blaze and socks from the destrier, the only way I can be categorically identified is by the armour. It is, as you say, more or less unique in England."

By the time Richard had changed into his buckskin breeches and green, quilted tunic, Mary was beginning to stir. He helped her to her feet and stroked her hair, "Come along my dear, we must hurry. Can you ride?"

She steadied herself on his shoulder and said dreamily, "Richard, you came for me." He tried to keep the urgency out of his voice, "Yes, we can talk of that later but we must go now. The pursuit cannot be far behind."

Mary took a step back and blinked two or three times while she gathered her wits, "Yes Richard, I can ride. My father used to take me hunting when I was but a child. I will not slow you down."

Soon they were cantering along the Ipswich road together, leaving Thomas hidden in the forest clearing until the pursuit had passed by. They left the main road just before Halesworth and cut across country to the Yarmouth road which they joined near Frostenden. Mary, cloaked and hooded, was still trying to come to terms with her unexpected reprieve. She looked wistfully at the track that led to the

Lollard settlement as they rode past, but Richard told her there was no time for even the briefest of visits. He did not want her to see the sorry remains of what had once been her thriving community. They only stopped once to water and rest the horses at Hopton, and when at last Caistor Manor's flint walls came into view, the large, red sun was setting in the cloudless, winter sky. There would be another heavy frost this night.

When they clattered across the open drawbridge, Millicent Fastolf was ready for them and Father Hugh had already arrived with Joan. So far Richard's plan was going well.

"Richard, I will look after Mary," said Millicent as they tethered their horses in the courtyard. "Dinner will be served within the hour."

"We threw off our pursuers between Shadingfylde and Brampton," said Richard as he munched through a thick slice of smoked ham, "I should think Tom Riches will be back at any moment." A huge log fire kept the hall warm against the frosty night, and for the present all seemed well.

"Painting white markings on your black horse was a good idea," said Hugh, "At least he cannot be identified now."

Richard nodded, "That was Tom's idea not mine. I owe him a great deal as I do you all. You have risked much by helping me."

"If Richard is indebted to you all then I am doubly so," said Mary who, after a bath and a change of clothes looked radiant.

"Nonsense," said Millicent. "It is every woman's duty to ensure that stupid laws made by stupid men, and there are plenty of them, are flouted whenever possible. No woman would pass a law to burn people who hold different opinions from the majority."

Richard raised his eyebrows, "But your husband is a magistrate."

"He is also a Norfolk squire with a strong sense of natural justice. He will no doubt grumble when he hears of my part in this, but provided there is no proof you rescued Mary, he will come round to my way of thinking. He usually does, eventually."

"I am glad to hear it," said Richard. "He once warned me against helping Lollards."

"Really," sniffed Millicent. "That was no doubt before you saved his life at Agincourt, which far outweighs any debt you may feel you owe to either of us."

"When do you plan to leave?" asked Hugh.

"Tonight," answered Richard. "It would not be wise to tarry longer."

"I'm sorry you cannot stay in England."

"So am I Hugh, but Normandy will be much safer. There are no Lollards there and no persecutions. It is also where the war is. Anyway, I have you to manage Calveley Hall for me while I am gone. Millicent's lawyer says you will be able to take possession in my name in a matter of weeks."

"Provided your part in Mary's escape remains secret," warned Millicent.

"Quite," agreed Richard. "Apart from us, Tom Riches and Father Anselm, no-one can prove anything."

Millicent said, "Your ship's master is my cousin. He will keep our little secret. His crew are all Gascons recruited in Bordeaux. I doubt more than a handful speak any English. He asks that you arrive at his ship any time before midnight so he does not miss the tide."

"We have already packed the few things we will need for our journey," said Richard. "Most of my ransom money is still with your husband at Harfleur, so we will not be short of funds when we get to France."

Millicent suddenly sat up, "Strange, the dogs are barking."

"Tom Riches perhaps?" suggested Hugh. But before Millicent could answer the heavy, oak door opened and William entered. The old steward had been running and was obliged to pause to recover his breath.

"What is it William?" asked Millicent.

"We are under siege My Lady. I was doing my final rounds along the curtain wall when I saw in the moonlight about twenty men approaching from the direction of Yarmouth. They were dismounted and leading their horses to be as quiet as possible. I was not sure what they were up to at first, but when they left the road and started to surround us I knew we were in trouble."

"The sheriff of Beccles' men," said Richard quietly. Geoffrey must have anticipated where I would go. If they find Mary here we will all be incriminated."

A powerful voice, which was audible in the main hall, boomed from the far side of the moat, "Lower your drawbridge at once. I demand entry as an officer of the law!"

Millicent spoke calmly to William, trying to steady the old man's nerve, "You say they have already surrounded us?"

"Yes My Lady. All exits will be cut off by now. What's to become of us?"

"But if they are Beccles men they will not know about the Pickerell Fleet will they?" William's anxious face relaxed. He even smiled, "Indeed not My Lady."

Turning to Richard, the Lady of Caistor Manor issued her orders like a veteran commander. "Richard, gather your things quickly and meet me at the barge house. Mary, bring Joan with you. Father Hugh, would you clear the dining table so no-one can deduce how many people have been here. William, hold off the Beccles men as long as you can. Request identification and be even more grumpy and long winded than usual. Then show them in here. When they have searched and found nothing they shall feel the sharp edge of my tongue. Now let us be about our business."

The barge house was located adjacent to the west side of the curtain wall which enclosed the manor house gardens. It was connected to a narrow, man made channel called the Pickerell Fleet which was used for bringing provisions to the house by barge from Yarmouth. One of Richard's duties as Fastolf's lieutenant had been to supervise the clearing out of the fleet the previous autumn. Without that fortunate coincidence, the sheriff of Beccles would have had his prey neatly bottled up.

Richard and Mary left the manor house by a side door and hurried through the gardens to the barge house. The shock of the cold, frosty night after the warm hall nearly took their breath away. A half moon shone through the orchard apple trees casting weird shadows across the herb garden, and the white frozen ground reflected the silver light rather too brightly for fugitives wishing to evade capture. There was no wind and the sound of their feet crunching along the gravelled path seemed to echo all round them. Much depended on the slumbering Joan, for if she were to waken and cry out, all would be lost.

Millicent had already untied the barge when Richard and Mary arrived. She whispered, "There is a slight current when the tide is on the ebb, so you should be able to drift downstream quietly without using the oars. The River Bure is about half a mile away. It will take you straight into Yarmouth harbour. My cousin's ship is called the *Fair Wind*. His name is John Tiptoft. Give my love to my husband when you see him. I intended to write to him before you left but the sheriff of Beccles determined otherwise." Shouting at the drawbridge cut short Richard's thanks; William could not stall much longer, so the fugitives got into the broad beamed, snub nosed barge and cast off.

Ducking below the low, brick lined arch in the curtain wall which connected the barge house to the Pickerell Fleet, Richard eased the barge out into the open. The flat, treeless landscape provided no cover, and from his position crouched in the rear of the barge, Richard could already see motionless black figures standing like ghostly sentinels at regular intervals outside the curtain wall. The nearest of these was only ten paces from the fleet. They would have to pass almost under his nose.

The freezing night had caused small flows of ice to form on the water which bumped against the bow of the barge as it drifted downstream. Each time this happened Richard was convinced the noise would attract the interest of the nearest sentinel, but as they approached him, his attention seemed to be diverted by the furious row at the drawbridge between old William and the sheriff's men, which was echoing across the Norfolk countryside. Baby Joan, wrapped up snugly inside Mary's cloak, slept on and as the manor drawbridge creaked slowly into place across the moat, the barge passed through the cordon of Beccles men unnoticed.

An hour before midnight two hooded figures presented themselves to the master of the *Fair Wind,* a cog of some substance which had ferried sixty fully armed men at arms across the channel for the Agincourt campaign.

"Your cabin is aft," said John Tiptoft. "Bertrand will take you there." Richard glanced sidelong at Mary but she seemed perfectly at ease about sharing a single cabin with him.

A little later the *Fair Wind* was slipping out of Yarmouth harbour on the last of the ebb. There was hardly any wind and the sea was calm, but the tide would take the cog far enough out of Yarmouth's lee to pick up the offshore breeze which usually developed during cold winter nights. Mary joined Richard on the quarter deck and together they stood arm in arm watching the lights of Yarmouth growing more distant.

"How is Joan?" asked Richard.

"Still sleeping," replied Mary. "She has been sound asleep since we left Caistor Manor." They stood in silence for a while, listening to the comforting creaks and groans of a ship in motion.

At last Mary said, "Are you happy?"

Richard smiled down at her and kissed the top of her head which nestled comfortably below his chin, "Of course, but …"

"But what?"

"I have unfinished business in England. Geoffrey might have lost his inheritance but he has not been punished sufficiently for what he has done. And there is still Titus Scrope. He has yet to feel my vengeance."

"I agree your cousin has escaped lightly so far, but Titus is a different matter. Of course he must face the full rigour of the law, but if you had seen the look in his eyes when he begged my forgiveness in Beccles market, you would understand he has suffered much already. The love Titus bore for me revealed a previously unseen side of him. You and I both know what a powerful force love can be. It even changed Titus Scrope."

Richard shrugged, "He can change into the Archangel Gabriel for all I care, I shall still tear his throat out when I get hold of him."

Mary said thoughtfully, "I see Titus more as a Judas than a Lucifer. He may well fail to cope with his remorse."

"Until he discovers you did not burn after all."

Wisely, Mary decided to leave the subject of Titus Scrope until another day. She tightened her grip round Richard's waist. "Will Millicent Fastolf be all right?"

"Have no fear for Millicent," chuckled Richard, "it is the sheriff of Beccles we should be worried about. Of course suspicion will be aroused when it is found that my disappearance coincided with yours, but that would not stand as proof in a court of law without corroboration. And now we have the rest of our lives to enjoy together. We must make the most of the opportunity fate has given us."

"Fate and Father Anselm."

"What do you mean?" asked a perplexed Richard.

"Who made sure we would meet when you wanted to swear your oath of vengeance? While you were talking to Millicent earlier this evening, Father Hugh said that Anselm had recently admitted it was always his intention to pair us off after Ann's murder. Things did not go as smoothly as he had hoped, and it was when I was condemned to burn he opened his heart to Hugh for he felt responsible. But by now news of my escape should have reached him. His purpose has been fulfilled."

Richard thought back to that terrible day when he had implored Anselm to solemnise an oath of vengeance. It had always seemed odd that a Franciscan should send him to a Lollard.

"But why would Anselm want us to be together?" he wondered aloud.
"I too have thought about that. Anselm could never have combated my faith with the power of theological argument, so he used the love of a brave and mighty warrior instead. My faith has not altered but I am no longer free to preach as I once did. At the same time he has brought happiness to you whom he loves like a son."

"Then I have much to thank that wily, old priest for."

"And I too."

The cog lurched as the sails billowed to the first gusts of the offshore breeze. Mary shivered and looked up at Richard silhouetted in the silver moonlight. In her eyes he was at least as noble as all the great lords and knights she had seen, and certainly more handsome.

"Richard."

"Yes my dear."

"You will forgive my inexperience in these matters, but amongst the many duties a man must bear for his woman, is not keeping her warm at night one of them?"

He smiled, "It is one of his most important responsibilities."

"Well, it is night and I am cold."

"Then let us go to our cabin."

Neither that night, nor for many more nights to come, did Mary feel the cold again.

THE END